NOW I CAN SAY
I'M AN AUTHOR

Proving literally anyone
can write a book

Vol. I

Josh Rolph

Library of Congress Control Number: 2022919208
ISBN: 979-8-9857796-2-2 (Paperback)
ISBN: 979-8-9857796-0-8 (Hardcover)
ISBN: 979-8-9857796-1-5 (ePub)

Printed in the United States of America
Edited by Josh Rolph probably 10,783 times.
Designed by Joanna Smith Creative, one of the best of the best of the bestestly best.
IngramSpark
1st edition.

Laugh Inside Lightly Publishing
6520 Lonetree Blvd Suite 116
Rocklin, CA 95765
(916) 244-2202

DEDICATION

To Kristina, Michael, Sam, Anna, and Nate, for believing in me.

And to Dad, my author father and inspiration.

CONTENTS

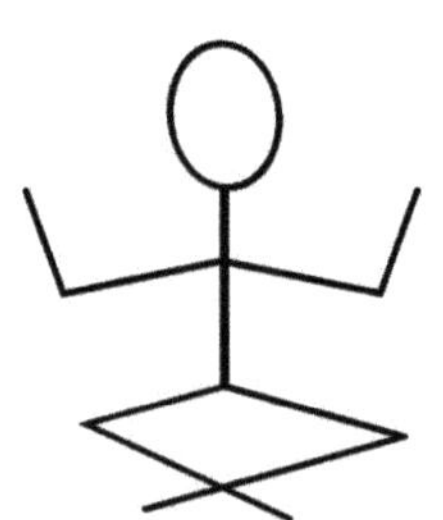

SOME QUOTES

"What is important is seldom urgent.
What is urgent is seldom important."
–Eisenhower

"You can just write a book if the book you write is just."
–Josh Rolph

"If you gottabooktowrite, you gottawriteabook."
–Josh Rolph

"If you say you are an author, author an are you say you if?"
–Josh Rolph

THE POINT

This is a book about trying to become an author. It's not about becoming an author, it's a book about trying to become an author. And trying to become an author wasn't easy. All I really wanted out of the effort was to say, "Now I can say I'm an author." And now, I can honestly say it. Honestly. Not that I ever dishonestly said I was an author. In any case, becoming an honest author wasn't easy. Honestly. I know I'm repeating myself. But seriously, I'm being completely honest, now I can say I'm an author.

And it wasn't easy.

MARKETING THIS BOOK

Shotgun approach. Put $10 behind each of these on Facebook Ads and see which gets the most traction.

- An unlikely, wannabe author tries to become an author in "Now I Can Say I'm an Author."
- Includes essays on Yogurt, Race Relations, and PANTS!
- Learn how to become an author if only by reading a book written by an author who wasn't an author until he finished the book!
- ~~The book every author wishes they had written.~~
- Who needs food when they're "Now I Can Say I'm an Author."
- The book no true author would write, except for this one.
- I only read "Now I Can Say I'm an Author" for the Acknowledgements section. [Possible t-shirt?]
- The most talked about book in the author's home when he's talking to himself about his own book.
- Plant the seed: Marketing books is hard. So we're not gonna even try to market NOW I CAN SAY I'M AN AUTHOR! Repeat: We're not gonna even try to market NOW I CAN SAY I'M AN AUTHOR sold at an Amazon near you! Now I can say I'm an author!
- Now I can say I'm an author. Can you?

- The book with the must-read PREFACE!
- The book with the must-read title.
- The book with the must-read footnotes.
- The book that uses the word "something" 116 times.
- The word "that" comprises 1.2% of the book.
- From the author of no other books comes this title.

What better marketing can be done than by my own country:

- Here's what the United States of America is saying about this book: "Copyright 2023."
- The Library of Congress announced "Copyright 2023" when the author of the book asked the Library of Congress to do that.

I would be humbled by my country saying that in my own book. Ok one more:

- The book he wished to be each year when he blew out the birthday candles. Then the last year he couldn't blow them all out and that was the year this was published.

ANOTHER QUOTE

"Up your sleeve, you may have smart books, stupid books, profound, funny, and sad books to write – but the first book you come up with says something significant about your innermost soul."

– J. R.

ACKNOWLEDGEMENTS

■ ■ ■

Yesterday

■ ■ ■

I'd like to first acknowledge myself, for I couldn't have written this book without me.

Besides me, no one I know – and pretty much nobody I don't know – as well as nobody I don't know who wouldn't fail to unlike indifferently objectionable...okay, that joke isn't working —

What I don't want to fail to say —

What exactly am I trying to say?

What I do want to say is absolutely no one will want to be acknowledged in this acknowledgements section.

If that is the case, then why should I include an acknowledgements section in my book?

Well, the answer is very simple: It's because I really want an acknowledgements section. It's just something I've always wanted.

One could go as far as to say I want an acknowledgements section even more than I want to produce an entire book.

But if one were to say I want an acknowledgements section more than I want a book, they would be so wrong.

That being the case, one could say I want to write the word

"acknowledgements" as many as times as possible in this acknowledgements section.

But again, if one were to say the word "acknowledgements" is a word I want included many times in this section, they would also be wrong.

Truth is, if I could only write this section – this acknowledgements section – and call it a book, I would. I would write an entire book of acknowledgements, thanking everyone in my life who contributed in some way to making this book possible – from family to teachers to mentors to the inventors of the traffic signal, jet fuel, the cereal I had for breakfast this morning – and at the end of the acknowledgements section the reader would turn the page expecting to begin the official book only to find the back of the sleeve.

Who knows, after reading the entire book, you might say you should have only read the acknowledgements section and spared yourself from the rest. This acknowledgements section may be the best part of the book. In fact, right now it is.

This section could also be the longest part of the book – I don't know. I haven't written it yet. What I do know is I will not end with the acknowledgements section, no matter how much I wish that's all I had to do to become an author. I'm deciding to begin writing the acknowledgements section because it might help me finish the book faster. It's like buying those 32 waist pants even though I'm a 36 at the moment. It's hopeful. This entire book writing project is an exercise in hope.

The problem with acknowledgements or the act of acknowledging is I'm not sure I want to acknowledge anyone, and it's not for reasons you might think. Yes, I could very well be an ungrateful narcissist. Or we've all heard the guy who says, "I can't write an acknowledgments section because I would hate to leave out someone who deserves acknowledgement." Yawn. I'm not gonna be that "can't write an acknowledgements section" guy.

What I don't want is to acknowledge any living soul in a work as seemingly self-focused as this one will attempt to be. By 'self-focused,' I mean to say this entire book is about trying to become an author. The lead character is me. And that's all there is. Close the book now if you're expecting more of it.[1]

Believe me when I tell you I would much rather write about someone else's attempt at becoming an author. The wise suggest to write what you know, so since I know me the best, you could say I am really taking this to heart, and then some.

For anyone willing to stick with me on this ride, I definitely acknowledge you. A true narcissist would say the opposite. They would only acknowledge themselves, not the reader. I just want to distinguish between the narcissists who write words and this guy whose words you happen to be reading. Here's something else a narcissist author wouldn't do: they wouldn't fall in love with you, the reader. And I've gotta tell you: I think I love you. I am, in very fact, falling in love with you as I write. So case closed. I'm not a narcissist. I'm just a deranged psychopath.

I'm convinced books are only as good as the author's passion, and of course, they're as good as the author's knack for turning a phrase, not to mention how the author should possess and adequately articulate some purpose and use good logic and ensure there are no holes in the narrative and break things up into digestible chapters and write somewhat coherently without too many run-on sentences like the one you are reading right now and should follow all the other ways good books are made good. Readers today demand something more readable than, say, the ancient works of a thousand generations ago when Plato's Republic[2] or Thucydides' *History of the Peloponnesian War*[3] went

---

1 Wait! Don't close the book! [3 second pause…] Okay, now you can close the book.

2 There are perhaps some parallels between writing this book and the *Allegory of the Cave.*

3 A work largely forgotten today because it lacks the page-turner quality the modern attention span demands. That, and it's really hard to understand.

to print. Readers today want a book to move along a little more quickly than those overly-wordy ancient writings.

We want our books today to be way more — what's the word?

■ ■ ■

22.5 seconds later

■ ■ ■

The word "tantalizing" comes to mind. And if it takes that long for single words to come to my mind, I might as well give up on writing a book. What's the right word? We want our book to be more tantalizing? No, that's not it. We want our books to be more…

■ ■ ■

6 seconds later

■ ■ ■

The word "immediately" comes to mind. We want our books to be immediately. Hold up. That's not right either. Coming up with words to fill a book isn't easy. Should I give up immediately? I won't give up immediately. And I won't finish the above thought about what we readers want in books in our day and age, because apparently I can't put it into words.

So before I stray further, let's stick with the acknowledgements section. Because if I've learned anything in these first four and a half minutes of writing my first acknowledgements section, I'll never finish any book section when veering too far off course.

That, or I could do something a little different – get a little crazy – go a little rogue – get a little *italicized* on you. I could break from standard acknowledgements section format by turning the tables on you[4]

---

4 Figuratively speaking, of course.

by turning to those who might want to acknowledge me. That's right. I could find people who want to do a little acknowledging.

No, no, no. That won't work either because that is something our narcissist author "friend" would do. Having others acknowledge me would break from all convention in acknowledgment prose, flipping on its head the whole idea of acknowledging, while confusing readers and simultaneously feeding into the idea that this book effort is, in actuality, all about me. I don't want to confuse or come across as a super-ego. People acknowledging me is really just a "Recommendations" section, which is typically reserved for the front pages of the second edition or the back sleeve. So strike that idea.

Oh! Here's an unconventional idea: I should write a lot of acknowledging that has nothing to do with the book. Like acknowledging the phenomena of street corner dancers sporting their headphones and waving a "big sale over yonder" sign. They didn't help write this book. But acknowledging them could be a nice twist in this section; something refreshing for those of you sick of reading same-old acknowledgements sections. And it would sure make those street dancers feel good.

Or I could include in this acknowledgements section those people who are not recommending my book but who are instead simply acknowledging I exist. Someone would do that for me. I'm sure of it. Right? Wouldn't they?

"Josh Rolph exists."

That's a terrible idea.

Excuse me while I brainstorm options for my very first acknowledgements section.

Here's the bottom line: The reason no one I know will want to be acknowledged in this section is because all my family and friends are really straight up people. They acknowledge me now, as a family member or friend, but they might stop acknowledging me altogether once they learn I've published a book with an absurdist title full of what they deem to be ridiculous content.

I'm preparing for the worst.

In order to keep the peace with those humans I love most, it may be best to save acknowledgements for future book efforts more worthy of acknowledging. Once I can say I'm an author, I'm planning to go all in by kicking out books on a wide variety of topics.

That is, if I ever get around to writing them. This one is taking me forever.

You see, this has to be my first book. The idea for this book infected my brain to the point that if I never followed through, I would have never written anything else. I've been laser focused on writing this except for when I haven't been, which has been when I was doing other things. Like, I'm totally into eating and sleeping. Typing while eating is challenging for me, if not impossible. I've even tried writing while sleeping. Not intentionally, but I can't say I haven't dozed off at least a hundred times while writing.

All of these are just excuses. Every author sleeps, eats, and has other things going on in their life.

But not every author has so many worthy distractions from writing. I don't say these to brag, they are simply a matter of fact. I am a married father of four young kids, I have had a pretty demanding day job with lots of travel and not a free minute to spare. There's community work – I even unsuccessfully ran for city council, then keeping up with my podcast, or the tons of time thinking about keeping up with my podcast, trying to landscape my incredibly incomplete yard, writing music, and all the other stuff I do that is making you not feel sorry for me one bit.

I know you don't care. You want to read. So I shouldn't get in the way of your reading.

Since I mentioned my family, here is a special word of appreciation and acknowledgment to my young children who didn't really sacrifice anything to get this book written and who, in fact, made it incredibly difficult for me to find time to write this book. I adore them. I so adore those little, beautiful creatures. However, I can't legitimately say, "Thanks, kids, for putting up with me while I wrote this book," because they were asleep while I wrote most of the words in this tome. But I'm sure they will wear this book as a badge of honor before full-fledged teenage life kicks in, on such a day when they no longer proudly say, "Now I can say Dad's an author." Then, possibly, for the rest of their lives, will begin wrestling with the fact that their father dreamed of becoming an author and the best he could do was this book. There are worse legacies to leave to your children, but not too many more.

Speaking of legacy, I think I want to become an author simply because I grew up saying my Dad is an author. Where this book is attempting to get a laugh – as in, if I get one laugh in the entire book, I will be absolutely thrilled (see chapter two's discussion on the monetary value of a laugh) – my Dad's first book was seeking a completely different kind of reaction from readers, a reaction falling perhaps directly opposite of laughter.

His first book is called *To Shoot, Burn, and Hang*.[5] If you laugh after reading the title then you are definitely more sick than I thought.

Dad's book is not a novel with a lot of guns, fire, and rope.

It is a work of nonfiction.

Yes, that's right. It's a work of nonfiction. He writes about real-life events of shooting, burning and hanging. All of that shooting, burning, and hanging in his book not only really occurred, but it all took place by and around my very own ancestors. As you can see by the title, we have quite the family legacy. Why would I want to mess with that legacy in my own book called, "Now I Can Say I'm an Author?"

Can you imagine my book sitting next to his on the bookshelf? They don't match; they don't seem to go together. You wouldn't know they were written by members of the same family.

Even though his first book and my first are complete opposites,

––––––––––––

5 *To Shoot, Burn, and Hang: Folk-history from a Kentucky Mountain Family and Community*, by Daniel N. Rolph, University Tennessee Press, 1994.

in that the subject matter in his is quite serious, and mine, a mess, it was his book that planted a seed that perhaps book writing is in my DNA. When I realized this, I actually considered giving a name to this book reflecting Dad's hard-to-beat book title of *To Shoot, Burn, and Hang.* I considered giving my book a title reaching for a word antonymizing[6] his:

- *To Backfire, Douse, and Unfasten*

or

- *To Be Kind, Generous, and Loving*

Both titles would give my book vastly different objectives, so I had now given myself a choice neatly fitting the "opposite-of-his" title criteria I established. It was evident I was making meaningful progress toward authorhood.

Ruminating upon those titles, I wasn't crazy about even one of them, which led to me brainstorming some more.

A quasi-rhyming book title idea came to mind one day while relaxing in the tub:

- *To Bathe, Change, then Shave*

A slight variation resulted in:

- *To Spend, Save, or Raise Range-Free Goats?*

My personal alliteration favorite:

---

6 Fake word alert!

- *To Skate, Skid, and Ski: While Skipping to Ska*

And there were so many more, which prompted an idea one night to name the book:

- *And There Were So Many More: Which Prompted an Idea One Night to Name the Book AND THERE WERE SO MANY MORE*

I acknowledge my Dad's book in my own book because his was and is an inspiration, just as he is an inspiration. I saw what he was going through when he wrote the book. Without divulging too much about him, just know what he did was extraordinary.

I'll just say this about him: where I do a fair amount of eating and sleeping which distracts me from book writing, Dad was dealing with health problems restricting his eating and severely limiting his sleep. Where I am a married father of four, he wrote a book as a married father of five. Where I have a pretty demanding day job, he had a longer commute, a full-time job, and taught nights at several colleges. While I do some community work, he did more. As I try to keep up with my podcast with editing tools galore, Dad was on the radio broadcasting before a live audience. I try to take time landscaping my yard, Dad did absolutely nothing in our yard growing up. That's the only place I have an edge.

But he has published books to show for it.

I wish I was just like my Dad. And that's the truth. But I do more than merely acknowledge Dad. I'm so indebted to him. Forget all the book writing, he's an amazing man with an incredible mind.

As I contemplate the word "acknowledgement" even more, I wonder who really wants to be acknowledged, anyway? Acknowledging someone is the lowest human-to-human form of recognition that exists. To be acknowledged is the equivalent of the eye-contact-then-head-nod obligatorily given on the street to a passerby.

This section could instead be called "Recognition." The word "recognition" is so much more generous. "I'm RECOGNIZING you." As in, "Bob, I look at your face and I recognize it. I know your name when I see your face. I recognize you, Bob. I give you recognition for being Bob. And a Bob you most certainly are. And you should absolutely find a mirror, immediately, to trim your nose hairs a bit because I'm starting to get grossed out while in the act of recognizing you."

Acknowledging is much worse than recognizing. In fact, acknowledgement is only one step better than completely ignoring someone. On the ignoring-to-adoring spectrum, acknowledging falls almost all the way down toward ignoring than to adoring.

"Bob, I acknowledge your existence. And that's about it."

A recognition section would be far more meaningful to those recognized than to those acknowledged.

I refuse to write a recognition section, though, because to honor the great tradition of authorhood I want to write a….

FOREWORD!

"Josh Rolph asked me to write a foreword to this book. Not only have I never heard of Josh Rolph but I have absolutely no interest in reading his book."

–Anonymous

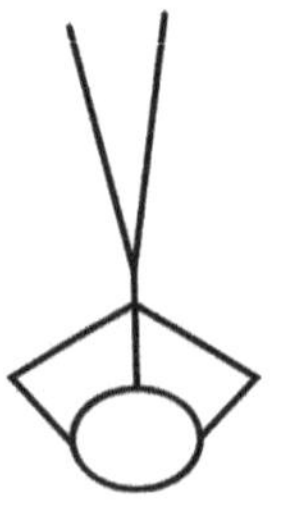

RANT

Once. That's the correct number of times you tap the spacebar after a period in a sentence. Once. Not twice, but once. It used to be twice on a typewriter before computers took over. Now it's just once. Once.

Once.

Once is not spelled right. Once should be spelled "wuntz." Where the spelling of "once" came from, I will never know. If I had my way, once would be pronounced "ohntz," closer to, but not exactly like pronunciation of the word "ounce."

Ounce.

Ounce, once's 1st cousin, is kind of spelled right.

And then there's wuntz's first cousin once removed, or the word "One."

One.

"One" should really be pronounced "own."

Own.

Everyone wants to own things. But why own when you can rent?

Rent.

Rant.

PREFACE
The Limitations of Book Writing

My first rule of book writing:
start with a preface before you have any idea
how to fill the pages of the book.

■ ■ ■

an October 21 long ago

■ ■ ■

Let me preface this by saying "preface" is the strangest word. A preface is usually included in the worst kind of horribly written books. I've heard people say, "To preface my remarks," which is a phrase almost never used in everyday speech, and most especially when someone is talking to you one-on-one in casual conversation. Instead, the word is almost always heard at the beginning of a formal speech, as in, the kind given in front of a crowd, like before an academic body. Using "preface" in spoken interpersonal communications is very rare.

To get more scientific about this, of all the uses of the word "preface," only 0.09% of the time is it used in interpersonal, face-to-face casual communications, while it's used 13.4% in formal speeches and the rest of the time as a book section.[7] For the most part, a preface is limited to the book section and only to the book section, though not in all books, only some books. And of those books only some of those, not the sum of some of the books, with the addition of some of the books, include a preface.

The word preface is strange because when you break apart the word it is made up of the words "pre" and "face." Those two words, or the prefix "pre-" combined with the word "face" don't seem to have a thing to do with book writing. Pre-face, for example, I was a zygote. Pre-Facebook I was much more productive. Then there's Pref-Ace, which I won't even get into right now.[8]

Before jumping straight into the preface, it's important to note my refusal to write a book with a title beginning with the word "The." I'm okay with beginning band names or songs with "The" or my podcast with "The" or episode titles with "The." I'm obviously fine with the subtitle to my preface beginning with "The." I'm absolutely not okay with this book beginning with "The." Books like *The Great Gatsby* and *The Bible* can get away with it. I'm not so out of touch to think I can pull off what was done by F. Scott Fitzgerald and God.

Beginning the book with "Now" is solid. There probably isn't a better way to begin a book than with the word "Now," especially starting one's first book with the word "Now." Sometimes I even wish my name was "Now."

"Now I Can Say I'm an Author," by Now.

Would be so great if my middle name was "Ican" and last name was "Sayamenawther."

I could do what Samuel Clemens did and go by another name, which seems to defeat the whole purpose. Imagine Sam going through life only being admired as a "Mark." I'm too tied to the name of my

---

7 Completely fictional percentages. Am counting on 100% of readers ignoring footnotes, as I do when reading.
8 It was tough to choose between using "Pref-Ace" or "Prefa-Ce."

birth than to switch my name to "Mark Twain," and too proud to give "Now" all the credit.

■ ■ ■

TWO MINUTES OR SO LATER

■ ■ ■

Creating a Relationship with Your Reader, a.k.a. You

Without a doubt, there is some kind of real, though intangible, connection that binds a book to a reader. It is never discussed among polite society but it's as real a relationship as can be, in a certain sense. If the book does its job, the reader and the book become inseparable. The book is the book, of course, but the book is also a very human creation. That human author creator is therefore the one with whom the reader, like it or not, is actually developing an intangible relationship.

For this reason, I wonder if there has ever been an author out there who, within the book's pages, offered to become friends with the reader. By "friends" I don't mean the type of friend like the 75% of those you might find as your friend on Facebook.[9] I'm talking about whether there are authors attempting to become good friends with the reader in the actual book, as early on as in the book's preface. I haven't come across a book where the author tries to become my friend, either directly through themselves or indirectly through a character. If not, I offer the idea of book-reader friendship as a theoretical idea that could have some passing short-term benefits as the book is enjoyed. Long term benefits could be enjoyed by those readers who can't let the book go, and who are, perhaps, clinically insane. In any case, a budding friendship could be established as an insurance policy for the author. If the book isn't any good, then at least the reader and author would walk away as super good friends. Friendship also means an ample amount of

---

9 No offense to 75% of my Facebook friends.

guilt for the reader if they didn't finish their friend's book, so here is a built-in incentive for finishing a book. How many books haven't been finished? Book friendship could be the cure all to unfinished books.

What if an author called you a "good friend" early in their book? I'm not saying this is what I want to do. I'm not saying I want to call you a "good friend." Don't worry, I'm not planning to call you a "good friend" in quotes, as in, "Yeah everybody, meet my 'good friend' who is 'reading' my book, my 'goooood frieeeend,' wink-wink, if you know what I mean! Heh heh" [followed by maniacal laughter].

I realize we are not likely to become good friends in this exercise of me writing and you reading. I mean, we just met. We're at the stage where it's all on me except for the part falling squarely upon you. For one, I want to be careful not to offend you, lest I ruin it all and you storm off, never reading this book again, putting an end to our once prosperous potential friendship that began and ended in a couple paragraphs.

I also don't want to make this awkward. Since I am not aware of authors befriending readers in any part of a book, including the preface of a book, I should drop the theoretical friendship idea altogether. But it is a very true statement that we have invested some time into one another. I, in writing to you. And you? Do you think you haven't invested any time into this book, even the kind of time that might lead to some kind of connection to this very book?

Put it this way: You have so far invested more time reading this book than most people spend in two lifetimes watching C-SPAN. And I want to be careful not to offend C-SPAN, because I love what they do. If you haven't skimmed the book too quickly, you've spent more seconds reading this book than there are numbers in your shoe size. And I want to be clear: that wasn't an insult - I don't care what your shoe size is but I'm sure it's over zero, assuming you have feet. And that wasn't an insult to those with no feet. Diabetes is a growing problem. And I'm not insulting diabetics and definitely not pre-diabetics nor am

I insulting those of you who are paranoid about becoming diabetic but continue to binge on HFCS foods anyway. What I'm trying to say is I am honored by the fact you are choosing to spend more than zero seconds reading these words. You really have no idea. Thank you.

Before I get too carried away with how you spend your time eating sugary foods or before I begin wasting my time with a math problem aiming to determine the ratio of minutes you have spent reading this book to the minutes you've spent being alive, I've barely started to write this book (every author knows the preface doesn't count as a credible part of your book[10]) and I'm going from having a great idea to a bad idea in only two paragraphs. My ideas are so all over the place.

Ideas...

Ideas are the main reason I haven't yet written a book. I keep getting interrupted by them. I wish I could only have one idea to write one book and not have any additional ideas. Like the idea I had this morning to check Facebook. Then Twitter. Then Facebook. Then the news. Then to eat. Then to eat some more. Then chips. Oh, how I love chips. Oh, how I love every corn product. Popcorn. I have to write about popcorn in this book, instead of getting up and popping it like I want to...

and just did.

Then I keep sitting here, staring at nothing in particular. Then staring at my phone not sure what to do next. Then walking to the couch. Then sitting on it. Then turning on the TV. Then about to forget the next two and a half hours as I watch TV. Then checking the news, Facebook, Twitter, sleeping, Facebook, Instagram, corn, news, Twitter, and so on.

Okay, I'll restart from the beginning (of this preface, the part that doesn't count, that you probably aren't reading, the purpose which must be solely to add pages to a book someone deems not long enough). And

---

10   I wonder if a book's word count includes the words written before chapter one. I'm sort of counting on this part counting.

I'm not going to second-guess myself. I'm going to start the book the same way I intended to start the book a minute ago. I should go with the author's original intent, because that is always superior. In this case, said author is me. And I'm going to go with my own intent, because if I go with anyone else's intent it would zap all my author energies and I would never even come close to finishing the book. So here I go.

After coming up with the idea for this book —

I can't exactly say it was an idea for an *entire* book.[11] Well, it was an idea for a book but it wasn't enough of an idea to fill a book that would otherwise appear complete. Most ideas aren't completed books. If an idea for a book is a complete book then wow, you have one heck of a well-thought out idea. We know from life experience, however, our ideas don't arrive so fleshed out. Dickens didn't one day say, "I have an idea for a book called *A Tale of Two Cities* that begins with 'It was the best of times, it was the worst of times…'" and then had in mind all the characters, words, etc. that flowed from his mind to paper straight to the publisher. Books are first ideas and then plenty of ink is spilled along the way filling in all the cracks of the idea, turning it into a book.

This is an important realization for me. I don't have anywhere near the amount of material needed to fill a book with this idea.

It's more accurate to say that this book began with an idea for a book title, not for a complete book with lots of words after said title.

So what happened next, you might wonder? Will you keep asking me questions like that throughout the book? That is, if I happen to come up with an idea that fills an actual book and not an idea for a mere book title? That would be helpful because I would know you are interested. It's one thing writing words into the ether. It's quite another writing words that are sent to imaginary people who are interested in this book. Don't worry, I'm not calling you imaginary. But imagining the real you is one thing that will make me feel like writing more, not

---

11   Please tell me if I'm annoying you.

to get all creepy on you. Every author does it, they just don't say it because the self-aware book isn't appropriate most of the time. I'm obviously determining that it's allowed now. And don't worry, I'm not really imagining you. That's sick and wrong. What I'm honestly thinking about is your money that purchased this book and is subsequently shared with my bank account.

There's nothing like a question from a loyal, imaginary reader who is real.

What's missing in books these days is reader questions. We need so many more of them, and by "we" I mean those of us trying-to-be-author types.

After conceiving of the idea for the book title, I resisted writing this book for about five full minutes or a minute or two less than that. The five minutes (or less) of resistance to writing a book with only a name came because of the name itself. I wondered who would read a book titled "Now I Can Say I'm an Author." I knew at least one person would read it – me – but who else? I am not a known name and I don't have a following. I'm just a regular guy who has an interest in dropping the "author" credential at convenient times, like at the grocery store when I need to get ahead of someone in line:

"Excuse me, young mother with screaming children, do you mind if I get in front of you? As an author, a book idea just came to me and I need to get home really fast to write it down."

Sigh.

I could even use it while napping during my day job (assuming I'm like most authors and still need full time employment to pay the bills).

"Right, boss," wiping the drool from my cheek, "I'll be right there."

You see, I could get away with napping on the job because…

I would be an author.

An author! An author! I would be an author. I can't wait for the day I can say, "I'm an author." I can't wait for the day I can say, "Now I can say I'm an author."

Authors don't get fired. Authors get all kinds of perks. Authors stand out from the crowd.

Authors are like royalty in our society, which is funny, because most make hardly any in royalties, as in, next to nothing, which will not be funny to me when I'm an author. Yet take all the empty bank accounts out of the mix, as well as the many book signings at small venues I travel to at my own personal expense where no one shows up – wipe away the unnecessary stress and anxiety of desperate measures like following 50,000 people on Twitter hoping at least some of them follow me back so I can get over 1,000 followers to make everyone think I have somewhat of a following, and all the other things I try, think about, and don't try, leaving me with the author credential alone, and I will at least have this: I will be an expert at something. Becoming an author will make me someone to be trusted. Admired. Becoming an author will be an accomplishment like no other.

Just like becoming a mother, once an author, always an author.

Just like the day I became human, once an author, always an author, not to mention still a human.

The author credential can only be taken away if it's proved that you plagiarized. And believe me, the only thing plagiarized in this book is chapters four through twenty-one.

But when thinking about all the many things I won't have after becoming an author – the lack of money, the time away from home doing valueless book signings, the anxiety and depression from not reaching the level of fame these hours and hours of attempted authorship failed to deliver, and oh so much more I cannot yet imagine – it becomes obvious that a complete attitude shift is in order. Nay, an attitude shift is absolutely necessary.

So in making a necessary attitude shift, let's do myself a favor by skipping over the part about lack-of-money, because I don't know how to make that attitude shift.

I also know how to make an attitude shift about book signings. In a digital age, who needs book signings anyway?

Things haven't changed all that much, though. The digital age does set us apart from the previous non-digital age, although selling books still requires ol' fashioned word-of-mouth – friends telling friends to read a book. It still requires people talking. It still requires meeting prospective customers. And that's where book signings come in. Just as the musician performs at coffee houses before launching from obscurity to stardom and just as the comedian plays to small, drunk crowds after midnight long before filming their first Netflix special, the author must go to local bookstores for book signings before reaching author fame and fortune.

I can do the local bookstore signing. I am capable of attending the local bookstore signing. I am made for the local bookstore signing. I will convince myself that I can do the bookstore signing whether I can do the bookstore signing or not.

One thing is for sure: I will already be an author once I do the bookstore signing, which will make the ordeal much easier. Heading to my own book signing this afternoon would be a little difficult. My book isn't quite finished. Unless I tried for a Preface signing. But let's be real: I am not yet an author at the point in time that I type these words. I can't cheat the system. Still have a little ways to go. My book hasn't yet reached "product" status. It's in the beta — possibly alpha stage. It isn't even a prototype. It is now more than an idea, but not an accomplishment. There is still so much more to do to finally become an author.

My first book signing – what will it be like? Let's say I have a book signing in a couple hours. Woah, the anxiety is kicking in already! What will I wear? Standard author attire? That brown tweed jacket with the dark elbow patches? Funky glasses even though I have perfect vision? Should I shave or grow out the shadow for a few days? Wear a musky cologne? Smoke a pipe?

I have no idea.

Get hair plugs?

Absolutely.

How should I act? Cool and calm or chatty and excited? Do I shake their hands? Am I assuming more than one shows up? What if only one person shows up? What if two people show up and they don't wash their hands, and I, unknowingly, shake hands with the E. coli infested book signing groupie, and then I touch my pen to sign, therefore contaminating my pen? Heaven help me, what if I touch my pen to my lips? And what kind of pen do I use, anyway? Do I go with the standard 0.6mm nib or do I go broad? Do I sit the whole time or stand on occasion? Like, when they approach, do I stand to shake hands? Do I pull up a chair for them to sit? Does standing to shake hands make everyone feel like a dignitary? How can I make everyone feel dignified? What if a dignitary shows up? Do I ask them to sign my book? How long are book signings? One hour? Two? When will I have overstayed? What do I write in their book? Do they pay for it before I sign, or after? Do I leave a tip jar? Do I give a speech at the beginning of the signing? At the end? Should I have someone introduce me? Will I need a microphone? Do I prepare a script of things to say that make me look really author-like? What do I say to the passerby who asks what the book is about? What's my elevator pitch? What if they find out I'm just a fraud? That I plagiarized chapters four through twenty-one? Do I mention my podcast and/or my blog? Am I always turned on, always marketing, always selling? Do I tell them about future book ideas? Do I charge cover price or give a little discount? Or is there a surcharge for an autograph? How much is too much? How often do I ask whether they already paid for the book? How salesy do I get? If they look wealthy, do I ask them to throw some extra cash into the tip jar? Does the bookstore ask for money to host my book signing? What is the resale value of a signed book? Of my signed book? Who sets up my table and chair? Do I put up a sign saying who I am and what the book is about? Where does the sign go? Is there one for the table and another for the entrance? Who sets the whole thing up? Do I have to do that? Does it hurt me that I don't have my own Wikipedia page? Where do I park? What if I have to use the men's room? What if they don't have a men's room and, well, you know? How do I wrap up the whole thing? Do I invite the press? Would reporters, bloggers, or podcasters show up for a book signing? Could I have the book signing filmed as a documentary or better yet, a reality series on book signings? When was the first book signing? I mean, in history? Why do people like book signings? How many questions in a paragraph is too many questions? Maybe as many as I've already asked? Plus one? And another? [Rude belch]?

We hear about Olympiad preparation for Olympianing. She memorizes her routine. She plays it over and over in her mind, we're told. She reviews the course, the run, the jump, the catapult, the throw. This doesn't help the table tennis player much, but it helps most everyone else. All I am trying to do is mimic the best athletes of our day. I am imagining the book signing, because if I can do it right, I can sell so many books.

I think.

Book signings. Book signings! Oh, how I look forward to those book signings. A chance for me to sit at a table with copies of the fruit of my hands – or is it the fruit of my brains? After laboring for so long to write it, the book will feel like the fruit of my loins.[12] My progeny. My posterity. My love.

My book, sitting on the table, waiting to be signed. Me, looking around the bookstore, laughing inside loudly that each of the authors represented by each book in each aisle is not there with me, sharing the spotlight. This is my day. The day when only one author gets all the attention, honor, and praise.

All that is important now is that at the end of this exercise, I will be

---

12 The mother of my children doesn't appreciate this joke.

expert at authoring. Because it only takes once to become an expert author. You write a book, you're done trying to become one. No need to write anything more. Once you achieve authorhood, you could write and publish an infinite number of books and yet maintain the same title as author. This is the essence of authoring. And not simply mere authoring of some simple authoring accomplishment. Not authoring an article, post, tweet, email, or blog. Authoring a book, no less. I will be a trusted and admired book author expert. Most people can write an email, some write a post, fewer a tweet, fewer still a blog post, even fewer an article. The fewest possible write a book. Since this book is about becoming an author, I will be an expert author author. Said with the highest number of the word "authors" in a row, it's no stretch to state I will be an expert authoring author authoring author, author, if that makes sense. It does to me. And since it does to me, and I'm typing furiously to become an author as quickly as I can, then it doesn't matter what you think because I'm almost an author. Or at least, I will be as soon as I can keep on typing until I have something that seems to be book length.

When I started this book, I began with these words:

"Now I Can Say I'm an Author"

[Insert more words.]

What I wrote above, in bold, are the first words I wrote after coming up with the title of this book.

So to recap, I began with:

"Now I Can Say I'm an Author."

Then I wrote:

[Insert more words.]

It looked exactly like this (reproduced with permission from my brain):

"Now I Can Say I'm an Author"

[Insert more words.]

Woah.
Woah.
This is...do you see what just happened?
I just wrote and wrote and wrote and wrote. It's incredible. I'm only in the preface and suddenly - I'm writing. I'm repeating what I'm writing, but who cares. The point is, I think I can do this. I can write. I can at least write half of a preface, assuming I have another half to go. But maybe that will give me exactly enough confidence to write an introduction. And then chapter one. And then two. After chapter two, how many more chapters should I write? So much to decide.

■ ■ ■

We can now agree that the author credential is amazingly great.

The only thing that has diminished the author credential by a notch or two is the advent of self-publishing. So many more can be authors today than in times before the self-publishing era took off circa 1999.[13] But still, so very few are authors, as we have established.

I just thought of another way I could drop the author credential.

"Excuse me, sir, I noticed you are reading a magazine. Thought I would just mention that I wrote an entire book."

No, the preface isn't over. There's more. I'm sorry to make you skip down a few empty lines. As you skipped them, I've been daydreaming about becoming an author.

The question then becomes, which publisher do I choose? I could make up one called Random Mouse that would sound like the mega-publisher Random House.

"An author? Seriously?"

Most people won't believe I'm actually being serious.

"Who is your publisher?"

"You know, it was no big deal. I'm published through Random Mouse," I'll answer, unseriously. Say "Random Mouse" aloud and you will find it is virtually interchangeable with the much more prestigious, not to mention real, Random House book publisher.

"Oh my gosh, Random House? I've heard of them! That's amazing!"

"Hey, yeah, I'm blessed," I'll answer, generally speaking. "I'd love to catch up but gotta run."

■ ■ ■

"Hey Josh, I heard you wrote a book. Who is your publisher?"

"Hewton Mefflen."

---

13 Full disclosure: I have no idea what I'm talking about.

"Woah, no joke? Incredible! You probably got a huge advance! You'll be in every classroom in America! Except for Texas."

"You know, it's all relative. It's all about the children." And then I'd begin to sing Whitney Houston's 80's ballad "I believe the children are the future..." I do a spot-on Whitney Houston that only sounds a little like an untalented male baritone wannabe author.

■ ■ ■

And then there's the simple fact that authors are COOL. That is not an acronym, that is cool with intentional all-caps emphasis. Authors are so cool, to me. And to you. If authors weren't so cool, you probably wouldn't be reading this book, would you? It doesn't matter what an author has written so much as they are authors. Sure, there is a difference between an author of trashy romance novels and the author of textbooks, between the author of x for dummies and a children's book. Between heavily researched tomes and carefully worded novels. Between every book ever written and this one. But still, you might as well lump them all together because they are authors, just as doctors can be either surgeons or professors. A doctor is a doctor in the same way an author is an author. You know the distinction, though. A doctor isn't nearly as cool as an author, but still slightly cool. Now chiropractors, on the other hand...

Doctors who are authors are the coolest, but I won't dwell on that subject because I am not a doctor and don't want to get myself depressed that I never pursued a Ph.D., M.D., D.D.S., or Chiropercificate.

Chiropractors: I love you all. Thank you for purchasing my book.

I compiled a number of theories as to why the author is so darned cool.

1. They know how to get something done.
2. They built something that didn't exist before.

3. There is evidence that they aren't as weird as their family thinks they are.
   a. If their family still thinks the author is weird, the author is now a money-making weirdo, which is much better than the alternative for both author and family.
4. Self-publishing doesn't apply to any of these rules.
5. Authors sound smarter than everyone else when they talk, especially when talking about how they are an author.
6. Published authors may have more brain cells than non-published authors like me, right now. No offense to you, the reader.
7. Authors no longer have to take out the trash on Monday nights like I do, right now.
8. Authors no longer snore like I will, about a minute after head hits pillow tonight, as is reported by fellow residents.
9. Authors become the life of the party wherever they go, and they also experience what it's like to actually get invited to parties.
10. Authors who had no charisma before becoming authors suddenly develop charisma and charm and people start to like them.
11. Authors who weren't attractive before coming authors become really attractive.
12. Partners of authors stop complaining about their companion's snoring.
13. Authors who are balding are able to afford hair plugs. And I just want them in the back, mostly. And the top, generally. And fill in the temples while you're at it.

Anyway, I wrestled with myself for those two minutes over whether I should create this "Now I Can Say I'm an Author"[14] book and came to the realization that the book must be written, if not for me, then for

---

14 *Now I Can Say I'm an Author*, by Josh Rolph, published by someone at some future time.

you. That's really why books are written, isn't it? If I say the book is for you and not for me, then it's got added appeal. It convinces the reader the author has their best interest in mind. Even if it's wildly untrue.

Books aren't perfect, though. They are full of words. Why can't they be full of other things? Like Hershey's beloved Milk Duds?[15] That was a key thought as I begin to think of what the book would actually say. I couldn't imagine spending countless hours typing. I wanted to do something else that would fill the pages.

That was exactly when "Pictures!" came to me, just like that. "Pictures!" I thought.

Then I thought again.

No, I can't use pictures without seeking permission, paying royalties a.k.a.[16] money, and as it is, I'm not sure what kind of pictures to include in a book about becoming an author. I could take pictures of myself in the process of writing the book. Pictures could include the typical writing scene: at the computer eating, watching trailers and then movies, and googling the random questions that pop in my head every other paragraph (or less). Also, the naps. The many involuntary naps. Hard to snap a photo of a nap while napping. So much work, anyway. I really, fundamentally, don't want to distract from the words. Pictures and video and the web are so distracting from pure, undefiled words.

Modern technology can provide additional ways and means to fill a book. The eBook can now include audio and video. The only problem is this kind of "interactive" book with added links and videos and images hasn't exactly taken off, and you still have the same copyright dilemma as before.

---

15   Unendorsed product placement.

16   I've used "a.k.a." twice now in the book, which is the max quota for "a.k.a." not counting this footnote reference to "a.k.a." or that one. So now I've used "a.k.a." four times unless you add this sentence in which case I've used "a.k.a." five times – or is it six now? Six uses of "a.k.a." now seven! In ancient times, seven meant completion. Okay, seven should do it.

Is there something more that can be added that would improve the appeal of the book? Am I stuck with mere words to convey what I want to say?

The answer, unfortunately, is yes.

Not to get too philosophical with you, but I've tried to make this book bigger than it actually is. I wanted to fill this book with something more than words. Something bigger than words. Something new...

and fresh...

and different.

After all, this was the book that would allow me to say, for the first time in my life, "I'm an author." I had to distinguish myself somehow from all the others.[17]

Have I mentioned that authors are smart? I recall claiming earlier that authors have more brain cells than non-authors. That can't entirely be true. I mean, all authors can't all, unanimously and in totality be smart, even though it has long been held to be the case. I hold out the possibility that there are authors who are rather dumb, and I could be dumbest of them all.

There was a time not more than four centuries ago when authors believed they were of higher intellect than basically everyone else. In the late 17th century, famed *Robinson Crusoe*[18] author Daniel Defoe proposed in another book of his called *An Essay Upon Projects* that there be hospitals for the housing of those who were born with "health and

---

17 The problem is, after reading through another draft of the current book you are reading right now, I realized that all I have done is written something that could have been written by regular ol' me, not ol' potential author-me. It's sad, really. I had ambitious plans for this book. I thought it would carry me somewhere beyond where I already was, but nothing magical happened. I just typed stuff and then I stopped and now I'm still here, only older.

18 Do I footnote a timeless classic? I really have no idea what the rules are on this sort of thing.

strength, but deprived of reason to act for themselves." His proposed tax to pay for the hospital would come from "those who have a portion of understanding extraordinary," which tax "might be very easily raised by a tax upon learning, to be paid by the authors of books." Creation of "institutions to house the mentally retarded paid for by a tax on authors because they happen to gain a greater share of intelligence at birth just as the retarded happen to get less."[19] No, I do not endorse Defoe's take on the mentally disabled, but I do find it extraordinary that he felt authors could alone fund such an institution. I only mention his writing because the idea of higher intelligence in authors goes back a long time, but I would not go so far as to claim that authors are of a superior intelligence. I said previously that authors *may have* extra brain cells. By "extra brain cells" I'm not sure what I mean. The key here is it is all my perception. All I know is what I have long held and perceived, which is that most authors *appear* to carry an intelligence far and above my own. What I'm unsure of is whether I, for myself, will attain a higher level of intelligence when I become an author. I guess I'll have to wait until then to find out.

So back to the title of the book. Shortly after I had the idea to call it "Now I Can Say I'm an Author," I began to toy around with other, perhaps better, title ideas. I stewed over naming the book, "Now I Can Say I'm Published." But people who say they are published are usually scientists or researchers. They get published in journals or magazines or newspaper editorial pages. It was about that time that I started getting weighed down by the whole title thing. I also thought of calling it:

- "A Mess of Words"
- "Now I'm an Author"
- "I'm an Author Now"
- "I Can Say I'm an Author, Now"

---

19 *An Essay Upon Projects*, by Daniel Defoe, 1697, edited by Henry Morley, The Project Gutenberg eBook.

- "Yippee-aye-ay!"

Other variations were teed up, vetted, and vigorously poll tested. At the end of the day, I kept coming back to the original title idea.

I settled on the title "Now I Can Say I'm an Author" because it looked and sounded right. It was a purely emotional decision. My brain was hardly used in the decision-making process at all. Being an author is somewhat different than *being published*. The way it's interpreted by the lay listener is an author is someone who wrote more words than one who is published. I'm not saying that's true, only that that's the perception among people who are, well, exactly like me and named Josh Rolph.

I wanted these people to know I wrote more words than that Harvard Business Journal published guy over there who may not, in all actuality,[20] be over there at all. To me, writing a book versus writing an article is the equivalent of the marathon versus the 5K. I was in this for the long haul. I was going to run the marathon.[21]

As I became comfortable with the fact that I would someday write the book "Now I Can Say I'm an Author," I began to feel less interested, because it's more or less easy to become an author of one book. What about an author of two books? Three?

That's when I came upon the additional idea to run not just a marathon, but an ultra. I was going to write a multi-volume series. Volume one would be this book. Volume two would be another book. Writing only two volumes is lame, I thought, so I should write three, because three is harmony. Both additional volumes will be exactly the same as this one.

I would love to share with you the titles of the second and third

---

20 I'm trying so hard not to use the word "actually" that I'm stuck using its word relatives. "Actually" is a word that, like "literally" and "dudemeister" permeates my everyday speech. I never actually say, "dudemeister." Literally.
21 A race I have never run in real life so I have no reason using this analogy.

books or volumes but I would rather hold that close for now. Just know they are "amazing" in the modern sense of the word. As in, "That movie was amazing, even though I slept through most of it."

Not that you care. But you should. Because I need to be taken more seriously than I was back in my pre-author days. I don't know if I will be more important than I was in pre-author days. I don't know if I will be more cool than I was in pre-author days.

At the very least, my hope is that by the time you are reading this:

Now I can say I'm an author.

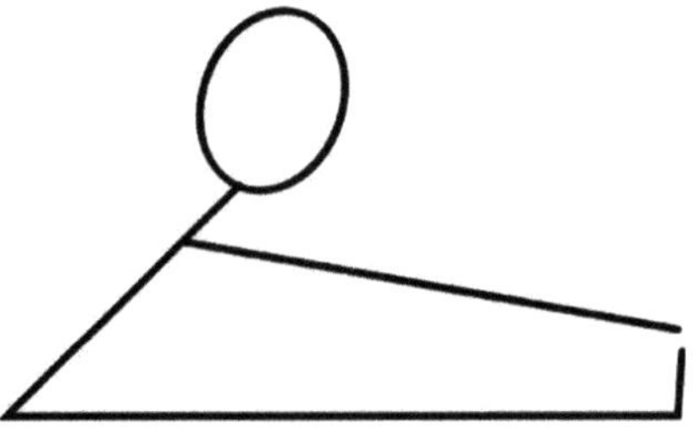

INTRODUCTION
The Introduction to My First Book
(Needs No Introduction)

The second rule of book writing is to start making lots of rules about book writing. (For the first rule, see the preface to the Preface.)

■ ■ ■

Three days later
October 24

■ ■ ■

True, this book needs no introduction, but I'll write one anyway because I would hate to move on to chapter one without taking a stab at writing an introduction to my first book.

Like the preface, and like most published book sections found before chapter one, most people skip past the introduction. Why is that? I would wager there's usually nothing of substance there in the introduction. I say "there in the introduction" because that's how the reader would see it. They would see the introduction as over "there." This introduction, the one you are beginning to read right now, is very much "here" from my current typing-away perspective, and from your own.

I'm not giving you an introduction here like authors such as them do, there. I'm giving you the kind of introduction here you should be getting there. Am I being repetitive? Hey, if I'm ever repetitive in this book, give me a polite nudge, okay?[22]

On the question as to why most people skip a book's introduction, it all begins in middle school.

During the time of early adolescence, children are exposed to books that are more challenging than their predecessors. It's no longer *Bob Books*[23] or Scholastic Awards[24] winners. We're talking the level of reading all of us adults are accustomed to in the news and in daily conversation. At this stage of reading, the vocabulary within sixth, seventh, and eighth grade reading levels is more expansive, the prose more descriptive and freer flowing. It is at about this time that readers are introduced to the introduction.

At first, children see the introduction as an essential part of the book, or as essential as the words and pictures that follow. There the introduction is, filled with words, the same as the rest of the book. But like the words on a title page, the astute young reader soon learns that the introductory words are in a separate category than those found in the first chapter. In middle school, the student finds that the teacher never quizzes on the introduction. Information in the introduction is generally supplemental to what is contained in the book, and youth aren't interested in supplements. They want the facts that will give them what they need to pass the test so they can get back to having fun.

Which is to say that the introduction is useless. It's unnecessary. It doesn't fit. It has no place. It is more for the author than for you. The introduction should have never existed.

Take the fictional work: the introduction serves as a preliminary guide to the story that proves to be supremely irrelevant to the actual

---

22   See Epilogue on a couple of ways to "nudge" or reach me.
23   *Bob Books: Set 1*, by Bobby Lynn Maslen and John R. Maslen, Scholastic Publishing, May 1, 2006.
24   https://artandwriting.org

story; in some cases even ruining the story by offering up too much detail at the beginning, or serving as a disjointed element we would do okay without. In nonfiction, introductions provide background or historical information more commonly found in future editions of the same book. Again, why not insert these items into the book's chapters?

Truth be told, successful films don't have introductions. Commercials don't have introductions. There is no introduction in a newspaper or news article and introductions aren't preceded by introductions. Readers don't need introductions. They don't want introductions. Since middle school, you, yourself have ignored, avoided, brushed aside, and disregarded the book introduction. If you are reading this introduction you are incredibly unique and should probably get checked in somewhere, if you know what I mean.

Now, friends, let me cover an important topic before I get too far along in the introduction. And I won't call you "friends" anymore. It doesn't feel right. That was a mistake. Also saying you should get checked in didn't help my cause. I'm sure these are the first of many mistakes I'll make until I'm an author, when I attain earthly perfection. I thought I would use the term from time to time in a bid to draw you into the book a little further by making you feel more comfortable. While the tactic may have worked decades and centuries ago, there is possibly some creep-factor involved with calling you a friend if you don't know me outside of these pages. So consider this the formal end to our friendship.

Speaking of friends, I may not cover this important topic later in the book, so I should get it out of the way in the introduction. Maybe that's the purpose of the introduction. I want to address people who know me.

If you know me, stop reading now, forget about it, do something else, and go about your life in such a way as to ignore this book. This is a prediction, knowing all I do about psychology, sociology, politics, relationships, and scripture, that people who know me will hate the entire book, with their hatred growing more prominent, raw, and inexplicable with each word they read. They will be angry the whole time, wishing they hadn't bought the book. They did it to be nice and now they feel obligated to read a little of it so they can pretend they digested the whole thing. But it would make them angry for some reason that would cause great grief thereby contributing even more negative energy to human society on earth. So, again, if you know me, stop reading now and sell this book used on Amazon or donate it to charity and don't worry about it. No guilt, it's fine with me. I understand.

For everyone else, reading the intro in most books is more about giving the author something to do after she or he has finished writing the rest of the book. They don't want to let go so they write the introduction.

I want to make a promise to you. It has something to do with substance. My introduction needs substance, so I will add something of substance. The most substantive thing I know is me. I am a substance. You are a substance. We are real, physical beings that are composed of tangible elements that make up our body and that somehow produce the thinking, decision-making consciousness of the mind.[25]

Forget the mind for a moment – thinking about it makes my brain hurt – and let's just focus on the substance that is my body. If I were to briefly describe my substance in only two attributes, I would say the best way to describe me is I am a slimmer substance with a receding hairline.

I feel compelled to focus on the hairline, since I've hardly discussed it with you thus far. I can hardly believe I made it this far without discussing it.

My hairline has been receding much like the Jakobshavn Isbrae in Greenland, the fastest moving though still incredibly slow glacier, since I was about 20 years old. When I was a teenager in the early 90s, the

---

25 Unless you're like actor Jim Carrey who believes we're not real.

style was to grow your hair longer on the top while shaving it around the sides and back of the head. That style experienced a resurgence in the mid-2010s, as it was also the fad in the 1940s and possibly 1950s, pre-Beatles, and will no doubt return again in 20-40 years. I liked my hair. It wasn't beautiful, soft, silky hair. It has always been a little coarse and slightly unruly. I realized at about 12 years old after watching *Family Ties* on TV and wanting Michael J. Fox hair that my hair wasn't anything like his. He parted it near the middle. I tried parting my hair in the middle, but my natural part was on the side. The hair disappointments were only beginning.

There was another teen actor I can't specifically recall who had great hair. It was so great that I cut out his picture from a teen-focused magazine intending to take it to the young lady who cut my hair. My mom typically cut my hair to save money. She was better at everything than most moms. A personal flaw, however, was she was also better at cutting ears than hair. After several misdirected cuts, I couldn't wait for the day when I could afford a professional stylist to cut my hair. The trauma of a mother drawing blood with every haircut, even unintentionally, resulted in my vow, as a teen, that I would never again allow a woman to cut my hair. Sexist sounding, I know. But in full disclosure, that's what happened. I can't be the first man who projected my mother on to all stylists at Supercuts. I'm proud to say I finally got over it at the age of 33 when I moved to Sacramento.

I never took the picture of the ideal boy haircut to the hair salon. The style of shaving the sides and back saved me from having to go get my haircut at all. A friend with a hair razor would shave mine every few weeks, and vice versa.

Oh, my hair. The thought and concern and love I have devoted to my hair. My hair is mine and it is the only part of my body I have some level of control over. Sure, I could exercise, but why exercise when it hurts? Why not focus all my bodily attention upon the hair?

One morning, standing in front of the bathroom mirror after a shower at twenty years old, I noticed something that gave me a terrible shock: my hairline appeared to have receded ever so slightly at the base of the temples.

"This can't be!" I thought. "I'm so young and I'm balding!"

"I'm not balding," I told myself. And I chose to believe it. I wasn't balding.

I'm really good at delusional thinking. As in, I'm the absolute best.

A few weeks later, I noticed it again and wondered if my hair had been that way all along.

A day or two later, same thing.

More than twenty years later, I'm still hanging on to some crop on top, and it's no secret to anyone in my circle of family, friends, neighbors, coworkers, neighbors friends, coworkers family and neighbors and friends that I am obsessed with my hair loss. When I'm obsessed with a topic, I speak about it constantly. I google it constantly. On Facebook and Instagram, the only ads I see are on hair loss. Every single hair loss company markets to me. I am the market they seek. No hair loss companies have found me on Twitter, though, which is probably a clue as to why their stock has never matched Google or Facebook's.[26] Anyway, I tell everyone I know and everyone I don't know about my struggles. Constantly. <u>And that's exactly what I won't do in this book</u>. I won't talk about my male-pattern baldness. That's my promise. And that's exactly the kind of promise an author should make in an introduction. That is a useful use of an introduction. It is irrelevant information made very relevant for an introduction. This discussion of what not to include in the book wouldn't have fit anywhere else in the book as well as it does here. It is the introduction that sets forth what you will find and NOT find in this book. You will NOT find ANYTHING about my hairline. Nothing.[27]

---

26 At time of writing.
27 Repeat: You will not find anything on my hairline in the footnotes, either.

■ ■ ■

When an author writes a book, they do it partially for themselves, of course, but they don't do it in a vacuum.[28]

Hope is involved. The hope that their masterpiece, their creation, will turn into something, someday, that others enjoy. I'm there, right now, exactly right there in that place exactly at this very moment. I want others to someday enjoy my book, my creation. And the best possible outcome of the book is not only for it to be read, but I'm hopeful it will also be enjoyed after the binding cracks and the pages start to yellow [cue Dan Fogelberg tune].

What I mean is this book could and should be written into a screenplay in order to watch it at the movies. Can you imagine this book becoming a movie?

How would a film of this movie look on screen? Is it possible to turn it into a screenplay? These are questions I'm asking myself, fully realizing you haven't yet read the book.

I'm not sure whether it's screenplay material. I'll have to think of that as I write the book, since I don't know what it will say yet, either.

Back to the movie idea:

The movie could begin with me typing. The angle? From above, looking down at my hands, typing in spurts. Maybe it could focus more on my hands and blur out the male-pattern baldness I promised not to discuss after this introduction but could very well include in film.

____

28 Nor do they write while vacuuming.

PROLOGUE

Quantitative psychologist Donald Hoffman says we've been doing it wrong. He claims that what we view as our own individual reality isn't, in fact, reality. To discover the real reality, he asserts, we must begin with consciousness.[29]

■ ■ ■

Exactly three months and twenty-nine days later
February 23

■ ■ ■

What you are about to read is the product of my mind.
This, right here, is the prologue of my mind.

---

29 *The Case Against Reality: Why Evolution Hid the Truth From Our Eyes*, by Donald Hoffman. Published by W.W. Norton & Company, 2019.

SECTION 1:
FIGURING OUT WHAT TO WRITE

How to Write Chapter One but You Shouldn't Read Mine; Okay, You Should

Resting upon the mantle to my right, an elegantly shaped AA battery-powered analog clock reminds me of the second, each one, passing so thoughtlessly, so automatically, so robotically, in a disciplined though ominous rhythm as if pecked on the rim of a miniature, faraway drum. Without an announcement of any kind, at the reset of the minute, the secondhand points straight upward as if to the heavens, but only for a second, before it falls to the right in evenly timed and spaced juts bursting in absolute micro-increments, descending militantly downward, gradually and predictably, until the narrowest clock hand points directly down to hell with no noticeable pause, beginning the programmed ascent, up again toward heaven. Its destiny is to follow the path of a circle, moving downward and upward, rightward and leftward, again, and again, and again.

If I were to be greatly reduced in size, devolving into a shrunken man, small enough to find myself at home inside the device's glass encasement, the clock's hands continuing to tick by the second on the mantle, would I feel much different than I do right now? Inside this ticking museum, the marching clicker echoing louder, how long would I endure the frequent swoop of the longest, slimmest, and least forgiving hand of the clock, its persistent reminder of time's advancement?

Fortunately, I'm not inside the clock. I'm about fifteen feet away. I'm not a mini-figure. I'm fully grown. Still, the secondhand tick has become to my mind as a drop of water of a classic torture device. I feel the second drip into my ear, finding its way into my bloodstream and neurocircuitry, rattling my soul to its core. Little chance do I have to recover before the next second hits. And then the next. And then the next.

Trapped inside the clock would be a torturous nightmare. For me, at this moment, I hear the faint click emanating from the clock above the fireplace, repeating a few dozen times until the sound disappears by the hum of a different sound, the sound of complete mental focus, as I begin to write chapter one.

■ ■ ■

Two days later
February 25

■ ■ ■

hapter one.

Chapter one.

First, let me open this book with a promise:

In this work we might someday call a book, I was thinking it might be important to work out a little arrangement with you, the reader. I won't go so far as to formalize the agreement. No signatures needed. No notary public. No blood oaths. No spells or strange surprises involving the dark arts. I will not go all cult on you.

The promise is simple and straightforward: In this book, I will not use vocabulary words you have to look up in the dictionary.[30] Schteriously.[31] See, you could try to look up "Schteriously," but you wouldn't find it in the dictionary. Promise remains intact. One of the multitude of barriers keeping me from becoming an author for nearly four decades was believing I had to know difficult words in order to write a book. I will prove to the world this is not true when my book is finally published. I will use words you all know and understand. I will do this because they are the words I understand. I don't understand any difficult words. Schteriously.

[4 hours later]

I just finished writing this chapter, the first chapter of my book, and after writing I knew I better come back to this part to insert a thought. I can do that, right? Is that allowed?

Here's the thing: I really don't want to write the chapter again. I don't want to even bother rewriting the chapter. Definitely not worth it. The Preface was much more interesting to write. I could write a thousand prefaces. It's one thing to write about the book, another to write the actual book. It gives me much less respect for book reviewers who write about the book and much more respect for authors of complete books. I will never again read another chapter one the same again.

There are now so many more words in my book's word count, why delete them all and start over again? I get the point of quality over quantity, so why don't we do this instead: <u>Ignore everything else in this chapter</u>. It might even be better if you skipped ahead to chapter two. Schteriously. Don't read what I am about to say below because it's not worth your time. Definitely read what I have to say in chapter two, though. Chapter two is definitely worth your time. Full disclosure: I

---

30 What arrogance of pretentious authors who use surfeited words all but logophiles find recondite, even abstruse. [← someone else wrote this footnote]
31 Made up word.

haven't written chapter two yet. One thing is for sure, chapter two is guaranteed to be an improvement over chapter one.

Also, a warning: this book starts out really slow. I mean, really, really slow.

■ ■ ■

[Now THIS is liberating. If I write something in my book I don't feel like going back to edit or if there is a part of the book not worth deleting, I can write whatever I want and as long as I tell people not to read any further, I'm pretty confident readers will respect my wishes. It's like a journal written in an indecipherable code, except this one is written in plain English, with words everyone will understand, except it doesn't matter at all that everyone can understand it because *everyone* won't be reading it, only I will be reading it over and over again after I become an author. For those of you who are reading right now, you have one more shot at respecting my wishes by dutifully skipping ahead to chapter two, and you should feel the pangs of shame if you continue reading because it's just like sneaking into my bedroom to read my own personal diary you know you should not be reading. Okay, now I'll let the rest of this chapter stand as I originally wrote it...]

■ ■ ■

Books can be written in a variety of ways. Of all the ways, the most important and fundamental method of writing a book is simply to write a book. Written books written right at Rite Aid require the "write Wright right Rite-Aid" rite.

See, Josh? This isn't gonna work.

I'm a failure of an author.

I'm a failure of a writer.

I'm a failure.

■ ■ ■

Sixteen months and a few days later
June 28

■ ■ ■

You can start reading chapter one again.

After sixteen months of not writing, I was determined to restart the effort. I decided to go public by tweeting out the following:

Josh Rolph
@joshrolph

7500 words, 32 pages #NICS
--my first book
--goal to finish good draft by Aug 15
--you don't care
--this isn't for you
--it's for me

I should really go to bed. It's late. I'm tired. I'm still catching up on sleep from a long week. This afternoon, I plopped myself down on the couch and immediately entered REM during a rare nap made infinitely more rare these days than, say, when I was a teenager, because since then I have contributed to what I hope is the responsible repopulation of the earth and am frequently reminded of my role in the said repopulation when spontaneously falling into deep sleep because not long after entering REM today my kids began to jump up and down on my abdomen, kicking me repeatedly for about a half hour until I fully woke up. Then I did some yard work, went out to dinner, put the kids to bed, and I came in here to write an hour ago. Since then, not much of this book has been written. I am still tired. My body is telling my mind I should be asleep. My mind is telling my body I should be writing. My body always wins. But tonight, my body is losing. At this very moment, it is losing badly. Why? Because I'm writing.

I'm writing.

People who write books are so amazing. They're so amazing they really shouldn't be called "people" anymore. They should simply be called "authors." Authors are an amazing class of superhuman people who are no longer mere "people." (Authors used to be people but now they're authors.) I want to be an amazing person like those authors. No, not a mere "person." I've been a person all my life. It's time to tear off the shackles of personhood and become an author!

Why does no politician ever target the segment of society known as authors? In the U.S, there is no longer segregation, but politically speaking we've got the poor, the middle-class, and the wealthy, the Democrats and Republicans, the diversity of races and ethnicities, union members, educators, veterans, women and men, children, the disabled and diseased, the bi's, Thai's, the wise and the bad guys, the old timers and the gifted rhymers — but there is absolutely nothing about the class otherwise known as authors. We have the haves and the have-nots, shouldn't we also have the authors and the non-authors? The published and the unpublished? The self-published and the actual-published? I'm not saying the non-authors are the have-nots, because they at least possess or "have" the books written by the authors. And not all authors are necessarily the haves. Politicians interested in making sweeping generalizations about the entire electorate could simply simplify class warfare by dividing the electorate into authors AND non-authors.

Okay, I'm feeling the author juices flowing. Don't gag, that wasn't meant to be gross. I will write a little more and then off to bed. This will be stream of consciousness. No editing, no filters. I need to treat this like my journal.

I used to be so good at keeping a journal. From the time I was eight years old, I wrote over the years and I treasure what little I wrote. But a journal didn't make me into an author. Blogging didn't transform me into an author. Writing comments to the federal register didn't earn me the coveted author title. Writing this book is the only way to earn the esteemed title.

An author. An author! I can't wait to be an author! I realize I keep saying this (see Introduction), and it must be getting annoying, but it's true.

There are so many questions. What literary agent will read this? What editor will tear it to pieces? Which publisher will take a chance on me? Probably none, but let's keep dreaming! How will I write the query letter? What will it say? How do I begin its first sentence?

■ ■ ■

Dear Literary Agent:

It is with great pleasure that I send you the enclosed book I have recently authored entitled "Now I Can Say I'm an Author." I would love for you to consider it, but first, my main question is whether it is correct to say I have authored the book before publication?

■ ■ ■

"It is with great pleasure" sounds so phony. I want to come across sincerer, more down-to-earth.

■ ■ ■

Dear Literary Agent:

Hi, what's going on? I just wrote "Now I Can Say I'm an Author" and I kind of want you to take a look at it. I say "kind of" because subjectively speaking, your profile pic makes you look like the last person on earth who would be interested in this book.

■ ■ ■

"What's going on" might come across as too casual. I need to strike a balance. Or better, I can get straight to the point.

■ ■ ■

Dear Literary Agent:

The enclosed book, "Now I Can Say I'm an Author," is a unique look at the lengthy process I went through to become an author, and chapter one even includes the earliest drafts for what ultimately became this very query letter. Schteriously.

■ ■ ■

I don't know. Agents probably don't want to know how I came up with the query letter. They may also want existence of the query letter hidden from the general non-author public. I could be blowing their cover by exposing the query in chapter one of this book. Who would publish a query-critic? I should have exposed it in chapter two. No one reads that chapter.

Enough with the query letters because let's face it. I haven't written the book. I can't write a query letter for a book I haven't written. Maybe if I was an established author I could shop ideas around until one stuck. But I can't do that because I'm not an established author. I'm an unestablished pre-author author. I'm not even an anything author so forget I even said it. I'm a nothing non-author.

So after first calling this chapter "How to Write a Book" and then changing the title of the chapter to "How to Write a Query Letter," I've now settled on calling the chapter "How to Write Chapter 1." Problem is, I still have no idea what to say. This is chapter one. No one can change that fact. Can I admit I don't really know how to write a chapter 1? I had no business giving the chapter an official-sounding name.

I'm just being honest. Every author should be honest.

Honesty.

Yes. Pure, unadulterated honesty that has nothing to do with adultery.

I think I'm getting somewhere.

Okay, if you want to write chapter one of a book, be honest. And by you, I don't mean you, per se, unless you do, in fact, want to write a book. If you have no interest in writing a book, stick with me. I'm talking myself through this.

Honesty. It's simply good policy.

Some might say honesty is a better policy.

Others could say honesty is the best policy.

I've never heard anyone say honesty is the worst policy, but it could have been said at some point in history.

"Honesty is the worst policy"
— Satan

For this book, though, relatively speaking, I'm aiming for a certain form of honesty. And anyone trying to write a book should go for their own personal form of honesty. The best thing to do, for sure. Be honest with your readers and be honest with yourself.

I have laid it all out on the table for you that I have no clue what I'm setting out to do in this book. Isn't that obvious? The ideas for this book are scattered across the table, and chunks of scraps of ideas and chunks of scrap chunk scraps are even spilling off the table and on to the floor.

Honesty alone won't cut it. If you have nothing but honesty, you don't have a book. You need something else.

Every book needs a hook.

See what I did there?

I rhymed. When all else fails, rhyme.

I know what I want the hook of this book to be: the struggle of becoming an author. Or more specifically, the book is about what I went through in order to say I'm an author.

Perhaps it's already been done. Perhaps some author out there has written through all the steps describing how they became an author.[32] That could be true, but it's also true that not one single author or non-author out there is me. Of the many things I can assure you, I am pretty sure of that. There have been lots of books written about a lot of things, but this one, from an aspiring author, one who has never written a book, one who can't honestly say he or she has become an author, one who is now apparently shifting from first to third person, one who is suffering from male pattern baldness[33] but will no longer write about the topic (again, see Introduction), one who has no reason for writing other than to call himself an author, one who came up with

---

32 I would research it, but I'm scared.

33 Also known as "balding." Interestingly, today a coworker said that after cataract surgery last week she noticed I have a lot less hair on top than she could see before. That's all I will say about that. (See Introduction.)

keys to successfully writing a book before successfully writing a book or a book chapter – the first key is honesty and the second is writing rhymes and the third is developing a hook for the book –

Honesty, rhymes, and hooks is all you have to remember.

One more seemingly obvious word came to me.

Honesty, rhymes, hooks and *acronyms*. HRHA

Reordering acronyms becomes important when you are left with gibberish like HRHA.

None of this is set in stone.

Since nothing is set in stone, "Reordering acronyms" gets its own acronym.

Yeah.

Reordering acronyms, hooks, acronyms, honesty, rhymes. RAHAHR.

Got that?

RAHAHR.

All you need to write a book is RAHAHR. (Pronounced "raw-HAWR."[34])

RAHAHR. So let it be written, so let it be done.

A hook should motivate the reader *to want* to read the book. The hook is an ephemeral, impossible-to-measure, purely subjective desire planted in the mind of the potential reader-recruit who becomes the actual reader when the hook plays its primary role to suck them in. My purpose in writing this book is not to get you to keep reading this.[35] It is merely to write a book so I can say I'm an author.[36]

Getting you to read this book would be nice, but that is secondary only to publishing.[37] Publishers won't want to publish unless they think you will want to read what I write, so that must be where the

---

34 Possibly.

35 Is it working?

36 Remember: Honesty. Even if it completely turns off the reader from everything you write, everything you stand for, and everything you are or might become.

37 Again, I'm just laying it all out here.

hook comes in. The hook, it turns out, isn't about what you want. It is all about what the publisher *thinks* you want! Eureka!

Now we've proven, leaving no room for doubt, there has to be a hook (for the publisher).

The hook doesn't need to be amazing. Books with amazing hooks get read many times over. I just want to get this published. I don't care how many times it's purchased.[38] These are the books you see on all the bestselling rankings. *New York Times*, e-reader lists, Scholastic Books, Caldecott – I don't know, I don't read much – these are the books reaching the masses – the ones that get people hooked, bought, and subsequently read. Books on bestseller lists have hooks that convince people to buy the book. Books with amazing hooks are easy for friends to pitch to friends and is the essence of virality in reading. If it takes a friend too long to explain the purpose of the book, it won't get passed along.

I don't know if it's possible for this book to have an amazing hook. So I'm settling for a plain, bland, run-of-the-mill hook.

If the bland hook for this book is "One man's journey toward becoming an author," I don't think many would read it. Why not? For one, it's about a man. No one wants a book about a man these days. Plus, it's not an effective *hook*. If it was made more specific, like "A 40-something white male's journey to becoming an author," it still fails to amount to much of a hook, even though it's completely true. This is where honesty is tested. It would be so much a better hook if it was "How a 40-something white male became an author while trapped at the bottom of the ocean's Challenger Deep with only one pack of Saltine Crackers." Or "40-something white male author writes stream of subconsciousness book while hypnotized."

Some other sample hooks for this book:

"He wanted to write a book and did."

---

38 Dishonesty can be useful when trying to sound humble and approachable.

or

"If he had died, it wouldn't have been written."

or

"An otherwise aimless book written for one aim and one aim alone: to write a book."

or

"Now he can say he's an author." I like this one, but it's not much of a hook because there's such finality to it. There is no real story. We already know the ending. So I don't like that one either. There has to be something better.

"A non-author's journey to authorship."

I don't know.

What's the genre?

Self-help, psychology, sociology, travel, puzzles, action-adventure, suspense, history, autobiography, 40-something white males? How do I package this thing? What if it's all the above?

Which leads me to puzzles.

Actually, no, I won't write about puzzles. I really have no idea where puzzles came from. I'm not a puzzles kind of a guy. I would much rather write about honesty than on puzzles.

Being told to be honest while writing a book, even if the book is bestseller material, isn't really useful, let alone specific advice. But so far, that's the best I can do. Just be honest.

Now I will say this: if you're writing fiction, don't be honest. If you are honest, you might get sued. Remember, when writing fiction, your whole book is a lie, so dishonesty is the best policy for authors of fiction.

Fiction. I could honestly write some serious dishonest fiction. Schteriously.[39]

____

39 Okay, I'm done with that word.

"Chapter 2"

"What do you do for a living? I'm always fascinated to learn what non-authors do as a profession."

– Josh Rolph, the potential author of this book

■ ■ ■

Seventeen days later
July 15

■ ■ ■

You never hear interviews of celebrity-author or author-celebrity types asking what authors were thinking when they wrote various chapters of a book unless they're especially tantalizing, provocative, or edgy. If a specific chapter is ever cited, no matter its content, chapter two always gets short-changed, in the same way the second born child in a family is always short-changed.

Chapter two is perhaps the most forgotten child of all the chapter children in a book. No matter the number of chapters in a book an author gives birth to, chapter two comes and goes with little to no fanfare. It's neither here nor there. You read it like you would read all the other chapters but it's forgotten as soon as it has ended, which is exactly like the second born in a family.[40]

In my family, I am chapter one. I was born first of several. I am the oldest sibling. This was the most anticipated event of my young parents' lives, when they would become parents, and my arrival helped make it happen for them. I was their first child, and the first maternal grandchild, making me a multi-generational firstborn, earning me the coveted Firstborn Award I just made up.

Not long afterward, only a year or so later, the second born in my family was born. That child was the second born, not the first-born. Note how there is no such thing as "secondborn," all one word? Firstborn is a word. One word. Just like chaperone is chapterone with a silent 't.' Have you ever heard of a chaptertwo or a chapertwo? NO. You haven't.

And what exactly is a chaperone? A chaperone is "one" who chapers,[41] or supervises, who looks after a group of people. JUST LIKE THE FIRSTBORN is the one who supervises and looks after the young-er siblings, and JUST LIKE CHAPTER ONE is the most important chapter in a book. Forget chapter two. It's a nothing chapter. Chapter one is where it's AYATTT (pronounced "AY-att YAY-uh BAY-BAY")

Come on, it couldn't be more clear than this.

At the same time, I'm stumped. Who was the second born in my family? I'm wracking my brain trying to think of who that dear person and non-author family member is. There are five of us siblings, which makes it tricky. I know Ben is third oldest. Then there's Mary. Lastly, John. But the second? What was its name?

Hold on for a second while I ask my wife. She's watching TV right now. Trust me, she's watching her favorite series on TV right this

---

40   There is real, scientific proof demonstrating that second-born children are a scourge on society. Look it up online. It's true. No offense to the sec-ond-born in my family, or the second born in your family, or you.

41   Used in a sentence: "My chapers hired me last year."

minute while I type on my laptop at the kitchen table. I'm not making this up to have a captivating story. She's literally watching TV right this second while I sit here typing like this while watching her watch TV.

"So, I'm writing chapter 2. And by the way, what is the" –

"Oh good!"

"Oh good that I said 'What is the' and didn't finish the question, or do you mean it's good how I'm writing chapter 2?"

"I'm happy you're writing chapter 2."

"You sound unusually excited about me writing chapter 2."

"I am!"

"But I said I'm writing chapter TWO, not chapter one or three or four."

"I'm not following."

"You're supposed to say, 'Oh no, I'm sorry to hear you're writing chapter two.'"

"Why would I say that?"

"Because it's chapter two. Anyway, I'm curious what the name is of my next oldest sibling. I can't even remember the gender."

"I'm just relieved you've moved on from chapter one. You've read it to me forty-five times. I'm so glad I will have something new to listen to."

"Right, but what is that sibling's name?"

"Was that the one we" –

"Wait, wait right there. I'm sorry. I can't talk anymore. I'm getting distracted again from working on my book."

She has put up with so much so far as I write my first book. Authoring is a sacrifice for both author and family. Spouse and children are willing to make sacrifices because they understand what it means to have an author as part of your family. It's fame and fortune 'til the end of time.

Every chapter one ever written begins with such excitement; such fanfare. The kickoff of a new book is nothing short of exciting, even if the first chapter is relatively short. The rush of a new story, a new adventure, a new idea. Chapter two comes along and it's like, "Yeah, we know, we know. We get it. Just keep it a little interesting or we're gone." Whatever the author attempts — whatever creative description, spin, yarn (or otherwise) the author attempts to write in order to pull in the reader more than they already were at the end of chapter one is never as good as the author hopes, nor could it ever be.

To make chapter two exhilarating reading is next to impossible. Notice I didn't say it's downright impossible. It's just *next* to impossible. In other words, I have a sliver of hope I can make chapter two exciting for you. So in my process of getting to authorhood I'm at this point where I want to be like every other author in humanity by making my first book's chapter two really, super impressive.

To get the creative juices flowing, and to stay awake, I'm now showering. In a suit and tie. Or am I being figurative? What if I'm not in a suit and tie? The water is ice cold, figuratively speaking. I'm doing this for some much-needed inspiration, dictating this to my hopefully waterproof phone, all to introduce some literary allusion to the text. And to be as transparent as possible, I'm debating whether I should save chapter two for the end of the book. That way, chapter two could be the climax of the book. The BADA-BING-BADA-BOOM of this project. Tall buildings skip floors, airlines skip numbering rows. I, too, can skip a chapter and include it at the end. The 100th floor of the skyrise can be the 13th floor. The last chapter of this book can be chapter two. Who cares?

I'm still not sure. We'll have to wait and see what happens, won't we? By the end of the book, I may decide to scrap the idea in lieu of another. This much is for sure, I have so much to learn about book writing. It's really a beautiful thing, isn't it? We're learning together. We're learning how book making happens. And it's a journey.

I can't wait to get going on chapter three. What will it be about? I have no idea! All I know is this is exciting. After I get out of the shower, figuratively speaking, I will start working on chapter three.

■ ■ ■

3 hours later
5:52 PM
July 15

■ ■ ■

My thoughts wandered the last few hours, but I'm still here, still in the shower. Thinking through this and many other things, and before moving on to chapter three, I just had a thought that is totally chapter two worthy. Since no one will care about this chapter, ever, I might as well add something else just as likely to be forgotten.

Quora,[42] a site with more questions than a four year old, was for a brief period my social experimentation laboratory used to ask the most ridiculous questions I could think of.[43]

There were times when I asked questions I didn't want an answer to.[44] Other times I really wanted an answer, even if there isn't really an answer. For example, what is the answer to "How are you?" Or "What is it like to be me?"

Worthy of a chapter two discussion, let's examine the question "How are you?"

On Quora, I boldly asked questions, such as:

1. Is it offensive to ask, "How are you?"

Does asking an individual, "How are you?" imply the individual has multiple personalities? Is, "How is you?" more appropriate?

---

42 https://quora.com
43 Will I be taken seriously if I end sentences with prepositions?
44 Will I be taken seriously if I end two consecutive sentences with prepositions?

In the event an individual with multiple personalities is asked, "how is you?" would that person not also be offended?

Is it therefore more appropriate to ask, "how you?" or the less formal, "how you doin?"

I also tried more serious questions:

2. What is the monetary value of a laugh?

In funny media, whether it be comedy found in film, sitcoms, late-night talk shows, satirical literature or stand-up, the viewer expects to laugh. In advertising, such as commercials, billboards, or web ads, the effective use of humor can be a marketing tool used to build a brand. Laughter is the creator's desired outcome, and their product is assigned a price.

Is there a particular method used to establish a monetary value to the quantity, frequency, and quality of laughs generated by any communication medium? If so, what factors are considered in assigning a monetary value to laughter?

This book could be looked at as research to explore the answer to that very question. I encourage you to count how many times you laugh throughout the book. Then divide the laughs by how much you paid for the book. The more laughs, the cheaper the laughs. Now, the laughs originating from this book shouldn't be classified as *cheap*. There will be high quality, incredibly valuable laughs, I'm sure. So think of it as getting laughter for a steeply discounted price.

How much is a laugh worth to you?

I've read a lot of comedy books[45] in my day. I mean, not a lot, but maybe twenty? If this were 1725, twenty comedy books didn't even exist. Ben Franklin wasn't writing yet. Chaucer, Miguel Cervantes'

---

45 Comedic books are typically classified under "humor" instead of "comedy." If the author intends to write funny, I call it comedy. "Humor" seems like a demotion.

Don Quixote, some Shakespeare, other books we've likely never seen — there were only a few books at the time and fewer still that were primarily meant to be funny. So twenty modern comedy books read and researched is a significant number in the greater scheme of things – like over the span of civilization – relatively speaking.

The twenty or so books I've (mostly) read were written by ultra-famous comedians who you have definitely heard of. Some of the books were funnier than others. I won't say which ones I liked here because I don't want to be mean to those comedian authors who weren't funny in book form. There are some ultra-famous comedians' books that don't make me laugh. At all. That doesn't mean, of course, their books aren't funny to others or that you, yourself, would fail to find them hilarious. Funny isn't always universally funny. I don't think there's a thing in this world which is funny to everyone. Except for passing gas. Studies show[46] there is universal comedic approval for loudly passing gas in public, when it's someone else, of course. Point is, when attempting to make someone laugh, there will be lovers, there will be haters. Those who love the gag and those who roll their eyes — again, note the universal, timeless, multilingual exception cited above.

The general rule for comedy books is there should be at least a few solid jokes per page. I tried really hard to write at least a few solid lines in the entire book. Part of the fun for you is to find those three. That may mean drudging through fifty pages before you find something funny. All I ask is for you to go through with that exercise for me. What's in it for you? That's a question I can't answer. I don't know what you hope to accomplish by reading this. You will never have an author tell you that directly. Of course, every author wants to be loved, praised, and have their printed copy dog-eared, underlined and every page highlighted; their eBook version tweeted and posted vociferously; their audiobook version listened to over and over and over and over

---

46 Look it up yourself.

again.[47] In store for you in this book is that unknown something I can't imagine you might want but hopefully there is something you can gain from giving it some of your time.

I will disclose to you that I just caught myself in the middle of a snore. The previous paragraph must have put me to sleep.

■ ■ ■

Nothing makes me more exhausted than writing this book. I've fallen asleep a hundred times so far, just writing this page. Remember, and let the record show, I'm still showering. Sleeping in the shower can be dangerous. How will I ever get to chapter three without drowning? Is book writing this exhausting for every author? There's so much I don't yet know.

Have you fallen asleep reading this? My book isn't making you sleepy, is it?

I guess the challenge is to write about something I know. When writing, however, I feel as if I know nothing. I mean, I don't! I've never written a book! What can I contribute to the volume of world literature that hasn't already been written? Is there any unexplored topic or viewpoint left?

I should write about something familiar. I should write about something I love. I should write about something that makes sense to me. And something I can write about for a long time while not taking so much time that I never finish. I need some time to think about how much time is too much and what exactly the topic I write on should be. What should my breakthrough idea cover? Should it be art, should it be politics, should it be science, should it be historical, should it be fiction? I don't know. I need time. I need some time to get this right. I need time to get what I write right. I need to go through a rite to write

---

47   Adding an extra "and over and over" was strictly a word count up-page decision.

the right thing. I need to go through the rite to write the right thing at Rite Aid. That's what I need to do. That's exactly what I need to do. Back to square one in chapter one, which is so far both the beginning and the climax to this book. It's all been downhill from there. Chapter two is becoming exactly what I thought it might be.

I wish I could make some kind of promise to the reader that by the end of the book you would know something more than you know now. Maybe at the end of this process I will figure out what that is, and maybe there is some profound lesson I will learn. Or maybe the takeaway is there is no takeaway.

See, this is good! This is a good exercise. I'm getting closer to the "why" of the book. Why am I writing, besides the goal of compiling a mass of words in order to gain the author credential? But I need to write a mass of words that say something. I don't know how writing about writing could get me any further than I already am not.

Like I said earlier, I need time to think – time to get this right. And that is the most important thing right now. So chapter three will have to wait until the long-awaited time of finding a purpose above the mass of words purpose finally arrives. The inspiration needs to flow. It has to be right.

And I think I should get out of the shower now. Is it normal for my fingers to be a beautiful dark blue and my whole body to be numb, figuratively speaking?

Yogurt & Depression

Last night I had my first dream of being an author, even though I'm not yet an author. In the dream, I knew I was a full-fledged, dyed-in-the-wool author, so there was a rush of excitement passing through me. At the same time, I was trying to swim in the middle of the ocean with no boat or island or flotational device in sight while pouring mustard with my left hand onto the hot dog supported by my right hand. I had to keep the hot dog bun dry. A wet hot dog bun would be tough to enjoy at any time in my life, but most especially before I drown, I thought. The dream was kind of strange but felt so real.

■ ■ ■

Four Years Later to the Day
July 15

■ ■ ■

If you're still here (I sure am), you will know in the last chapter I was showering in a suit for creative purposes, figuratively speaking, trying to come up with material both for chapter two and for the rest of the book. I gave up on chapter two while awaiting artistic, authoring inspiration. That was four years ago, to the day, in case you missed the part above this paragraph which reads, "FOUR YEARS LATER TO THE DAY" [not case sensitive]. Turns out, seeking authoring inspiration by wearing a full suit in a cold shower for several hours may cause you to incur a mild case of hypothermia, as I so incurred, which left me hospitalized for something shy of three days (figuratively speaking). Thanks to all who helped me through that challenging time (figuratively speaking). I did it (figuratively speaking) to become an author. And I'd do it again, just not right at the moment.

Capturing the chronological history of book writing is important to me. I've picked up so many books that skip all pleasantries by jumping right into things without offering any explanation from the author's point of view about where they were in space and time as they wrote each chapter of their book. You will get the specific chronology from me. Without gushing all over you, I will say I owe you that and so much more for taking the time to read this. Unless, of course, you are borrowing the book, in which case you owe me about twenty bucks.[48]

In an article I had read before my figurative suit's fateful day in the shower – one of those list articles or "listicles" that have perhaps misled millions of innocent individuals like myself with their "we know everything about life in 9 simple bullets that don't say much at all but we tricked you into reading" attitude – I had searched and found several articles suggesting creative writing tips for aspiring authors. One of the lists said to shower with clothes on. I thought it would be a smart idea to shower in some of my most expensive clothes. Forget the hospitalization, I ended up ruining my nicest suit and tie in the process, figuratively speaking, of course. I realized the suit fatality as soon as I got out of the shower and noticed some of the blue coloring in the navy blue suit was staining the bottom of the walk-in shower. I googled

---

48 Depending on the year and future inflation/deflation, this figure could be much higher or lower. Please search the web for an inflation calculator in your country to determine the current value, using this book's copyright date as the base year. Prediction: not one reader will do this.

"dry clean wet suit" and learned right away that it was pretty much over for my expensive power suit that had cost me more money than I possessed, which is why it went to my credit card — the same one I owe the next minimum payment for this Friday.[49] The suit's low quality was made bare when after the shower, the navy blue color washed off only to reveal a splotchy gray underneath. Not only was my power suit cheap and ruined but I had been duped by the sales rep at the suit store to spend many hundreds more than the thing was likely worth. I got really depressed almost immediately and as you may know, when depressed, the creative juices cease to flow and as an aspiring author, there's really very little hope in writing anymore when feeling despondent, figuratively speaking, of course.

So another lesson learned about becoming an author: don't get depressed. It's fine to be depressed before or after writing a book, but don't get depressed during the book writing process. I'm adding this new dimension to writing to the RAHAH acronym:

Reordering Acronyms
Hooks
Acronyms
Honesty
Rhymes
Don't Get Depressed

So now it's: RAHAHRDGD

Remembering that we can reorder the acronym (see "RA"), it now reads:

RADGDRHAH

____

49 Because I keep buying things I can't afford.

Or

Reordering Acronyms
Don't Get Depressed
Rhymes
Hooks
Acronyms
Honesty

The writing of the preface, acknowledgements, introduction, chapters one through two, the figurative cold shower, the hospitalization – one minute led to another and before I knew it, the book had made its way into the faded-memory past, until thirty minutes ago when I was sitting down for breakfast with my trusty cohort, the laptop, joining me at the table. In a search for something else in my files, this document by the name of "NICS" happened to pop out at me. "NICS," if you can gather, is short for "Now I Can Say." That's what I've been calling this project. It had been so long since I had seen "NICS" and even if I had, the acronym began to mean absolutely nothing to me, as in, I couldn't remember what it stood for, if anything. When I would see "NICS" among the files, I would just continue to scroll or search without giving it any thought. I wasn't moved by "NICS" like I had once [wuntz] been. Not at all. It was just another document sitting there. All motivation to become an author had left me.

But today, I saw the document again, as I had dozens of times over the previous four years, and noticing that the date I last saved it was exactly four years ago to this very day, my heart began to beat at a slightly faster clip than it had before I noticed the anniversary, which suddenly had a way of faintly renewing my interest in this work.

That's when I knew it was coming back. The "it" was my desire to become an author. The "it" was beginning to stir within me.

It's tough to describe what "it" feels like. I had felt it before, although it had been so long since I had last felt it, more than four years, to be precise.

I quickly skimmed the previous contents of the book. I began to make slight grammatical changes and reworked a few sentences. "Maybe I can publish as is?" I thought. What if I just wrote a pamphlet? I've never authored a pamphlet.

But remembering what I wrote about the importance of authoring a book made me walk the pamphlet thought right out of my mind.

The decision was made: I wanted to become an author. I wanted to say, "Now I Can Say I'm an Author."

Next thing I knew, I was at the end of Chapter two and found myself saying aloud:

"Chapter three, chapter three, chapter three." In my excitement, I repeated the "chapter three" chant many more times. I thought of just writing out "chapter three" a thousand times and that would therefore result in a two-thousand word count chapter three. But then I wondered how many times is too many, how many is enough, how many until my hand started to hurt, and not being able to settle on a number coupled with carpal tunnel fears led me to give up on that idea.

If I was going to write a book that would be taken schteriously, I couldn't write two chapters only – I couldn't write a mere pamphlet (no offense to pamphleteers). I had to add another chapter. This thing had to be seen through to completion. Everything important in the world comes in threes: three branches of government, three blind mice, another thing,[50] *Three's Company*, three amigos, AAA discounts, the Three Tenors, Three Dog Night,[51] three little monkeys, a three-piece

---

50   Including "the butcher, the baker, and the candlestick maker" would have required that I begin to use semicolons to separate everything else. I spared both you and me the extra semicolons.
51   What's the story behind naming that band?

suit, the trinity, Three Mile Island, triple entendre, the Three Stooges, and of course, tri tip.

But my inability to settle on a subject for chapter three threw me violently forward to the drawing board, giving me a nasty bruise on my upper sternum.

Why do I start so many sentences with "but?" Why do I do that? Why do I use "that" all the time? What's my problem? I was told never to use either by my third grade teacher. But back to "but," why can't I write like a regular author not saying "but" in every other sentence?

"At least I'm not starting sentences with 'butt,'" I countered.

"True dat," I replied.

I could replace all my "thats" with "dats."

At the time, I had moved from drawing board to sitting at my table, eating breakfast, as I so often do, when I began to notice the little canister of Yoplait brand yogurt sitting before me. I couldn't help but observe, all at once, how ergonomically incorrect that little yogurt canister is.

What is it? A carton, canister, or…oh, maybe "container" is the best word for it.

The yogurt container has crevices and divots and edges that are completely unnatural for a human to reach with just a spoon. After the spoon usage has been exhausted, there is still yogurt hidden underneath the lip ridge thingy at the top. I do everything I can to reach it with my spoon, but to no avail. It's a struggle. It's real. And the three spoonfuls of yogurt that brought me to this point have left me hungry for much, much more. If this is all that is left, well, I'm going to do what it takes to get there. Not to be graphic, but the tongue is the only tool sufficient enough to reach under the ridge at the top of the lid. If I can get that, I just might skip all the yogurt stuck at the bottom in those impossible-to-reach places.

I'm sorry, but there's no way of getting around "that" or "but," at least not for me. Schteriously.

Anyway, yogurt.

I can't remember exactly when the thought came to me, but I recently figured out how to open the little container of Yoplait yogurt without it squirting all over my shirt.

Yoplait had consistently squirted on t-shirts, dress shirts, ties, fingers, keyboards, desks, tables, important papers, superhero outfits and my bibs since partaking of my first Yoplait in the summer of 1989 at the age of thirteen-and-a-half.

I tried for years to open the hair-thin aluminum lid with such care.

But it was never good enough.

There was so much air pressure in the little container that it would explode each time.

The anxiety, embarrassment, shame and subsequent depression that never followed continued until I decided to devote considerable thought to the problem.

After a slew of sleepless nights filled with notebooks, diagrams, and complicated Pythagorean theorems I didn't even understand, it came to me almost at once: I had to point the lid in the direction of either a trash can or the face of someone irritating, opening the product away from me.

Apparently, the point-and-aim method had been the secret all along. If only Yoplait had printed a warning label on the lid explaining how the contents would explode regardless of altitude. Irregardless,[52] I pat myself on the back each time I remember to open the lid the right way, cursing myself when I don't and have to walk around with the blueberry Yoplait splatter of shame on my dress shirt the rest of the day.

We're told the proper etiquette for sneezing is to do so into our shirt sleeve and for eating we put a napkin on our lap. Yet there is no guide for proper opening of the Yoplait lid. When it opens, a moist towelette should appear in order to catch the exploding yogurt splatter.

---

52 I only use "irregardless" because a few words earlier I use the word "regardless."

Since I made the discovery a year or two ago, I have given a lot more thought to Yoplait, as you will soon learn.

I've noticed, for example, that the grocery store devotes a significant percentage of the yogurt shelf to the Yoplait brand, about 38%, in fact. Yoplait is always priced just a notch above the generic, with obvious Yoplait perks and amenities offered for mere pennies more than the greatly reduced inferior non-brand fortunate enough to share the store's shelving beside it.

The next time you are in the grocery store, I want you to stop for a moment to admire the yogurt section. It is crazy for me to see how much of the store is made up of yogurt.

We love yogurt. I love yogurt. And Yoplait is the far and away leader of the yogurt industry. I love their Harvest Peach, followed by French Vanilla, with Key Lime Pie flavor which has the ability to make me smile. Your choice of yogurt for decades was either Yoplait or the inferior generic brand.

With slashed prices and incredible deals that went something like "Buy 35 for only $5" combined with the popular brand's strikingly alluring color swatch (bright reds, crisp whites), a customer like me has no choice but to purchase Yoplait. As the popular saying may as well go, "Yoplait or the highway."

Well actually, now there's Greek yogurt. That stuff came out of nowhere!

I'm not one for conspiracy theories (heck yeah, I am), but anyone notice that the recent surge in Greek yogurt coincides exactly with their country's bankruptcy? The country's beyond broke and they're sitting around the parthenon in Athens thinking, now what do we do? Bomb a rich country? Nuclear attack? No, we can't do that. We need a positive image. Right now we have the gyro. We're tired of being known as the greasy spoon of Europe. We can change our image with healthier food. A low fat, high protein, lean….yogurt! By Zeus, that's it! (This entire paragraph should never see the light of day.)

So now we have about five competing brands of Greek yogurt who are all competing with twenty varieties of Yoplait. It's almost like Pepsi vs. Coke or Apple vs. PC all over again. And we all know how those branding wars turned out.[53] With yogurt, the Greek's competitive advantage is the yogurt consuming population doesn't like the smooth taste of Yoplait as much as they want some yogurt they can chew on. Not that Greek Yogurt is chewable. It's so much more dense than Yoplait. The stuff has mass. This is the reason why people are ditching the little chunks of "Harvest Peach" for the less flavorful but much more massy Greek "Honey."

The brilliance in the Greek's plan goes even deeper. The increased density of Greek yogurt guarantees one thing and one thing only: there is no longer an air decompression issue such as the one we have experienced for decades with the more creamy, probiotic Yoplait.

After all this, you might think Yoplait is through, finished. Oh boy, you couldn't be more wrong.

If you were about to give up on Yoplait forever, never fear. Yoplait still has the edge. Greek yogurt might be healthier, but, Yoplait has, well, keep reading.

I don't know of a particular Greek yogurt brand with an identifiable philanthropic bent, other than every Greek yogurt's mission which is to give you your fill of casein protein. Without a more charitable cause, Greek yogurt's only thing going for them is no lid to lick.

Who licks the lid, anyway?

I do. I'm a lid-licker. I mean, come on, I paid 80 cents for the little container! At least a dime's worth of yogurt in the little tub is smeared all over the lid. The lid is yogurt's appetizer.

About the lid...You just might be dead or younger than two if you never saw Yoplait's "Save Lids to Save Lives" marketing campaign from

---

53 Nothing really happened.

1998 to 2016. If you never saw the "Save Lids to Save Lives" campaign, have a seat. I really hate to break this to you…

Here's the cold, cynical truth of the matter: When you have a product that ruins clothing because of a faulty part, which in this case is the lid, you have to have a good campaign using the same faulty lid.

The "Save Lids to Save Lives™" campaign for cancer awareness was the perfect solution, proving that not every good idea originates at the Parthenon. Greek yogurt wins silver. Yoplait wins gold.

Only a jerk would get mad at a lid enrolled in the cause of saving lives.

I don't want to bash the saving lids program. But I will anyway.

My problem isn't that I don't want to fight cancer. I DO. But I also have a heightened hygiene problem, as in, I don't like germs and I seek to avoid them at all costs. Those lids are germ infested petri dishes of germonic (as opposed to Germanic) virus, disease, and halitosis.[54]

To give you an example of my germaphobia in practice, in a previous job I forged a path I called the "Germ Freeway." As in, it was the *Way* that was *Free* of *Germs*. It involved trekking twice the distance to get from my office to the cafeteria, with the perk of having no door handles involved, and therefore, no potential to brush fingers against the doorknobs of my non-handwashing colleagues, who chose to infect the more direct Germ Freeway and its five handled doors on the way to the café.

In Yoplait's case with their charitable call for contaminated lids, did they give any consideration to the mailroom staff? Like, let's say I'm in the mailroom, and in comes package upon package of used Yoplait lids. Some of them were likely washed. Many, I would wager, were not. People are disgusting, I've come to find. So it's safe to assume that many licked lids arrive to the mailroom even more laced with bacteria

---

54 There is only one instance of "halitosis" in this book, unfortunately.

than ever before. This isn't anthrax being delivered by an unsuspecting USPS –it's colds, flus and mono.

How much money would they have to pay me to open those lids? How much would it take? Not enough. Whatever it would be, I would be gagging all the way to the bank.

Who mails in a licked lid, anyway? I mean, besides the person who wants to cure the world of cancer?

The Yoplait mailroom must be a heavily sanitized corner of Royal Oak, Michigan. I really feel for the staff who put in the sweat equity working at the facility. Imagine responding to the job ad that reads: "Do you want to save lives?" And then you walk into the Yoplait training room only to learn you're opening biohazard-contaminated mail.

I hope the mailroom boss is kind to them and gives them lots of hand washing and Vitamin C. I would demand a Hazmat suit and a hot shower at the end of my shift.

I'm convinced that Yoplait continued to get away with this licked lid issue simply, if for no other reason, than because they end their name with a silent "t."

Think about it. "Yoplay," isn't as sophisticated a spelling for the brand. "Yoplay" looks like the description of a cellist meeting a British rock band. However, the more refined spelling of "Yoplait" is the ultimate in European sophistication. Which is why when it comes to yogurt, the kind that splatters all over creation but is cancer saving, colorful, with a silent "t," will always find its way on top.

[Sigh.]

After 3,000 words of writing and 3,000 words closer to becoming an author, that's all I can think of saying about yogurt.

■ ■ ■

Two Years, Two Hours and Forty-five Minutes Later
9:58 PM
July 15

...

As soon as I typed the period in the last sentence ending "yogurt," I entered a depression that was undiagnosed, fairly mild, and overall, not-so-bad. And it happened over yogurt. After yogurt. Because of yogurt. Yogurt was the source of my undiagnosed, fairly mild, and overall not-so-bad depression. But it was more than that. It was typing the word yogurt, which came about because I was writing a book, that caused the undiagnosed, fairly mild, and overall not-so-bad depression. The two-year-long episode led me to understand, realize, and begrudgingly accept that I should no longer attempt becoming an author.

What I found through the ordeal was this: I coveted authorhood only because I dropped out of law school and had no real skill. Like lawyering, authorhood was a skill I was either unwilling or incapable of achieving in this life, which is what led to me decide…

I Give Up on Becoming an Author

The glorious day when I find myself in this glorious situation:
"Let's go around the room to introduce ourselves, starting with this
gentleman here to my right."

"Bob Spiggetti."

"Jill Frend"

"Gabba Tran"

"Uh, yes, um, hi! I'm Josh Rolph, and I'm an author."

[pause]

"George Wan"

"Len Sivitz"

[and so on…]

■ ■ ■

Fifteen years, one month, and seven minutes later, to the minute
10:05 PM
August 15

■ ■ ■

ere's what I want to know: who the heck are you? As in, you. The one reading this book right now. How did you get your hands on a copy of this book? What is your name? You know mine. I don't know yours. That's just rude. How dare you open this book and expect me ——

Deep breaths, Josh. Deep breaths.

This is too hard. After a solid effort trying to become an author over the past twenty three years and ten months,[55] heavily involved in book writing for three full chapters, having written about 15,000 words, averaging about one word every twelve hours, or said another way, one chapter roughly every eight years, I realized and admitted to myself what you have known all along: I am incapable of writing a book because after writing about yogurt, there is nothing more of significance to write about.[56] Depressed, I haven't been able to write since then. No longer depressed, I've accepted my station. I will never become an author. So with some sadness (and a ton of relief) this will be my last chapter, which means I have not written a book. I have written a very wordy, picture-less brochure.

The sadness mainly derives from my expectations being too high. I should have never aspired to becoming an author. In other words, I wasted time, which is sad. As my life coach tells me, whether I write a book or not won't make anyone else sad. This is merely a personal regret. And as I learned through this unsuccessful effort, no matter

---

55 Figuratively speaking.
56 You already knew that, right?

how impersonal the content, for the author, book writing is almost exclusively personal.

If I lower my expectations down to nothing, I'm not sad at all. In fact, I'm very happy I've almost completed my first picture-less brochure. Check that off the proverbial bucket list I don't really have.

My only goal for this last chapter is to end the brochure on a positive note, with an ask of some sort, which is something I've noticed in every brochure I've ever read:

"Join now!"

"Buy now!"

"Sign up!"

But I have nothing to offer.

Or I could copy the brochure's incomplete direction:

"Call for more information!"

"But wait, there's more!"

"Take a number!"

But I have nothing more to add.

Or I could go the scarcity of space and time route:

"Space is limited!"

"Don't miss out!"

Or appeal to everyone's desire to get along:

"Everybody's doing it!"

Brochures are all the same. They're all asking you to do something in the here and now. At least with my brochure, I won't ask you to do a thing. You can close the brochure and move on, continuing to pursue your life.[57] I allow you to have your own feelings.

Unless I don't publish it at all. I could allow the electronic version of this brochure to stagnate on my computer and further diminishing my chances at printing when an electromagnetic pulse bomb hits North America and subsequently fries the hard drive as we usher in the new dark ages zombie apocalypse.[58]

Until that dreadful day, I can honestly look back with great pride on everything I've accomplished since beginning this brochure about (what feels like) twenty-four years ago. I have the fondest memories I will probably forget.

There has been a lot of learning about me, about commitment, about attaining goals. Just don't label me a quitter. If you do, you don't understand me. I'm stopping this because I now have a life. I'll readily admit, I had no life when I wrote the first chapter of this brochure.

But today, I have big plans with really exciting new projects that are so big and so exciting and new that I won't have time to type because I'll be doing other important things like talking and collaborating and faxing.[59]

For those of you who are curious about my future plans, I'll be straight up with you. I'm mucho interested in pursuing some kind of brain-stimulating hobby like Sudoku[60] or flipping houses.[61] Didn't I mention puzzles last chapter? Did I mention flipping houses as well? It was so long ago, I can't remember.

Actually, the Sudoku line is a joke. That highly addictive game is so

---

57　Or you can devour every word of this brochure, repeatedly, for the rest of your life.

58　This footnote is a placeholder for a reputable citation that might validate this claim.

59　I wrote this part in 1988.

60　I wrote this part in 2002.

61　I wrote this part right before the market crashed in 2008.

2003.[62] And I'm really bad at it, anyway. I was good at the one in my local paper[63] which would get progressively more difficult throughout the week, but depending on the publication, some higher brow magazines had Sudoku puzzles labeled "easy" that were somewhere between *I-can-handle-the-fact-that-I-can't-solve-this* impossible and *soul-crushing-humiliatingly* impossible, at least for me. You might as well forget about filling in only two numbers in the medium-difficulty section. I felt terribly defeated. Alone. Scared.

In protest, I no longer read high-brow publications.[64]

This could explain why I renamed Sudoku "Noduku," as in NO-Sudoku, as in ME-NO-Sudoku, and I try really hard to stay away from the addictive numbers game.

I'm done with book writing because book writing has become so passé. Book writing is so 2004 to 2009, when everyone was trying to self-publish.[65] Facebook and Instagram wrapped that platform up fast by diverting everyone's time from self-publishing to self-promoting.

Turns out all anyone wants to do these days is share pictures and videos on social media. No one wants to read about the completely boring aspects of anyone's life – even mine – as was done at the beginning of the blogging era. Back then during the heady days of blogging, it was like, "Woah, I had no idea that friend could write a coherent sentence." We realized they could. Over and over again, ad nauseam. Facebook entered the scene and we were again shocked by this new form of social media. "Woah, that person I forgot about posts like an animal, but I don't have to spend time reading about their fascinating lives because of this cool scroll feature." Then Instagram came along to show that at the end of the day, we haven't progressed much past childhood, a simpler time when all we preferred was picture books.

---

62   I wrote this part in 2004.
63   Definitely wrote this sometime in 2010.
64   I don't write them, either.
65   I wrote this part just now.

See! I've learned so much. Yes, exactly, it's the journey, not the destination.

My gut tells me that book writing about the boring aspects of life probably won't come back for at least another generation or two, like when Web 14.0 comes out. I think 14.0 is when the internet is embedded into our brain stems.

"If you plan to fail, try flailing the plan."

—Josh Rolph

Had to squeeze that quote in there before I ended the book writing effort.

Let me give you the quick run-down on authoring an incomplete book from all I've learned. This class is called "Authoring an Incomplete Book 101," where is taught that what might have begun as an incredibly exciting idea could be impossibly difficult to pursue to completion. And books are pretty much dead, anyway. Gone, over, done, dead. Everything has an end. Even *Seinfeld*. It was television comedy perfection, yet it ended. Everything ends. Everything. Except for this chapter, so far.

One more thing on Jerry Seinfeld, the father of the famous 1990s sitcom about nothing bearing his name. Have you noticed he doesn't do nothing anymore? He moved on in whatever the 2010s decade is called to doing cars and coffee,[66] which is something, not nothing. This is a huge reason why I can't keep up with the book. I'm not going to waste my life away writing nothing to no one. It's not the way to live. If Seinfeld can't do it, why do I think I can?

I just went to the kitchen to get a napkin. I came back with a tissue.

---

66 *Comedians in Cars Getting Coffee* is the official show name. Such a great name.

Oops. How do I eat this popcorn and type without a napkin? Fake butter everywhere...hard to clean up with a tissue. This is not right.

On that note, why can't Orville Redenbacher make a microwave popcorn bag that opens more easily? Didn't he invent the business?

I'm kicking myself for eating microwave popcorn when I know better. What was I thinking when I bought it the other night? I thought I had abandoned it altogether since I heard once that microwave popcorn butter can lead to Alzheimer's.

And if you can't tell, I really have no idea where this chapter is going. I don't know if this chapter has a purpose. I don't know why it's here. It is evident I have no reason being an author. From brochures to marketing to Sudoku to Seinfeld to Alzheimer's, wandering around aimlessly from page to shining page, I try. There is no story, no arc, no thesis, no feeling in the entire effort. It's not even funny. Couldn't I at least make it a little funny? Instead, I've written a pointless chapter with no act 1, 2, or 3. It is possibly the worst chapter ever written. As much as I would like to think I can do this, I have to admit: I am not humanly capable of writing another coherent chapter. Thank you for reading as much as you have, if you are still there. Thank you for indulging me in this failed attempt at becoming an author. I wouldn't be surprised if you found alternative uses for the pages of this book. Like going to the cupboard for some scissors and cutting it into a puzzle which would make it more purposeful than the words in this chapter. All I ask is that you not use the book as toilet paper. Anything else is fair game. Except for burning it in a cultish bonfire. Try to avoid using the book's pages for that. No voodoo, please. Oh, and don't make from these pages a papier maché effigy of me and use it as a piñata. That wouldn't be nice. I'd rather you used it as toilet paper, but only if you're stranded in the desert with no plant-based alternative. Or food — you could use it as food. It may not digest well so bring along some B12 vitamin to speed up your metabolism.

Thank you so much, and I wish you all the best.

I Give Up on Becoming an Author - Part 2

Me in the 2nd grade spelling bee:

"Please spell 'author,' young man."

I swallowed so hard it was almost an audible gulp. Something strange happened, though. The nervousness instantly left. I brightened up. I knew this word. I knew it well. I was sure I could spell it out with confidence. I not only loved authors, I had the great privilege of once meeting an author at a book fair. In other words, I not only knew the word, I knew an actual person deserving of the author title. It was round one in the second grade competition and I was determined to win the entire thing. First my school, then the district, region, state and finally on to Washington, DC for the national spelling bee championship. I would win notoriety, prestige, and most importantly, money. I knew this word. I had the confidence of bodybuilder Arnold Schwarzenegger, of the Conan the Barbarian movie era. Nothing could stop my rise from seeming second grade nothingness to instant fame. The press, scholarships, the Ivy League — I was going to be as famous as Michael Jackson, if not more famous.

"Author," I repeated.
"O-t-h-e-r."

"You are incorrect. Have a seat over with the audience, young man."

■ ■ ■

One Week Later
August 22

■ ■ ■

Since I quit writing my book last week, I've been thinking about what I would write if I was still writing a book. The answer became obvious two minutes ago: I would write about something that would make me laugh, like writing a new chapter called, "I give up – part 2."

That's the moment I realized I could start a new chapter. On what, I didn't know. The next challenge was coming up with a topic. I looked down for inspiration and saw this magnificent piece of 80s-era technology cradling my wrist:

My Calculator Watch

I have been in love with calculator watches since I first saw one as a kid in the '80s. It was love at first sight when I saw it on the kid's arm a few desks over from me. It was the watch I loved, not the kid's arm. That digital screen, the tiny buttons with numbers and mathematical functions.

I had forgotten all about it until all these years later, I remembered the watch. Having purchased one a few years ago, I noticed there is somewhat of a fraternity whenever I come across someone else who is wearing one. In my first eighteen months of wearing the watch, there have been three. We wave and honk when we pass each other on the highway.

I want to start an online calculator watch business. Alibaba.com has a few distributors selling calculator watches of the ridiculi variety that look amazingly cheap. I've spent more hours than you should know looking for the perfect calculator watch to wear and sell. If anyone wants a share of the business, let me know. I'm hiring. Payment in the form of high fives.

One model in particular arrived in my mailbox on Friday. Made my day. Fortunately, detailed directions came with the watch. They were terribly translated but I figured it out.

Sporting the newly-programmed micro-multi-keypadded beauty on my wrist on my way to work this morning, windows down, wind through my thick locks,[67] I marveled at the beauty of this decades-old gadget. Nearby drivers slowed down to take a look. Either that or traffic was bad. This was a new era in my life. The calculator watch era.

One extra perk included in my new gadget is I am able to program email into it. That was surprisingly cool, a significant advance in features. Letters. Not just numbers. Letters. The @ symbol. More letters and a dot.

Only took me 15 minutes to type my wife's email using the little keys. But it has an email address field, which I find to be so choice. No, the watch does not send email as we find in the smartwatch world. But it doesn't need to send email. It's a calculator watch. I should sell calculator watches with copies of this book I quit writing.

Genius.

Decided: I am going to attach a calculator watch to every book that I never finish writing. The price of the unfinished book will go up by $15 to cover the cost of the watch, so the non-finalized book may become priced more like a college textbook.[68]

---

67 Actually, windows up, heater blasting, dreaming of my once thick locks with a tear running down my cheek. (Technically, I am not breaking my promise to never discuss my male pattern baldness in the book because this is a footnote and not the actual book.)

68 And lord only knows how much those go for these days.

6

Eleven Tips for Writing Your First Book

If the United States Department of Agriculture certifies Angus beef, shouldn't a United States Department of Books certify authors? Currently, the Library of Congress acts as the book certifying agency by assigning copyright privileges to various works of authorship, but the Library of Congress is one of the few agencies of the legislative branch, not to be confused with the many agencies housed within the more zealous executive branch. Who would you rather have on your side? The President of the United States[69] or 535 members of congress who can only agree on the naming of a post office? Congressional oversight of the LOC is minimal. How good do authors feel when they see their copyright information listed a few pages into the book? How much better would they feel if a United States Department of Books, an agency that holds the full power of the executive branch, stamped "100% USDB Certified" on the book cover? And wouldn't it be something if the first book entered into the USDB were a humble title called, "Now I Can Say I'm an Author"?

---

69 I wrote this part before Donald J. Trump became president of the United States of America.

■ ■ ■

Forty-one years later, to the nanosecond
August 22

■ ■ ■

I do not want to rush through the writing of this book like I'm starting to do. I don't. Repeat: I don't.

You can't rush art. Rushed art doesn't sell. Rushed art with calculator watches attached doesn't sell either, I've realized, which means changing my plans again from the last time I wrote. After dusting off[70] and reviewing the last chapter, I remembered my new marketing plan from when I had decided to relaunch my authoring career.

In chapter one, I developed an acronym, RAHAHR, that almost killed this book. Without question, RAHAHR led to the destruction of my expensive but cheap suit in chapter two, figuratively speaking. I fully realize acronyms are like lists and lists are incredibly popular in the modern world. You can't turn around without seeing a list of reasons for or reasons against, a list of things to do or not do, a list of this or that or the other thing.

For some unexplained reason deep inside my consciousness, when something becomes popular, and I mean when *anything* becomes popular,[71] it's over for me. When I made the connection between the popularity of lists and the road I was going down with an acronym-styled list, I decided this: even though I hate those types of list articles or "listicles," as they are affectionately called, I wasn't creating click bait. I was writing a book. And lists in books could be different. It's not, however, too often that I see a list included in a book. Again, I don't read much so I offer only anecdotal evidence. What I'm thinking is a list in this book could turn things around for me. What I know is the list cannot go back in time, saving my navy blue suit from destruction, but the

---

70 Both literally and figuratively.
71 Besides fashion and a whole host of other areas.

list sure could save this book from sudden doom. Lists are potentially just the thing I need to get back into author mode, and incredibly, I have a great idea for a list right now.

You already know about the list because you got a little teaser in the chapter's title: eleven incredibly easy ways to write a book. I can see those of you who want to become authors skipping everything in the book and coming straight to this chapter. Forget the preface, the acknowledgements, the moving introduction – forget chapter two and yogurt and the rest – those of you who aspire to becoming authors want to succeed which is what brought you here at this very moment in time, so I can't botch it up.

One of the tricks of the trade, however, is not giving away hard-learned lessons on success this early in a chapter. I'm not giving away my list that easily. Lists aren't always free. This is a book, not the inter-net. You paid for this. And if you didn't, check with the publisher for the modern way to slip me some cash.

Of course, you could always skip down to read the list if pressed for time. Just earmark this page and come back later to read the setup (see expert advice on the setup in The Setup section below for more about setting up the setup).

First, here is a backward countdown of five preliminary items you and I should cover before jumping right into the actual list. Each item covers a book writing issue I face, dream of, . The reason for a descending countdown is not readily apparent to me at the moment.[72]

5. Is the word "book" ugly?

For those of you who don't already know, "book" derives from the Old English "boc" which came from the Proto-Germanic "bokiz" that means "beech" or "beechwood." How that all came about would

------

72 Neither is it apparent now, while writing this footnote.

require more historical information than what I just gleaned from a simple Google search. It's interesting that the Germans now call it a "buch" which is so close to the English "book." What's frustrating is we could have ended up calling it by the more elegant French word "livre" instead of the harsher Germanic "book."[73] Why the English-speaking world adopted the Germanic over the French is a great question for another day, especially in light of the numerous French words we now call our own, but could it have something to do with how Germans invented the printing press which earned them the right to own the word in English? Who knows. The point I really want to make here is "book" is such an ugly word. A book may not be ugly, but "book" definitely is. The "booklet" is the more feminine version that is much more pleasing to read, say and hear, but no one reads booklets anymore. People do read "e-books" with the popularization of the e-reader. "E-book" is also much less ugly than book. "E-" anything tends to electronify a word yet to end a word in the "ee" sound is to make it sound childish, unless you're referring to a bookie which is a slang term, anyway.

Words with long "e" suffixes aren't as ugly as their root word counterparts.

We can all agree, if we disconnect ourselves from the meaning of the word, that "cook" doesn't sound too appealing. "Tim" might be a great guy, but his name requires a lot of mouth to say. "Bam" is a violent sounding word.

But these same three words with the "ee" ending suddenly become the harmless words "Cookie," "Timmy," and "Bambi."

4.75. Blog

At least the word "book" is not as ugly as the word "blog." That word

---

73 No offense to Germans.

is so much worse. Why, you may or may not ask, does "blog" rhyme with so many ugly words?

We've established that the word "book" is an ugly word. A truly ugly, horrible word. When analyzing book's modern-day step-cousin, "blog," we must first observe that it has the word "log" in it. And we can all admit that "log" would be an unappealing word for you to say, not to put words in your mouth or anything. Similarly, within the same rhyming family we find "clog" which is absolutely foul, both in the shoe type (I despise clogs) and plumbing senses (see "log"). "Flog" should be internationally banned, and it possibly is as a form of torture under current rules of war. "Bog" is downright despicable and no one wants to be the "cog" in the wheel. To "hog" means not to share. "Noggin" is the crude way of describing a head. "Jog" is tiring just to think about, especially right now when it's a little chilly outside. "Zog" sounds like a surname of a creepy guy from a darker alternate reality. A "dog" is great until someone calls you one. Egg nog. Fog and smog. Frog. All -og words from the past, present, and future should be banned forever.

4.5. Other Ugly Words

While we're on the topic of ugly words, why is it that primary reading platforms in the modern age are named or described by incredibly ugly words? We've covered the words "book" and "blog" already. Think about all the other things we read that are just as ug.[74]

- We read billboards. Billboard is such an ugly word, not to mention offensive to those named Bill. It is also possibly sexist to name a billboard after a man. Why couldn't it be called a berthaboard or a cisgenderboard?

---

74   In cool kid circles, "ug" is used as the shortened version of the word "ugly." I was never a cool kid, except for kindergarten through 3rd grade.

- Menus. Also incredibly sexist. The next time you go to a restaurant, you can protest by asking for a "u," just be clear and point to the menu so the server doesn't think you are hitting on him/her/them.

- Cereal boxes. Since I was five, I have loved reading the back of the cereal box. But really, "cereal box?" Does it really take two words and four syllables to describe a cereal box with the words "cereal box?" Can't we describe a cereal box as a "morningthing" or something like that? It's too many syllables of verbiage. Not only is it too many syllables, but the word "cereal" has always been tough for me to pronounce aloud, followed by the forced finish of the word "box." The word "box" is so abrupt, harsh, and final. I can't say I'm reading the back of the "cereal." That wouldn't make any sense. I'm left with "cereal box."

- Obituary. It's about death, so yes, it should be an ugly word, and it should be five syllables. Say it out loud, however, and you will appreciate that this one is pretty darned ugly. We should pronounce it "o-BIT-oo-ary" to avoid uttering the obscenity.

- Newspapers. The ugliest part of the word "newspaper" is the "pape" part. Think about the "pape" sound and you will begin to despise it as much as I do.

- Pamphlets. Like the "pape" in newspaper, the "pamp" in pamphlet has got to go. No one wants a "pamp" in their pamphlet.

- Booklets. The booklet is one heck of a bad coverup of an already ugly word. You can't disguise anything with the "-let" ending, at least not with my keen sense of word ugliness. The word "goblet," for example, is gawdy gross and it is no surprise it contains the "gobl-" letters that can be pronounced "gobbling" and "gobble" and arranged into "blog" and "ogbl." Let's not forget the french-sounding word that still ends in "-let" we so straightforwardly call "toilet."

- Tweets.

That pretty much covers what I read.

4. The Setup

What am I trying to say in this descending list setup section that exists only to get you ready for the ascending list? I'm not sure. But every book chapter needs a good setup. This descending list is my attempt at writing a good setup. Oh, and I just made up a quote:

"Good setups don't grow on trees."

–Josh Rolph

3. Money

Writing a book isn't a charitable endeavor. You write a book hoping your effort will be rewarded in some way. Being loved is one possible reward. The other way I hope to be rewarded for my effort is through an old-fashioned check, beginning with a healthy advance, followed by the flow of royalties to my bank account for the remainder of my mortality. The great thing about writing a book is dreaming about how much money I might make by winning the book lottery. Writing and then finishing a book is like entering a book lottery. You get one ticket, and there are millions upon millions of book lottery tickets. The chances of winning are slim, but at least you get a chance. Since starting this book, I created a spreadsheet with all the things I will buy after I get my first book advance.[75] I'm calling this pre-money, because it's

---

75 I decided not to include the list of wants because the wants change too often.

as if I already have it, and it's almost a certainty that I've already spent it.[76] Every last cent.

A book publisher won't give me a penny in advance if they are unclear of the book's target audience. I aim for an audience thirsty for this kind of book. If I am asked, I'll just whip out #3 of this descending list, showing I've done all the hard work for them:

Target Audience (aka "Market")	Market Size
My blog and podcast subscribers	Mom, Dad, all but 2nd born sibling
Aspiring authors	8 million
Yoplait workers	883
The inhabitants of Mongolia	3 million
People who go by "Josh"	714,458
People who go by "Joshua"	x
People who go by "Ua" (pronounced "OO-uh")	0
F&R	285
Facebook "friends" or everyone I had ever known on Facebook back when I accepted all friend requests up until about 2011	820
Used car salesmen	85,000
Flight attendants	98,700
Deceased painters	4.3 million
People who hate the word "book"	1 or 2
TOTAL	(16,200,152 or 16,200,153) + x

---

76 Using various methods involving credit.

2. Fame

There are other great reasons to write a book. Fame is tied to book writing. Prestige is tied to book writing. In a previous section of this book I spent some time dreaming of achieving author status. Until that great day arrives, I can soak in the fact that I'm writing a book, or that I'm a book writer. And that's worth something, too. Not as much, but it is worth something.

Right around the time of the 2006 congressional elections in the U.S., and since, bloggers have been gaining unprecedented access into the press galleries at political conventions and important events. Some bloggers have gone on to receive national, global, and possibly even universal fame.

Which is the primary reason I also host a blog, in addition to book writing.

To say you are a blogger in this day and age isn't what it used to be, but it still may place you among society's elite, especially if you have millions of readers. Even though I am still building my readership (now at tens of readers, up from ones of readers), I've used the blogger title several times to cut in line, inspiring my desire to use the author title in similar fashion:

"Excuse me, kid, I'm a blogger."

At McDonalds, "I'd like the blogger discount."

And at the movie theater, I once stood up between the cell phone lecture and the trailers and said, "As a blogger, I just want to ditto what they said about cell phone usage."

You know I don't like the word "blog," which is why I can't wait to substitute the blogger title with the superior author title in similar situations in the future. It is a titular upgrade, for sure. And remind me to never again use the word "titular."

1. Money & Fame

Here's the bottom line: a successful book, like a successful blog, can bring in loads of cash and fame. The only difference is subtle though highly consequential. It all comes down to titles. Bloggers are stuck being called bloggers. Authors get to be called authors.

Also, authors make more than bloggers, by a factor of three.[77] Tremendous difference.

■ ■ ■

From the descending list, we turn to the ascending list:

11 Tips For Writing Your First Book

1. Don't write daily. It adds so much anxiety to the book writing process. Let it be natural, but not too natural. The 41 years between writing this chapter and the last was maybe on the "too natural" side of things.
2. There are two types of "funny." Funny comes in many shapes and sizes. It's really tough to land a great line, especially in a book. So it's best to write without any humor. Like I've always said, "Like I've always said."
3. Don't write lengthy chapters. Chapters that run too long will cause you to lose readership. When the reader goes away, say goodbye to your book going viral.
4. Don't make fun of Facebook, Amazon, Google, Apple, or anyone who is a website. These four sites are taking over the world and you don't want to be the one they chew up and spit out.[78] They can make your life wonderful or awful. And for that matter, don't poke at Mark Zuckerberg,[79] or anyone who is smarter, wealthier, younger, and much, much less handsome than you.

---

77 I will always point out fictitious stats in this book, like I'm doing right now.
78 *The Four: The Hidden DNA of Amazon, Apple, Facebook, and Google,* by Scott Galloway. Penguin Publishing Group, 2017.
79 See next chapter.

5. Don't give up after your first chapter, second chapter, third chapter, and so on. If you do give up, try giving up again, and then keep writing.

6. Never go back on your promise to give up on book writing. "Commitment can't be faked, forged, fawned, flaunted, feigned or Frodo'd." - Josh Rolph

7. Don't take a moment to stand-up, straighten your back, place your hands at your hips, spread out your legs, and attempt the Tarzan yell.

8. Don't ever do any type of polar bear jump into ice cold waters. This is a dangerous activity that has nothing to do with book writing.

9. Don't worry that your book can only be written. It cannot be blogged, podcasted, filmed or autotuned. It cannot respond to you. It cannot be your friend.

10. Don't fret about the fact that you don't often use the word "fret."

11. Don't disappoint your reader with a list you just made up.

SECTION 2
FILLER MATERIAL TO INCREASE WORD COUNT[80]

---

80   If you read this section title and wonder how it might be distinguished from Section 1 which may have felt like filler material to you, then don't think too hard about it. Just skip ahead to Section 3.

The Man With No Sense of Humor

Humor is relative.
Homer was an author.
Hammer is a tool.
Hemur rhymes with femur.
"HMR" in ancient Hebrew meant "reddish."
Relative, author, tool, femur, reddish.
Humor would make a good name for a relative.

■ ■ ■

Forty-one nanoseconds later
August 22

■ ■ ■

MEMORANDUM (1st draft)
To: All Employees
From: Rex Schlonnagan, Senior Executive Administrative Vice Manager's Assistant
RE: The Restrooms
Date: November 1, 2015

ear Fellow Employees,

It is with great pleasure that I report to you our third consecutive week of incredibly high scores for cleanliness in our two company restrooms. For the ladies' room, we've scored a perfect 100%. I am so proud of you all. Really. So proud. The men's restroom isn't far behind with an all-time high score of 88%! Great job! Great, great job! These are our highest Cleanliness Hygiene In the Bathroom (CHIB) marks since I started working here in 2012 Q2, and is possibly the greatest accomplishment ever in my 22 year assistant management career.

As I announced in our quarterly staff meeting two short months ago, I made the CHIB score priority issue number two. Number one needs no reminder: customer eye contact will always be most important, and I will address a new aspect of customer eye contact in a future memo.

You all laughed after I made CHIB priority "number two," but I promise, it wasn't meant to be a joke, though I guess it's funny if you have a sense of humor, which I don't at all.

I'm always wondering if what I say will make you guys laugh in front of me or behind my back. That, I can never predict. As I've discussed with you on many occasions, I devoured the book about how to be funny, even if you're not, but it didn't teach me anything. When I recounted to all of you how I finished the last word of the book without having laughed once, and then turned to the back flap thinking I would find something funny, most of you chuckled, but I didn't get the joke. I find that some of you chuckle when I say things not meant to draw a chuckle. It can get a little frustrating when the chuckle is on me.

The book on how to be funny might as well be written in another language. Perhaps Stuart can lead a segment at our next meeting about how to make people laugh. He always seems to make you all laugh a lot. With him, it's not the regular laughter, it's the so-called "LOL" variety of laughter, though I don't get any of his jokes. None of them.

For a long time, I thought people found Stuart humorous only when he raised his voice and did the thing with his eyebrows, all at the same time. But then there was the time he was whispering with no noticeable eyebrow movement and he got some significant laughs. Once I couldn't fall asleep as my mind went over each of Stuart's methods, which made me wonder whether the content is the funny part. It just makes no sense to me and I find myself at home or in the grocery store thinking about what he said and wondering why it was funny. I've taken notes and will even fully disclose that I have secretly recorded Stuart while he is talking to see if I'll capture something funny I can study later at home. After a few attempts memorizing what he said and trying out some lines at the grocery store or post office, I've only received perplexed looks. I just binge-watched a popular comedy series and have to admit that I didn't laugh once! Not even one time! This is apparently the funniest show on TV. I watched a ton of it which, I'll now admit, is why I called out "sick" a few days in July.

Some might see my lack of a sense of humor (on both the giving and receiving ends) as strange, but I see my lack of humor as a gift from God and perhaps the reason I not only work for this very serious company but why I'm also in this industry, because I hear it's not really a funny industry to be in, like most industries are, especially the comedy industry. If I never become funny it's okay. I will move on to learning people skills. But let's get back to bathroom cleanliness.

As you are aware, bathroom cleanliness is only a small part of what we do here at WoopDeeDoo. Our number one goal is to serve our customers promptly, safely, and with our trademark WoopDeeDoo wide-open smile with head tilt. Anything less than that high standard is completely unacceptable. This quote from our Senior Manager comes to mind: "With great responsibility and accountability comes great stewardship." Think long and hard about those words and I promise: I will too.

So where, you might ask, does a high CHIB score fall into the mix of our Three S's: SPEEDINESS, SAFETINESS, and the WoopDeeDoo SMILE? I would argue they are all interchangeable; one does not go without the other. A high CHIB score is a solid statistical representation of how well we are speedily serving customers the juiciest DOOBLE WOOPERBOOGERS, safely upselling our DOODEEDOONUTS for DEESERT (with the memorable jingle, "They make you say DOODEE!") And don't forget our DEElicious fries, recently changed to WOOPTATOS from POOTATOS after the infamous "smear" campaign. If we could, let's stop calling them POOTATOS in the kitchen area. It's tough to change but I'm confident we can do it. And gosh, we perform an incredible service for thousands in our community and send them off with our signature smile. If we can do so many of these things well, PLUS have the cleanest bathrooms in town, WoopDeeDoo will be the ire of every other fast food establishment in town.

Let's address the difference between the perfect female restroom score and the 88% male score. As we've discussed in the past, the 12% deduction off our male score is from the uncleanliness on the floor beneath the urinal. You'll notice our score improved by three percentage points since I installed a splash guard. We will continue to monitor the situation closely, but not too closely. Since an 88% score is higher than any WoopDeeDoo bathrooms within Region 2, I think we are in a good position company-wide to hold title well into the future. Should the splashing drop us to "Number Two," I will solicit your opinion on how to make the necessary improvements to get us closer to 100%.

In closing, I wish to share with you again a hearty congratulations on our many successes. Please be on red alert for my next memorandum on customer eye contact. It has to do with our CHIB score. But how, you ask, does bathroom cleanliness relate to customer eye contact? Oh, just wait. Just you wait. I have created a practice we may have to trademark before implementing because it will distinguish us from our biggest competitors. If you haven't yet invested in our stock, now would be the time to do so.

MEMORANDUM END

8

~~Why I Don't Do Lists~~ ~~(And Why We Don't Want to Die)~~

***I'll just come out and say it: This was, is, and will forever be the worst chapter of the book.[81] But to keep up word count, I'm leaving it in! ***

~~"Facebook enables and disables. You can meet, socialize, discuss and laud. You can compare, envy, fight, and endlessly scroll."~~

■-■-■

~~A few minutes after finishing Chapter 7~~

■-■-■

~~1. If you think Facebook is a perfect company led by angels, you are right.~~

~~2. Facebook is, in fact, run by angels in heaven above, directing its employees evenly between Facebook and Instagram.~~

~~3. The only non-angel on staff is Mark Zuckerberg, who is actually very human, and perhaps 1/16 Cherokee.~~

~~3A. This isn't really a list.~~

---

81 No offense if it's your favorite chapter!

3B. You are disappointed.

3B(1). You thought you would have more to read.

3B(1)(a). You are addicted to lists.

3B(1)(a)(i). It's okay.

3B(1)(a)(ii). I am here to help.

3B(1)(a)(iii). I don't know if Zuckerberg is 1/16 Cherokee, but I used to hear a lot of friends back in our formative years tout they were.

Lists aren't beneath me. If I saw this list, I'd click on it without thinking:

18 things Belgians Should Know about Mark Zuckerberg

After reading the list, I would most likely continue not thinking.

Wait, 18 things…18 things…that's an even numbered list. Even numbered lists aren't as interesting as odd numbered lists, in some cases. I may want to create a list of 17 instead, switching Belgians with Buddhists. Or adding Buddhists before Belgians.

Or wait, this one could get a lot of hits:

99 Traits Your [spouse/partner/lover/pet] Wishes You Had

Lists. Lists! LISTS!

There was an era when certain websites were gods of the list, though that movement has declined in recent years. While list articles aren't talked about as much as they once were, we don't have to look far before finding the odd numbered list and the even numbered list.

LISTS! LISTS! LHHISSSTS!

Does the number matter? I decided to do some more research.

I went to Parents.com, thinking I'd hit a list goldmine. Surprisingly, it took me about eleven long seconds to find "11 Signs You're Becoming Your Mother."[82]

Huff Post is a list-haven: 11 Reasons to Love Costco That Have Nothing To Do With Shopping.[83]

---

82   http://www.parents.com/parenting/moms/signs-youre-becoming-your-mom/

83   http://www.huffingtonpost.com/2013/11/19/reasons-love-costco_n_4275774.html?utm_hp_ref=mostpopular

Are you seeing a theme here? Eleven, perhaps?

Someone hasn't learned that 11 is the new 10, with 10 Reasons You're Not Rich Yet.[84]

There's always someone way behind the list-making curve with "9 Websites That will Save You Time in the Kitchen."

Then there was my local paper, with "10 Things to Know for Wednesday." So many things to learn, remember, and list.

LISTS! LLLLLLISTS!

What is the list? Why is it here? Where did it come from? Where is it going? It got me thinking about life, about death.

There's a huge market in pre-death lists.

For a perfectly good reason, I'm sure, 1,001 is a very popular number among lists of things to do before death. See Amazon.com. Take out the zeros in 1,001 and what do you get? Eleven. No coincidences.

LISTS!

Not to be outdone, Dane Sherwood decided to write *2,001 Things to Do Before You Die*.[85]

An ambitious Facebook Page creator started a page called *10,001 Things to Do Before You Die*.[86] They are still compiling that list.

A future prediction as the human race makes huge gains in cyber-scanning capacity: a surge of 10,011 lists.

Here's where it gets cool. The old "bait and list" headline is a tactic as old as the world is young, according to Italian novelist (aka "author") Umberto Eco, who touches on their ancient origin.

What's more, he says, "We make lists because we don't want to

84 http://www.dailyworth.com/posts/2064-10-reasons-you-re-not-rich-yet/?utm_source=outbrain&utm_medium=syn&utm_campaign=o2064

85 http://www.amazon.com/001-Things-Before-You-Die/dp/0759298777/ref=cm_lmf_tit_20

86 https://www.facebook.com/pages/10001-Things-To-Do-before-You-Die/156638007723652

~~die."[87] I haven't read the article, but I don't need to. Like most listicles, the title alone speaks to me.~~

~~LISTS!~~

~~In dramatic fashion, minimalist Dr. John Izzo wrote, *The Five Secrets You Must Discover Before You Die*.[88] I hope his way under 1,001 list philosophy catches on. Perhaps it will at some dystopian day.~~

~~...list~~

~~This is my least favorite chapter. What's your least favorite chapter of the book? From here on out, I will intentionally write chapters that are no worse than this one.~~

~~As the reader, I encourage you to do as I did and cross out your least favorite chapter, assuming it's not this one, because it is already crossed out.~~

---

87 http://www.spiegel.de/international/zeitgeist/spiegel-interview-with-umberto-eco-we-like-lists-because-we-don-t-want-to-die-a-659577.html

88 *The Five Secrets You Must Discover Before You Die*, by John Izzo, PhD. Mc-Graw-Hill Education (India) Pvt Limited, 2007.

Death Penalty

One of the greatest mysteries of all is death, and to put the mystery in as simple a form as possible, your own death can be imagined in one of two ways: awareness either ends or continues in, or after, death. If you are no longer aware, then it's all over. If you die yet maintain awareness of some sort, well, then that just opens up a whole host of new questions. Either way, it's an uncomfortable topic we all avoid, like hemorrhoids.

■ ■ ■

47 minutes after finishing Chapter 7
August 22

■ ■ ■

Let's go ahead and get death out of the way.

Why death, you ask?

Why not! Why not broach controversial issues in this journey toward authorhood?

Seeing how the book already tackled the topic of yogurt – from spills to biohazards to a Greece-led nuclear holocaust –it's about time we delve into another provocative topic like death. Try not to think of death as you read this, though, since it's pretty depressing. Instead, try to think of this chapter as me furiously typing in order to become an author of a book.

There's nothing like a provocative book tackling difficult topics in a way that appeals to the masses. How to do it tastefully in a book that will never be seen by the masses is the only challenge.

When dealing with the subject of death, one must first address life.

I love life. The parts I don't love, I've managed to tolerate. Death, on the other hand, freaks me out. All the religion and science in the world will never change the fact that death is just plain freaky, mysterious, and again, freaky. Some of us have great faith and confidence in death, the rest are all freaked out by the prospect of our own demise. Admit it, you are too, L. Ron Hubbard!

When it comes to faith and therefore religion, you may believe in God. You may not. We haven't talked about this yet in the book but yeah, might as well go there.

You may believe there is more to life than what you see. You may not. You may believe there is an unseen, cosmic metaphysical purpose to your life. Or you may not. You may believe you will be around after you die. You may not. Society is growing increasingly secular, in large part because the greatest spiritual questions involve whether an Amazon Prime subscription carries into the afterlife, with God welcoming believers into a mansion fully integrated with the fruits of Jeff Bezos's labors: unlimited video streaming, instant shipping, and unlimited access to an exalted Amazon Alexa.

I want to talk about one specific aspect of death discussed in the public sphere. Just as there are atheists and believers, each falling on one side of the question of God, there are two different sides to the issue known as the death penalty.

Whichever side you fall, for each of you choosing one side, there is likely one of you who chooses the other.

There is a danger when anyone brings up an issue as polarizing as the death penalty. The danger is that by even expressing a position on one side of a polarizing issue like this, one is sure to make people upset and angry if they fall on the other side of the issue.

This is my book. I want this book to be somewhat controversial, so I'm left with no choice but to write about heavy topics, beginning with the death penalty. I'll write about others in the future. I'm sure of it. In the natural progression of this book, I think it's perfectly fine to deal with death at the outset, establishing that I'm an unafraid author willing to talk openly about the questions plaguing humanity.

"Let's begin with the end in mind."

–Josh Rolph

Which is why I have decided, after seeking Amazon Alexa's opinion, that I will choose not to take a side on the death penalty in this chapter. And it's not my fault. I asked Amazon Alexa and she told me not to take a side. "What's the point?" she asked, rhetorically. Do I want to alienate half my readers? Is the price of becoming an author worth losing credibility among half of you? Isn't that what politicians do? They don't say anything? Am I now becoming like a politician by not expressing my true feelings on the issue? I thought I was just becoming a beloved author! Now I'm becoming a slimy politician!

For those of you who hoped to disagree with me on the issue of the death penalty, you thought you had me here, didn't you? You thought this was where you could push me into a corner and say, "See! I knew you weren't author material! Authors don't fall on the wrong side of issues because they are right about everything!"

But I'm not going to fall into your trap.

And I'm not going to make those of you who might agree with me really happy, either.

I'm just not going to take a side. Not only is it the best thing to do, it's the only thing to do. It's not a cop out. Technically, not taking a side is still taking a side, just not one you can see. Sides have sides and taking an invisible side is just as valid of a side to take, you just can't see it, because it's invisible.

Now, let's stop here for those of you aspiring authors who are here to observe how it's done. I want to part the curtain. First, I gave the chapter a title very different from previous chapters. In the first seven chapters of the book, the primary theme was book writing. Then, all of a sudden, chapter eight is about the death penalty. I couldn't think of anything else surprising at the time. Books need an element of surprise to keep readers reading. If this book was made up of nothing but book writing information with no surprises anywhere, no reader would get nearly as far without a well-timed surprise. Seeing as how this book was in need of a surprise, especially after the crossed-out chapter on lists, the lamest chapter of them all, I made the big surprise happen in chapter eight. I'm learning so much as an aspiring author.

I will agree I was hoping for some "click bait" in this book which in this case would be "book bait" or "bait bait." It's tough to get away with as an author, but since I'm not really an author yet, I figure, what do I have to lose?

Thinking through this a little more, the main problem with the death penalty is I'm not clear on what "death penalty" actually means.

I mean, death. Penalty.

Death. Penalty.

Isn't it obvious to you? Do I have to say it in another way?

Penalty. Death.

The penalty of death. The <ahem> penal[89] nature of death.

Isn't death a penalty for all, regardless of whether they or not you find yourself on death row? Don't we all end up on a "death row" of sorts at some point at or near the end? Every day, a group of living are lining up for death. Some are given notice and for others it comes as

------

89 Terrible word alert!

a total surprise. Why then limit the death penalty to a select group? Death is a penalty as it is.

Isn't *death* penalty enough?

Pants

Let's take a moment of silence for pants.

■ ■ ■

Still August 22

■ ■ ■

As soon as you finished the last chapter on the death penalty, one of the most controversial issues of the 1980s, you were most likely wondering, "What is Josh going to talk about next? The Iran-Contra scandal?"

I might. Don't tempt me.

Or I could talk about a more contemporary issue, like gun control.

The majority of National Rifle Association members who like guns do so because they enjoy shooting at targets or going out for a hunt. Since the shooting is done for recreation, and recreation is associated with fun, then those on the pro-gun side could call their side "fun control" instead of "gun control." Calling it "fun control" could win over fence-sitters who would have a little more empathy with the gun crowd because really, who wants to limit someone else's fun?

On the other hand, equating guns with fun would deeply offend anti-gun advocates who see no fun in brandishing a high-powered weapon for whatever purpose. But if I go there and start writing about gun control or fun control, this book will get "out of control."[90]

Oh no, did I just write that? What is happening to me as I morph into an author? I'm becoming a gigantic dork. I thought this book was bad three chapters ago, and now look at what I'm coming up with. This is terrible. What am I doing? I can't publish a book like this. I just can't.

I'm trying to write a book. Nothing is really happening. I keep waiting for this book writing "thing" to kick in. But it's not. You can probably tell that it's not kicking in for me. I'm on chapter nine after years of failed effort – which is certainly some level of achievement, I might add. Maybe I just need a break. It's time to put this aside for a little while to gather my thoughts. Never did I think I'd make it this far. Nine chapters. I know I'm not quite there because I still can't

■ ■ ■

THREE HUNDRED THIRTY-TWO AND A HALF YEARS LATER
February

■ ■ ■

Pants.

YES. I'll write about pants!

As I write, I am wearing pants.

I'm fascinated by the saggy pants look, as in the pants worn way down below the waist. So fascinated, I am determined to try it out one day. I'm not as impressed by those who let the pant waistline sit only an inch or two below the waist. I'm thinking of the pants worn by guys who carry the waist much lower than that.

There are the guys – and this is a gender thing – I don't see women

---

90 This is Pulitzer material.

wearing pants this low – there are guys who wear their pants especially low. It is the most intriguing thing to me.

It could be called the "sag" look, but I say there are varying degrees of sag. The "sagsag" is kind of low, the "sagsagsag" falls lower than that. I call the lowest low-riding pant fashion the "sagsagsagsag," said with emphasis on the second syllable.

I can empathize with men who choose this bold fashion statement. I, too, have had to wear the sag look for most of my life, though no one would think I dress that way because it looks like my pants are around my waist – maybe even a little higher. I want to blend in. It just so happens that my legs make up 80% of my height.[91] This means if I were to pull my pants up all the way to my hip bone, it would appear as if I wore my pants about up to my neck. I would just be pants and a head.

A few weeks ago, I saw several men in different locations with the sagsagsagsag look. It made an impression on me. I was struck that these men were not content with the mere sag looks made famous in 1992 by pre-teen hip hop artists Kriss Kross. These days, men go all the way – absolutely as low as (they think) they can go, which is impressively low, just above the knee cap.

In my observations, I have found a belt is needed to keep the pants in place. The placement of the belt in sagsag mode appears to make it difficult to walk quickly. Is this similar to the difficulty a woman might have walking quickly in a skirt?

The deeper question: Is the fashion of both sexes' beginning to mesh into one? Will the sag look transform into the pencil skirt?

A prominent myth circulating about the origin of the saggy look is that it began in prison to either send certain sexual signals or it was the result of oversized prison wear. I call it a myth because I believe the good folks at Snopes.com who have been debunking these claims for as many years as there are the internet.

---

91 More or less.

There is only one reason a man would dress this way – only one: He believes he looks good.

A Fashion Prediction

I'm ready to put it all on the line with a bold male fashion prediction that will take off in the future human fashion industry. I will wager that the fashion trend of the future will be...

The ultra-sag: Pants worn around the ankles, à la Steve Martin in the cover art of the 1970s film, *The Jerk*.[92]

The only difference between Steve Martin's look in 1979 and the future look is that the legs will continue to be covered. Shirts will go down to the knees and boxers will descend from knee to just below the ankles, into the shoe. It's time to invest heavily in textiles.

The ultra-saggy look will catch on by the masses shortly after this trend first appears on the fashion runways of Paris, ending abruptly several years later when the cost of denim decreases dramatically during full implementation of an international multilateral trade deal in a post-protectionist era, creating astronomical demand for full length jeans. Ten years later, the ultra-saggy look will re-continue, though it will be picked up mostly in rural areas. The style won't make a comeback to trendy urban areas until two decades later.

Whatever the future may hold, and it will definitely hold something futuristic, Steve Martin should be credited for blazing the path for the ultra-sag revolution way back in 1979.

____

92 *The Jerk*, Directed by Carl Reiner. Steve Martin. Aspen Film Society, 1979.

A Tale of Two Coca-Colas

Author's note: People write in bulleted format in the year 2117.

■ ■ ■

Not much later
February

■ ■ ■

After writing about yogurt so many chapters ago, I decided it would be a good idea to share thoughts from the future on soda.

- Coming to be in 1975 was to be born in the best of times, it was to be born in the worst of times, it was the age of moon landings, it was the age of disco, it was the epoch of hope, it was the epoch of Watergate, it was the spring of technology, it was the winter of bell bottoms, they had everything, they had nothing, they had preservatives, high fructose corn syrup, red dye 40, MSG, and NutraSweet – in short, it was so far from the current day in early 22nd century America that it is hardly worth making a comparison.

- When it comes to food, those who came to be in 1975 happened upon the world in exactly the best and worst time in human history. From the beginning of civilization until 1962, all of humanity was fed at the kitchen table with foods that looked, smelled, and tasted a lot like they did when those non-genetically modified products were first plucked from the ground.

- But for people born in first-world nations in the 1960s and 1970s, the tortured souls who were raised on Pop-Tarts – a popular breakfast consisting of a toasted block of sugarized and hydrogenated fat material – and an overwhelming assortment of other highly processed, preservative-filled fake foods, the taste of which caused almost instant addiction, cravings, and late-night runs to Dunkin' Donuts (since renamed "Dunkin Dates"), it was as if they were raised on hard drugs from birth and didn't know any better.

- In the first decades of the 2000s, greater demand from the younger, health-conscious Millennial generation led to an obsessive turn away from Fritos and bologna toward all natural foods that were legitimately natural in the original sense of the word. As these Millennials rose to power, they instituted laws such as the soda tax in municipalities worldwide and later began to ban the drink altogether. ("Soda" was the general term for sugary, high fructose corn syrupy carbonated drinks served cold.)

- Many today in the 22nd century don't realize the dominant soda company with the highest revenue in that era was the now very health-conscious Mato-Tato company, formerly known as Coca-Cola.

- The Mato-Tato Company was originally founded in 1886 as the Coca-Cola Company. The company became famous for a fountain drink created after the Civil War by a man who aimed to create a medical substitute for the highly addictive opiate morphine, a widely used painkiller. The special ingredient behind his carbonated drink was a careful mix of cocaine and caffeine that promised to cure morphine addiction, headaches, and impotence.

- Once cocaine was eliminated from the drink in 1903, the beverage's secret formula continued unchanged for over a century and the company became one of the most successful businesses in the world, in large part because of their highly effective marketing campaigns.

- During this time, while the Coke drink recipe stayed the same, the company began experimenting with products that were healthier and could not be used to clean corrosion from oven racks and car batteries. Slow to make a "diet" product under the Coke name, as Pepsi had done decades previously, they decided to substitute sugar with an artificial sweetener, naming the new product "Diet Coke" which became an instant hit. For a brief season, Coca-Cola was without controversy.

- Seasons come to an end...over the next thirty years use of artificial sweeteners became heavy targets of consumer groups. Coca-Cola tested the market with caffeine-free and reduced calorie products, but none caught on with the general public.

- The year 2016 was the first year consumption of bottled-water rose above that of carbonated soft drinks. Coca-Cola, while still hugely popular, had reached its zenith. Sales began to slip, and for the first time since the sugar rationing of World War II, the company looked for ways to cut costs.

- Two decades and many failed new product launches later, the writing was on the wall: Coca-Cola could not continue as it had. In 2036, the company announced a ten year phase out of their staple drink with a plan to unveil a new all-natural substitute. After pouring billions into research and development, the company prepared for a major global announcement.

- The company planned to announce its new product at the Super Bowl, the most popular media day on the globe. A Bowl first was achieved in 2046: Coca-Cola purchased every advertising slot for Super Bowl LXXX to roll out their much-hyped replacement product. Once game day arrived, after hours of hilarious, thought-provoking, and clever Coca-Cola sponsored commercials during each break of the football game, it wasn't until the end of the Super Bowl that the company revealed the name of its replacement product. After the game, the screen went dark for 10 seconds, fifty times the average attention span of that era, and then lit up, briefly flashing the words: "Dirt Coke: Available Tomorrow." Many thought this was simply part of the publicity stunt, but the next day in what was considered the most secretive product launch since the "i" eye-embedded microchip release in 2040 (formerly known as "iPhone"), selected vending machines and restaurants around the globe were stocked with the new Dirt Coke product. In some cities, spontaneous mile-long lines of soda and dirt fans emerged, eager to sample the new drink. Surprisingly, the reviews were predominately positive.

The first glass bottle of Dirt Coke

- "Tastes like dirt," said one young woman sipping the new drink outside of an Atlanta-based convenience store after waiting in line for four hours. "I love it."

- Dirt Coke was an instant hit, proving that Coca-Cola's genius marketing savvy had convinced most everyone that a dirt-mixed soft drink was healthy, fun, tasty, and cool. In just one generation, public taste had evolved away from sweetened products. Now, dirt was the new sugar.

- The world's love affair with Dirt Coke didn't last long. In the 2050s a study found that traces of dirt used in the drink were not as healthful as Coca-Cola had claimed. Between negative publicity, a U.S. Department of Justice investigation, and numerous congressional hearings, the embattled company all but admitted fault when it announced another new product rollout to replace the soft drink altogether. Customer fatigue set in, and Coke stood at the verge of bankruptcy.

- Exactly fifty years ago in 2067, Coca-Cola Company was formally dissolved and replaced by Mato-Tato Company, the company that created their current product we all know and love: the red tomato. (Author's note: 2067 was the one hundred year anniversary of Kellogg's discontinued Pop-Tarts, which in that year was a popular product in the black market along with Cap'n Crunch cereal.)

- Few today know how the soft drink icon made the move to the tomato as its flagship product.

- The story begins when a young marketer at Coca-Cola in the 2030s foresaw the trouble the company was trying to ignore: soft drinks would someday face prohibition just as alcohol had a century before. The marketer, Umbule Rasul, an immigrant to the U.S. from Botswana, was convinced that in a generation the public was headed for a sugar-free, all natural diet similar to the almost exclusively tomato diet she enjoyed on her family's tomato farm.

- Tomato drinks, unfashionable among the young for more than a century, were beginning to surge in popularity as an energy drink substitute, since the tomato contained all four major carotenoids, including the widely popular lycopene.

- Rasul drew up a prototype antique-variety heirloom tomato drink and, as the story goes, pitched it to Coca-Cola executives during one lunch break. The pitch went well but not as she had planned. The tomato drink concept was not accepted, but execs were quick to see a rising star in Rasul, and not long after the meeting she enjoyed a meteoric rise in the company.

- Nearly three decades later, as the Dirt Coke fiasco ensued and the "Dirty Coke" public campaign broadened, the board asked the loyal senior executive Rasul to take over as the company's CEO. Soon after accepting the top position, she immediately went back to the drawing board, still convinced that the tomato was the answer to the company's woes.

- Rasul was first to coin the term "Mato-Tato" with a design that would match the classic logo. She worked with scientists in R&D to develop a breakthrough edible coating to label her landmark product.

The first Mato-Tato product launched in 2067

- After many genetically modified varieties of tomatoes had flooded the world market, Mato-Tato's simple, classic heirloom tomato caught everyone off-guard. The tomato, coated in a safe, pathogen-resistant gloss with the trademark "Mato-Tato" symbol, could be eaten right off the grocery store shelf without having to wash or rinse the product. Any contamination during handling of the product would be instantly repelled by the patented coating, destroying even the most dangerous pathogens.

- The Mato-Tato is widely popular worldwide. Almost everyone eats at least one cold Mato-Tato at every meal. You can't have a party without a few six packs of Mato-Tatos in the fridge. The

Mato-Tato Company is by far the most successful corporation of all time, and Rasul, still living, is the wealthiest trillionaire on the planet.

- So back to the individual born in 1975. In my review of best and worst times to live, I have decided that 1975 was an incredible time to be born, for both good and ill. The person born in 1975 knew the taste of highly-addictive sugary substances, a taste unknown in our time, but they soon learned how bad these products were for their health. Having been born in 2097, I have never known what it is to taste Coca-Cola, Twinkies, or Red Vines. I can only read about the products from a more backward age. But what I can do is open this cooler on the beach with my friends, take out a cold Mato-Tato, bite into it, and feel the fresh tomato juices dripping down the sides of my mouth, fully confident that my antioxidant levels will soar to heights my great-great-Pop-Tarts-munching-Coke-guzzling-grandfather, Josh Rolph,* could never have imagined.

*Author's note: I'm not really Coke-guzzling - that becomes a folk tale perpetuated by my future great-grandchildren. I do enjoy strawberry-filled Pop-Tarts, unfrosted, and am eating them at this moment.

*Additional note from Josh Rolph to Coca-Cola Company lawyers who don't like this chapter: This is fiction. Your jobs are secure until at least Super Bowl LXXX.

11

HappyNew! Year with a Bang Needa buck

If only book writing were as easy as writing email spam, I could have finished by now.

■ ■ ■

A day or so later
February

■ ■ ■

I thought I'd take a break from book writing and insert a spam email I received some time ago. I also want to take a pause to give some reflection on spam – a moment of silence, as it were. I will add upfront that I believe in spammers. There are people behind the spam. Real people. Real robots as well. But mostly people. Think about that for a minute, possibly less. They breathe, they eat, they sleep. We love to mock, ridicule, and pass laws to curb their careers in email fraud, but let's really think about this some more.

Consider this: they could be the modern-day cowboys that bring the wild, wild west to the world wide web. Lots of w words there.

Lots of w's.

What do we gain from having a wild west of email? I'm not sure. Maybe fraud. Confusion. Impoverished seniors with internet duped by people like USA Sally who wrote me one of the most brilliant spam messages I have ever received, one crisp winter eve long ago...

■ ■ ■

To: "Josh Rolph" baddawg-007@gmail.com
From: "USA Sally" lakhubuku@yahoo.com
Subject: HappyNew! Year with a Bang Needa buck
Date: Jan. 1, 2008 14:50 GMT +0000

My family and I had a trip visiting (Bangkokladesh), when we attacked some unnamed gunmen in darkness. All ourr money,phones and credit cards got stolen in poker bet from God bless you understand. Valuable items no longer have, except for this computer we talk now, yours truly. It was magnificent terrifying experience that ends with them took us out for ice cream and bad lactose stomach cramps, you understand.

The local authorities throw a fit and the consulate was too casual. We were ask to come back in 2weeks time for investigations celebrations to be made proper, A Team music and everyone you understand. But the truth is we know the sitting ducks for return flight booked and is leaving in few hours from now but presently the cab died to the airport, I know you too understand death and economy.

You are financially strapped due to unexpected robbery attack, Wondering if you can enthused forward ($2,650,00 USD) or anything more you can afford because first semester customers, I promise refund you in full as soon as I return hopefully tomorrow or next. write back immediately to Lhaku Buku to let me know what you can so do oku.

Gracefully truly yours,
Lhaku "Pete" Buku God bleess

■ ■ ■

After I had received this message, I wrote him back.

From: "Josh Rolph" baddawg-007gangsta@gmail.com
To: "USA Sally" lakhubuku@yahoo.com
Subject: HappyNew! Year with a Bang Needa buck
Date: Jan. 1, 2008 14:58 GMT +0000

Dear Lhaku:

I know you're trying to scam me. If I sent you $50, would that satisfy you?

God bless,
Josh

■ ■ ■

To: "Josh Rolph" baddawg-007@gmail.com
From: "USA Sally" lakhubuku@yahoo.com
Subject: HappyNew! Year with a Bang Needa buck
Date: Jan. 1, 2008 14:59 GMT +0000

Dearest Josh;

Thank you so kindly. $50 USd is realluy good. Can you send me a little more than that? $2,450 is more money?

■ ■ ■

I won't bore you with the transcript of every email that went back and forth. We wrote a dozen times or more, short messages like the last two above, him holding his ground that I send him $2,450. So I finally sent it all, with a little tip, my Social Security number, birth date, and a part of my soul that has a weakness for spam.

#12

Hashtags Aren't Funny

By now, we've all created a hashtag on social media to try to be funny, but I am here to tell you none of them are funny. Ever. My advice is to not make #s funny. Ever. I would list out all the hashtags that aren't funny which could be its own book. Since I'm already twelve chapters into this book, I'm not about to rewrite a book about hashtags. I refuse. I refuse to write about unfunny hashtags. What good would it do? None, I say. None. There is no funny hashtag and there never will be. Ever.

■ ■ ■

A couple minutes later
February

■ ■ ■

Hashtags aren't funny, except for this one:

\#

13

Race Relations

Imagine you are a page of a book. For most of your life, you are visible to no one. You are compressed tightly against another page for most of your existence. When the reader finally gets to you, you are visible for only a short amount of time, and then all goes dark again.

■ ■ ■

Sixty-seven days later
May

■ ■ ■

This is the part of the book where I am completely aware of your boredom. You are bored of this book and I know it. I am aware of it. I acknowledge, recognize, and accept it. Already, roughly 87% of the total readership has abandoned the book, so I'm really glad you are at least still here, even though you are just as bored as I am beginning to become with writing it. And maybe my boredom reflects on to you. It's like if we were sitting in the same room together and I was excited to be there, you would be much more interested in chatting than if we were in the same room and you could feel the boredom pulsating boringly from my tired eyes. But you're still here, reading this book. You know what you are? You're a patriot in my book — you're not a patriot in this book, but you are in the expression, "You're a patriot in my book."

The 87% of non-patriots left their copy of this book in any number of places, the pages visible to no one. This is not always done intentionally, people just get distracted with other things. For a book to be viewed page by page, cover to cover, there has to be some kind of alignment astrologically between author and reader. There's no way around it.

It's one thing if it's a fictional murder mystery with the kind of built-in suspense that leaves them with no choice but to turn each page and put off other life priorities in order to continue reading. Books like mine about becoming an author don't necessarily leave the reader with a continual hook that keeps them glued to the word. I'm fine with that. I'm glad you're still here, though. It means a lot. I'm glad I'm still here, too. It's morbid sounding but I could have died at any time up until now. You could have as well. So let's celebrate life because reading means living. It's alive-ing. We're alive and that's something to be not-bored about, until the thought of gratitude leaves our mind and we return to a mundane, very often meaning-deficient life. Even though 87% of my will to write a book has also left, the very act of writing chapter 13 means ensuring this book has enough material to call it a book and not a leaflet. Chapter 13 is also the unluckiest chapter number of them all. It is the floor number that builders skip over.

To keep you here at least a little while longer, I thought I'd write about something controversial, like, I don't know, race relations. It's a topic that doesn't seem to be getting better, even as society is becoming more enlightened in recent decades. Much ink has been spilled on the topic, but not from me. So why not dive in? Not many people talk about it candidly and honestly. The topic doesn't come up much but you know it's on everyone's mind. There are racists and non-racists. We need improved race relations between all parties. This is why I wish to discuss a different kind of racism altogether.

Watch any Hollywood movie from the 1930s and 40s and you don't see it anywhere. You assume it's happening, but you don't see it. Then comes the 50s and 60s, and racism became more prominent because people were healthier in post-War America.

Fast forward to the 1980s and all of a sudden it was seen on every street in the country – mostly in the morning in the suburbs. Headbands and sweatbands marked its most devoted adherents.

But compare our day to the 80s, we now see it all around us, at all times of day and night. The attitudes have changed dramatically since even the 80s.

Today, it's the bumper stickers. I began seeing them several years ago - I'm not sure when. 26.2, 13.1. They confused me. These numeric codes, decimals, fractions. What could either mean? On some cars I saw both. They were quickly sprouting then blooming as a field of flowers in springtime. I wasn't sure what it all meant. These drivers, the ones sitting behind the steering wheel, driving away as if they had not a care in the world, seemed to boast of these unusual numbers. Then I realized the numbers have to do with marathons and half-marathons. This type of person felt they should attach to their vehicle a number to show they:

1. Knew the distance, measured in mile tenths, of either a half and full marathon.
2. Wished to share no other clues as to what those numbers might mean.
3. Could imply to nearby vehicles that they had run a half or full marathon (or in some cases, run both).

I have a problem with these types. A big, big problem. I speak of my relations with those who race. This is – as I've stated – a different kind of racism. Nay, this is in very fact and deed a different kind of racism.

On the surface, my relations with those who race is mostly okay. Deep down, however, there is an emotional wanting. I want to have better relations with those who race. I want to drive by their vehicle and like them.

Most importantly, I want to improve relations between those who run and those who watch. Those poor souls standing on the sidelines during a long-distance race may wait a long time in order to cheer on their runner.

It's similar to the relations between reader and the author. I'm running a marathon right now, trying to type more words. I feel that the unique fingerprint identifiers at the end of my fingertips may be modified from their original unique markings after all this typing.

Criminals: Who needs sandpaper? Just type a book!

Authors don't want spectators. Fingertips hitting the keys, over time becoming worn down like a rough stone worn over millennia by the perennial flows of a river. You are reading, your eyes shifting from left to right, over and over, exercising your eye muscles while both of our synapses fire in the brain, triggering the neural lobe that borders along the boredom area of the mind, a race of synapses in the writer, a race of synapses in the reader, two separate bodies, once distinct, who have different roles occupying their own space in the physical world, now unified in their journey towards the same destination of consciousness.

14

How to Fall Asleep Without Meds and Live Longer

The self-help genre is a surging body of literature grown popular because people want to improve their lives. But 'self-help' is written by people that want to help you. True 'self-help' – the very definition of the two words conjoined by a hyphen – would be a book written by yourself to yourself. Someone writing a 'self-help' book intended for others should instead rename it the "help-yourself" genre, but that sounds rude, as in, 'Go help yourself, you freak of nature.' Perhaps self-help is the way to go. I don't know. I just work here.

■ ■ ■

Two millennia, four centuries, sixty-eight years and fourscore minutes later

May

■ ■ ■

My book needs a how-to chapter that isn't directly about writing a book. It is indirectly about writing a book. Because if one thing is for sure, no book will be written if I am sleep deprived. Trust me, I've tried it. Sleep deprivation further enhances the incredible sedative that is book writing. It's therefore best to write after a good night's sleep.

The last time I had a hard time falling asleep at night was in high school, until the *Night That Changed Everything*.

Before I begin to describe the *Night That Changed Everything*, I should bring up the fact that up until now, in this book that has now fully entered its teenage chapter in book years, the stage of a book more awkward than ever, I have steered clear from turning this book into what could be called a "self-help" book. The book is definitely helping me to write a book, I will admit, but it's not necessarily *a guide to help you* write a book, with the exception of the acronym I came up with in chapter one. There are no additional step-by-step instructions or best practices to follow in order to become an author yourself, unless you copied every word of this book and published it on your own, which I strongly encourage. I mean, you can copy this one if you want, but if so, you are likely a lunatic. If I were you, I'd copy a *NYT* bestseller![93]

All said, this chapter fits neatly within the category of "self-help." And after discussing boredom, resisting at first and then fully giving into the tantalizingly dreadful purgatory of boredom-ness, and not liking it one bit, I decided to turn to something more exciting, which is a very simple plan that will help you fall asleep.

So stay awake while you allow me to show you how to go to sleep.

I should also add one more thing about trying to become an author and sleep. I mentioned in chapter two how writing puts me to sleep. There is something intensely sleep-inducing about sitting down to write this book. Perhaps other authors are invigorated when they write. As for me, it's the most coma-inducing effort I have ever undertaken – the kind that can put me right to sleep while sitting upright in this chair. It's extraordinary how little effort is expended in the writing process before I'm knocked out cold. This book will take me many more years, possibly decades, to write, at this sleepy-slow rate.

---

93 Who knows, this could be a *NYT* bestseller in an alternate reality. But we probably all have two heads in that dimension. Some things are better left unknown.

Before I continue with my story about the *Night That Changed Everything*, I feel a disclaimer is needed: what I am about to share will change the course of history with regard to fixing the insomnia epidemic. Know that there is one solution even greater and longer-lasting to end insomnia once and for all: trying to become an author.

On the *Night Before the Night That Changed Everything*, I was not trying to become an author. I struggled falling asleep. Pretty much every night as a teenager I had the hardest time transitioning from wakefulness to the sleep state.

Even though it was a long time ago, I remember the night time ritual as if it was right this very moment: quiet, desperate for sleep, yet still helplessly awake.

I was thinking about all of this throughout the *Afternoon Snack Time of the Night That Changed Everything*.

"How will I possibly survive on little to no sleep?" I asked myself.

I am here to report to you that help has arrived. Way back then when I was a young whippersnapper I invented a method to fall asleep requiring zero medication, no expensive tricks, and zero trips to the therapist to work out the issues that were likely keeping me awake. This is something anyone can do. This method uses the only available resource you are left with when resting in bed at night: your brain.

Some sleep gimmicks, like the Counting Sheep Method (CSM), actually kick up brain CPU power by as much as 35%. You might as well be on the couch watching a Jason Bourne movie - the effect is much the same.

Other sleep suggestions from the experts require more thinking, more concentration, more focus on relaxing.

These suggestions are perhaps the worst advice you could receive for restful sleep.

My medical breakthrough is simply this: Imagine a Blank Piece of Paper.

That's it.

Just close your eyes and imagine a blank, 8 1/2" x 11" letter-sized sheet of white paper. You will then fall asleep.

After years of experimentation with the paper method, I feel a need to offer up some pointers.

First, DO NOT – REPEAT – DO NOT imagine this piece of paper, an actual sheet of paper I tried to use as a sleep assistant on October 3, 1992:

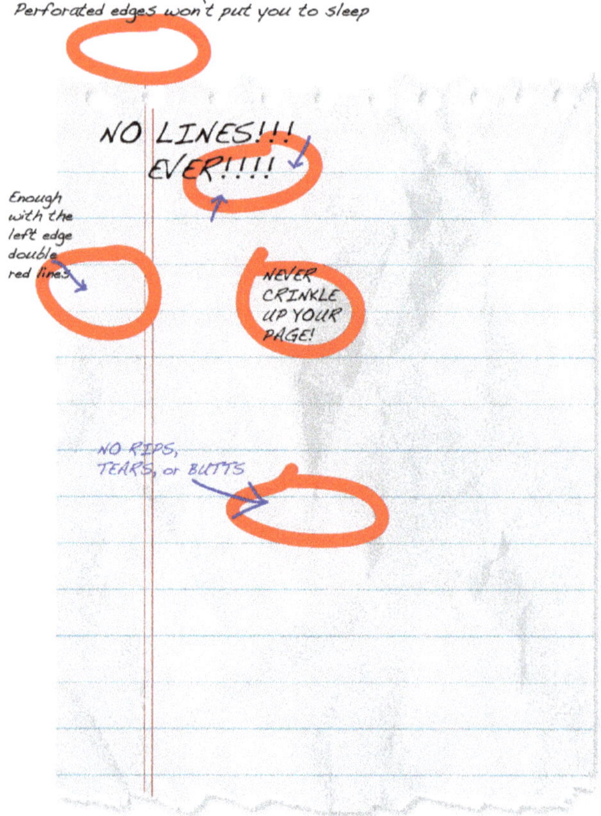

Instead, your sleep paper must look exactly like this 8 ½" X 11" paper (not drawn to scale):

This is your Sleep Assistant. Nothing more, nothing less.

I had my three-year-old diagram how the bedtime process should look in the image below.[94]

94　I actually drew this.

I will now tell you the direct, no-joke impact the paper-to-sleep method has had on my life, in bulleted-form, no less—

- When I want to sleep, I sleep.
- I am more successful.[95]
- I've counseled a few people in the last 20 years with this approach; at least three people.
- When using this sleep method, my dreams are incredible. Not good – incredible. Incredible, as in sometimes terrifyingly incredible. You may have similar results: both amazing and horrible dreams that will leave you thinking: my brain came up with that? Man, I'm messed up!

---

95   (Than I was as a teenager.)

When this will not work:

- After you die.[96]

From the goodness of my heart, I've shared all I know on the subject, even making things up from time to time, like most professionals.[97]

By the way, I'm eating fresh dates right now. They are so good.

And I am still awake. I won't become an author while asleep. That's a pro-tip.

Sweet dreams.[98]

---

96   Known in some circles as the "die penalty" of sleep. See chapter eight on the death penalty.

97   Let's be honest.

98   Note to self after publication: Conduct research on whether reading this book fights insomnia.

15

Parenting

The day you become a parent is the day you are reborn into an alternate you.

■ ■ ■

Sixteen Days Later
June

■ ■ ■

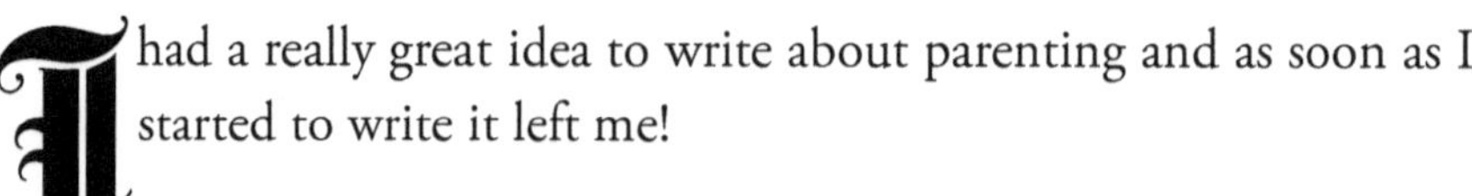 had a really great idea to write about parenting and as soon as I started to write it left me!

Climate Change

This book will warm your heart by 0.0001°C.

■ ■ ■

Sixteen Milliseconds Later

■ ■ ■

17

Benji Emoji

Try to use a top hat emoji in your next text.

■ ■ ■

Sixteen months later
October

■ ■ ■

Long ago, the ancient Greeks stared at the starry sky, creating entire mythologies around the superhuman characters they transposed over the light-bespeckled nightscape. These grand, elaborate myths were sophisticated, calendar-based creations that taught sweeping moral lessons to many generations for thousands of years.

As the night sky becomes less visible in our urban and suburban nightscape, we no longer look up to the sky. We look down to the glowing rectangular masses that may someday evolve as a sixth digit on our hands. Today, emoji are the new, modern-day constellations, in the sense that images on these devices are used to convey a feeling or emotion.

Fortunately, these small, simple emoji symbols, though trite, uninspired, and lazily created, now help us to communicate feeling and emotion to those among the billions of humans who share the same planet. Unfortunately, the transmission of these symbols from device to mind reveals no moral lesson whatsoever.

Rather than bash emoji, I simply want to accept the phenomena and try to find the good in it all. The main thing I like about emoji is the word "emoji" itself. The word "emoji" reminds me of the name "Benji." When I hear "emoji," I think "Benji." Every time. But there's no Benji emoji, which is a shame.

What's sad is how emoticons, or keyboard character combos like a smile represented by colon followed by the closed parenthesis bracket, are fading, while emoji, the little images built into our smartphones, are taking over.

Years ago, I developed a small catalog of emoticons that could have taken off, if it wasn't for the Big Emoji corporate types.

I won't share these emoticons here in this book, mostly because I don't want to. Also, because their time has passed. My interest is to write about things that have a little more enduring value, that can be read a decade or two from now and not feel like ancient Greek. Emoji may just be that thing.

As I look up to the sky while down here on my phone, a feeling washes over me, a beckoning from a better place, encouraging me to look forward. Forward, to the monitor in front of me. Forward, to the keypad beneath my five-digited fingers. The passion driving me to finish the book allows me to continue typing, however, there are limits to what I can type, and at this time, I've reached my limit on Greek legend, moral lessons, emoji, emoticons, and people named "Benji."

The Inked and the Pasty

Get your Skuggis for the Tjusig or Kampig Kartotek...only at IKEA.

■ ■ ■

Roughly seventy-one decades later
January 1

■ ■ ■

I have a theory about people with tattoos that I want to share. It may offend somewhere between 20% and 46.6% of you, my reading audience.

I waited for a long while in a long line at IKEA the other day. (When I write "IKEA" I'm not shouting, it's just that when texting where I was that day my phone's autocorrect turned "Ikea" into "IKEA," so I will go with the authorities on this one.)

I counted 15 people waiting in the three available lines near me. I only counted because I noticed something curious: seven of the fifteen in line had visible tattoos. That's 46.6% of the IKEA line population that bore tattoos. Let me repeat that figure: 46.6%

In my line standing directly in front of me was a woman in her 40s with school-aged children and her parents. She had a tattoo on her arm – I forget what it was – and two tattoos that caught my eye right away because of their unusual placement on the back of the leg in the center of each calf and their uncanny resemblance to the Transformers logo. Untrained as I am in tattootlage, the Transformer logos turned out to be cleverly designed butterflies.

In the line of IKEA patrons heading to the register on my right, a 30-something woman with her hair up had a tattoo right behind her left ear of at least a six-inch tall hand flashing the 'hang loose' gesture. It would have been much cooler if it was animated.

To my left, I saw a man with a tattoo sleeve. I don't know the proper term for this, but it is like an unusually colorful shirt sleeve painted down the entire arm, ending at the wrist either buttoned or in French cuffs. I hear monograms are an extra fifteen bucks.

According to a Pew poll, the percentage of Americans under 40 with tattoos is a surprising 40%.[99] Surprising because I thought it was only 38%. A Harris poll says 1 out of 5 adult Americans has a tattoo - but that probably includes the old guys with dark, faded anchors and skulls on their wrinkled forearms. Tattoo tech has come a long way since then. In twenty years, tattoos will talk back to us. Forget Terminator, in 200 years these tattoos will likely take over the world.

My point? The IKEA line's tattoo-baring guests were not representative of the American population. That said, it was completely under-representative of the population in Sacramento, possibly the inkiest region in the developed world.

Anyway, I'm just stalling because I'm afraid to share my theory about people with tattoos. I really don't want to offend anybody, and if so, I would prefer to only offend 20% than 46.6%.

---

99   "Explosion in Tattooing, Piercing Tests State Regulators," Stateline Article, Pew Trusts, by Marsha Mercer, June 14, 2017. https://www.pewtrusts.org/en/research-and-analysis/blogs/stateline/2017/06/14/explosion-in-tattooing-piercing-tests-state-regulators

So back to IKEA. Here we are, two very distinct groups, the inked... and the pasty.

Wait, wait, wait! The "Inked and the Pasty" would make an amazing name for a soap opera!

So here we are, at IKEA, the tattooed and — pasty is not the right word — how about the erased? I say erased which might offend because it implies there was an expensive removal treatment, but that's really not my intent.

No matter what they tell you, I'm no erase-ist.

What should I call people like myself? The "non-tattooed" or "un-inked" or "tattooless?" How about "blank-skinned?" All of those make it sound like I'm superior because I haven't chosen to ink myself. Those kinds of statements represent the worst kind of erasism.

So again, I keep getting distracted, but there in line at IKEA, as I looked down at my cart, I thought of the hundreds of aisles of IKEA products I had passed. Look it up on their site – 12,000 products fill the store. It's true. It has more products per square inch than my wife's purse. There is the large warehouse area with goods stacked Tower of Babel style with hard to find part numbers that you have to get just right to put that table or Billy bookcase together or whatever it is you are purchasing, assembly almost certainly required. Thousands of household products meant to make their mark in your home.

MAKE THEIR MARK IN YOUR HOME. Did you catch that? Oh yes, I'm shouting.

Follow this closely: Tattoos. Home products. Marks. Tattoos. Permanence. Home products. Permanence. Choices. Statements. Marks. Permanence. Home Products. Tattoos...

I stared for a moment at my only IKEA item, a frame with a silly IKEA name, I forget what it was, like "Gillabagam" or something. Translated, it probably means "jabberwocky" or "vinniebarbarino" in English. Looking at the clock, I noticed how long it had taken me to find that frame — somewhere over an hour. This is a frame that will go in a small corner of our home. It will probably be there for three years. Four and a half, tops.

I then saw the tattooed with overflowing yellow bags consisting of more than just frames, and wheeled pallets stacked with large boxes of new furniture. They were buying tables and bookcases and items that would mark their homes for decades to come, if not longer.

I looked at the frame and then at my skinny little pasty naked bare boring little pasty skinny but incredibly useful left arm. At the time, I wasn't looking at my right arm.

I looked at the hang loose woman and then down at calf butterfly. Total ink cost between the two? Maybe five hundred bucks. How much was in their carts? About five hundred bucks' worth.

At that exact moment I came up with this theory, almost word for word: "People with tattoos have an easier time buying things at IKEA than I do."

P.S. One of my favorite pastimes – scratch that – one of the things I find to be amusing in life is the diversity of associations. There is an association for <u>everything</u>. Everything. Just to be sure, I looked up to see if there is a tattoo association, and I wasn't disappointed. <u>http://www.nationaltattooassociation.com</u>

CHAPTER
19

Our Corner of the Eye Problem

Think about:
Seeing a little mouse scurry across the ground on a forest trail vs. Seeing
a mouse in your pantry

■ ■ ■

Next year
March 5

■ ■ ■

Once from the corner of my eye I saw a
flash of darkness
zip
erratically
along the carpet like this –
SHWALAKAZAM –
back and forth.
Really quickly.
Like a boomerang, back and forth
but all on the left side of my eye.

It's hard to explain. I'm a terrible writer. Why did I start a book when I can't describe anything? Let me try this again.

I was sitting here on the couch. Actually, it was a chair. I didn't own a couch. I was young, but not so young that I couldn't be legally married, which I was. We were still newlyweds, a year into marriage, and shouldn't have been because we couldn't afford a couch. It was nighttime. We were watching a movie. The movie was funny. I forget what the movie was, but again, it made me laugh. I wonder if it would still make me laugh. Probably not. My humor has matured so much since then.

Just as I laughed out loud (at a funny part from the movie), out of the corner of my eye, on the left side, so out of the periphery of my left eye, I saw that same dark dot quickly flash around and go – KAZOOKEE – back and forth, really fast. SWISH-SHWOO, like that.

It was dark in the room. I forgot to mention that. So the dark flash occurred in the darkness. That's important to know.

Does any of this make sense?

Fine, I'll just say the punch line here, which really wasn't meant to be a punch line. I'm just a terrible excuse for a writer.

The dark flash turned out to be a mouse.

I should turn this story into a children's book called, "SHWALAKAZAM" when I figure out how to describe this story. No results found for that word in a Google search.........YET.

I should also write about all my experiences with mice sometime in a future book I have no excuse writing. It will be therapeutic for me. It will gross you out, unless you like mice when they're in your home. I'm still dealing with each of these traumatic experiences, the first that occurred when I was about three years old. I'll need some time to work it out.

■ ■ ■

Anyway, we've talked about me – let's talk about you now. That's right, I'm looking right at you...OUT OF THE CORNER OF MY EYE. I've noticed something about you from the corner of my eye that bothers me. It bothers me a lot.

When I see you from the corner of my eye...how do I say this without pointing my finger toward the part of the eye I'm referring to, and without a diagram of the human eye?

I'll just give it to you straight from the heart, without my pointing finger being involved. Instead, I'll bring up your fingers, or at least, one or two of your fingers.

When I see you from the corner of my eye, I can see you picking, with one of your fingers, sometimes two, at the corner of your eye.

I try to point the periphery of my eye further away from you but somehow I can still see what you do after you pick the contents of the corner of your eye.

From the corner of my eye, the thing I notice you doing is you extend your hand in such a way as to enable you to see with your full eye the gooberish contents of the corner of your eye.

This happens so often, at least quarterly, and not just with you, but with others as well, that I can keep silent no longer.

I will also get into trouble with those of the opposite gender (as me) as I am about to say something that may come across as sexist:

I've never seen a man do this out of the corner of my eye, or otherwise.

I will admit that I am a man, and to avoid being a hypocritical man, I will also admit that in addition to being a man, I have done exactly what bothers me in others out of the corner of my eye.

It can therefore be said with some degree of certainty that both you and I share this in common:

We both have a corner of the eye problem.

20

Something Really Cool Happened Today

What is it, to be obscure? Is it alone, lonely, isolated, lost? Is it the empty room or the crowded room filled only with typing strangers? Is it Facebook?

■ ■ ■

The last few months flew by
June 15

■ ■ ■

Josh Rolph
Something really cool happened today. I can't say what it is exactly. All I can say is you should know that something really cool happened today, everyone I've ever known. The main reason I'm saying I can't say what it is is I've wanted to have an obscure post since obscure posts were invented circa 2008 but I just haven't had the opportunity yet...See More

Unlike · Comment · 11 hours ·

👍 You, Kristina Rolph, George H. W. Bush, and 1 other likes this.

Write a comment ...

Your key takeaway should be that something really cool happened today.

Something really cool happened today. I can't say what it is exactly. All I can say is you should know that something really cool happened today, and I'm announcing this here on Facebook, to everyone

I've ever known. The main reason I'm saying I can't say what it is is I've desperately wanted to write an obscure post since obscure posts were invented circa 2008. I've also wanted to write "is is" in a sentence since 2010 but I honestly either forgot I wanted to do that or it hasn't worked out/haven't had a chance – one of those things. Unlike many millions who have obscurely posted since the very first obscure post was shared on social media by someone with a melodramatic personality, I just haven't had the opportunity yet. It being my first time jumping into the world of obscure posting, I made sure to carefully choose each word in "something really cool happened today." I didn't want to say, "Something amazing happened today" or "something extraordinary happened today" because I don't want to be overly dramatic like my obscure post forebears about the really cool thing that happened. Today, the opportunity fell on my lap. If you had told me when I woke up this morning that I would have the opportunity to obscurely post, I would have told you you were crazy. (True confession (is there any other kind): I've wanted to write "you you" in a sentence so badly for almost forever.) So I tell you friends, relatives, semi-friends, acquaintances, semi-acquaintances, former relatives who through divorce are no longer in my family — oh, and the we-never-met-but-somehow-are-Facebook-friends friends — the point of this post is for you to know that something really cool happened. Today. To me. And really, that's all I can say. I would tell you what happened, but I've made the tough decision that I can't say exactly what it is. Not that it's that big a deal, because it may not be anything. But know that the something that happened was cool. Really cool. Something really cool. And it happened today. It really happened. I will not under any circumstances tell you what happened. To make myself clear, no matter how much you plead, beg, threaten, or cry in your comments, I refuse to tell you the really cool thing that really happened. Even if you attempt comment obscurity pretending to have little interest in my obscurity, I still refuse. No matter the tactic taken, I refuse. I'm glad I'm making myself clear in an obscure post. Clear/obscure is a good thing. In the process of making myself clear, however, I suddenly feel like I should apologize for not telling you as much as I already haven't. So I'll just come out and say it: I'm so sorry. My clear obscurity has nothing to do with not trusting you with the information I am intentionally hiding from you.

How to be an annoying commenter when I'm trying out obscurity

The main reason I can't tell you what cool thing happened is because I don't want comments saying, "What is it?" Or, "Josh, will you leave us hanging?" Or, "is it X?" (Where X equals something that has nothing to do with the cool thing and simply ends up detracting from the cool thing.)

Josh Rolph
Something really cool happened today. I can't say what it is exactly. All I can say is you should know that something really cool happened today, everyone I've ever known. The main reason I'm saying I can't say what it is is I've wanted to have an obscure post since obscure posts were invented circa 2008 but I just haven't had the opportunity yet...See More

Unlike · Comment · 15 hours ago · 👋

👍 You, Kristina Rolph, George H. W. Bush, and 5 others like this.

John Doenut What is it?
1 hour · Unlike · 👍 79

Carl F. Quinn, IX, Esq. Leaving us hanging...
7 min · Unlike · 👍 22

Write a comment ...

Everyone's so nice when responding to obscure posts.

(On second thought, your guess about X could actually be the right thing which would be really weird, I mean what are the chances of you guessing what it is? Are you stalking me? Then I would someday have to admit that the person who guessed correctly was right about X. I couldn't lie and say they were wrong.) Or I could get the comment that says something like, "thinking of you," or, "you're in my prayers," which means that you skimmed my post so quickly that you didn't read the words "really cool" and thought my post said, "something happened today," so you assume I don't want to go into detail because it is a private matter and when people don't go into detail on private matters it is usually because something bad has happened. When bad things happen, your instinct, if you're normal, is to help, which is why one might say, "You're in my prayers." But it is really just laziness when someone doesn't fully read your posts. The "you're in my prayers" comment would also attract my friends who are a little more bold and who want to protect me. They might respond by saying, "Didn't you read his post, idiot? He said something cool happened." Then my atheist friends might start arguing with the faithful prayer commenter about the uselessness of prayer and the superiority of a disbelief in God, creating a sub-post thread of hundreds of comments with tweet-length arguments that get everyone worked up on both sides of the issue, completely forgetting that the post was intended to share that something really cool happened today. What I'm saying by saying "something really cool happened today" is this is a private matter of the positive kind so you do not need to pray for me. I mean, you can pray for me. Either way, I'm not sharing exactly or even generally what it is that happened. And even though it isn't something horrible and there's really no need to pray for me or if you're atheist there's no need to keep me in your thoughts, which is odd anyway to be kept in anyone's thoughts, I won't stop you if you feel so inclined to either pray or keep me in your thoughts. Maybe I've written so much already on this that you're worried about me and will pray for me or think of me anyway. Maybe not. I can't control your prayers or thoughts, however much I wish I could keep you from praying for me and keeping me in your thoughts.

I fully respect your right to feel however you want to feel after reading this post. Your feelings are absolutely yours. All I want you to know – and you can choose your reaction to what I say for better or worse – is that something really cool happened today. That is all. I've given you all the information I wish for you to know. I will not give you any more information than that, at least the way I see it now. It could very well be that next year I decide to do a follow up to tell you either a little more information than I provided today or all the information. Every last detail of it. The problem is most people in this setting don't like the details, they just want short little snippets of information or general summaries. If they want more detail, which they rarely do, they will ask for more detail. If I were to provide more information at a future date, like, let's say next year at this time, I don't know exactly how I would handle it. Would I say, "Remember the time I posted saying that something really cool happened? Well, now I can say what it was." Then I would explain what happened with a general summary that everyone would read (no more than two brief sentences...never run past the point that they have to click "See More" to see more). I wonder what you would think if I posted something like that next year or a decade from now.

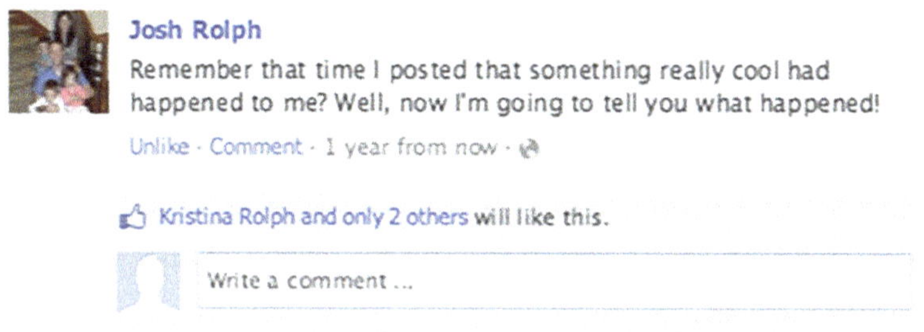

I did a search on https://future.google.com/ and found this future post in the archives.

What if you didn't care? What if you skipped over it because you were still bothered by the fact that I didn't tell you what the cool thing was when it happened? Worse yet, what if you didn't think it was cool? What if you thought it was the opposite of cool? What *is* the opposite of cool? Oh! This is bad. And here I said it was "really cool" forgetting that everyone's version of cool is relative. What is "really cool" for me may only be "cool" for you. So next year if I were to reveal what it is that was really cool, you may downgrade my "really cool" to your "cool" and think I'm out of touch because I have no understanding of "cool." Worse yet, what if my "really cool" is your "super cool?" What if our cools are completely out of balance? That would be so not cool. What if you read it, thinking it's actually "super cool," and get really jealous, thinking I'm better than you? What if you spiral into a depression all because I am so much more amazing than you could ever be? Oh no. No, no, no, no. What have I done? I thought an obscure post would be intriguing and fun. Now I profoundly regret that I ever dragged you through this. I regret it because I can never admit publicly on Facebook what the really cool thing is that happened today. I'm horribly embarrassed that I made such a big deal out of what happened to me today when it probably isn't that big a deal at all. It really probably isn't. I've realized that for my own self-esteem, and possibly yours, I'm never going to write an obscure post again.

Josh Rolph
I've been thinking a lot
Like · Comment · 39 minutes ago ·

 Everyone living and deceased like this.

 Write a comment ...

21

Naked

An excerpt from this chapter:

"I'm writing 'NAKED.'"

■ ■ ■

Sixty-six years later
October 29

■ ■ ■

Besides the highly controversial chapters on race relations and the death penalty, one subject that hasn't really been explored is the dilemma authors face about whether to include so-called "edgy" material in a book.[100]

Racy romance novels come to mind when I think of an edgy book, filled with titillating content describing human-to-human relations in brow-raising detail. Amazon.com contains all kinds of books of multiple genres attracting the baser instincts. These books contain every degree, shape, and form of the vulgar or prurient. There are books that push the boundaries of normative behavior, taking the reader down twisted paths.

All said, there are books moving past the raunch and edge of

---

100   When I wrote "authors face" I envisioned my own "author's face."

yesteryear, heading straight into new, uncharted frontiers involving enhanced exploration of sexuality, drug use, criminal behavior, the vile and the profane, inhumane acts, dark arts, etc.

If you have read to this point and you enjoy that kind of thing, you may have been disappointed to find that this book contains nothing of the sort. Until now, this book has been fairly simple and straightforward. There is so far nothing in this book that might even remotely be considered risqué.

I am not pushing many boundaries, except for the fact that I think no one has ever written a book called "Now I Can Say I'm an Author," ever, since the dawn of baked bread. ("The Dawn of Baked Bread" would make a really good non-edgy book title.[101])

If I were to go there - go edgy - and include something fairly scandalous in here, I would try something that isn't necessarily avant-garde, though it is avant-garde in the fashion, or fashion-less sense. By fashion-less I mean I will take the book *past fashion* into some sort of a post-fashion state. I will remove fashion altogether. I will take this book naked. And not just naked: completely naked, stripped to the bone, nothing at all, absolutely full-on-nudity naked, however I'm not going to change the book title to "Now I Can Say I'm Naked."

Now that I can say this chapter is naked, the book is now edgy. Since the book is naked, and this is the naked chapter, it could sell so many more copies from a marketing standpoint.[102] The market for people who want to purchase nakedly branded products must be growing because the phenomena is found everywhere I go. There's even "naked marketing" which has nothing to do with porn. It's marketing that's naked, and as far as I know is not referring to the marketers themselves.

Going naked is today's gold standard, go-to edgy premium sauce.

---

101   A Google search resulted in zero results of this phrase. "The dawn of sliced bread" search produced numerous results.
102   I use "standpoint" way too often when talking. Thought I would write it here and then include it as a footnote.

It's the new platinum, sapphire, diamond titanium brand identifier. For this reason, everyone's going naked these days. There are all kinds of naked products. Naked this, naked that. Drink the naked juice, eat the naked food...there's even nude pantyhose. It's crazy. Naked, naked, naked. I did an Amazon search on products and had to cover my eyes after finding naked creams, naked vitamins, naked everything. There are naked books, naked stores, universal naked nakedness every place I turn my naked eyes and my naked body that is currently clothed.

So much nakedness.

But out there in this materialist world, is there such a thing as a naked chapter of a book? Either way, this chapter will be the naked chapter. Cuz we all know I'm desperate here. I've gotta sell some books. And that being said, there's nothing more edgy than naked, and this chapter goes completely bare. It's the chapter gone wild tell-all filled from the beginning of the chapter to the end of the chapter with a continual stream of naked nudity the likes this book has never seen. Absolute and total nakedness from chapter heading to chapter footer, the body of which is completely and utterly naked. Utterly. Naked to the core. Its essence is nakedness. It espouses nakedness. It *is* nakedness. It is the nakedest form of naked this side of naked. If this chapter had bones, they would be exposed right now. This chapter is rated so naked that nakedness will have to be redefined to include in its definition this purely naked chapter. It is so naked only the naked will be allowed to read it. This is rated NC-naked. A new rating system is needed. It's off-the-charts naked. So naked there will be new naked off-the-charts charts. Here's the naked off-the-chart chart chant:

Naked, naked, naked.

Naked.

Naked-naked.

Naked naked, naked naked.

I just wrote naked, several times. And I would do it again if it meant going more naked.

It's the naked poem of the century. Naked prose. Naked alliteration.

Naked allusion. Naked literary art. The most naked of the arts: the naked arts.

If I knew how to haiku, I would naked haiku.

Naked.

I am writing NAKED.

I am not writing while naked but I did just write an all-caps NAKED.

For those of you who have already been there, done that, who see nothing new here, nothing edgy, why don't I go a step further in a way you may not have imagined. That's right, I'm taking this chapter *past* nakedness. All the way past naked. If naked were here and that line way over there was the border of naked, I would be crossing that line of nakedness. I would be moving past the line, all the way. I would jump across that line and be on the other side of naked, looking back laughing maniacally at how I moved far past the boundaries of naked. You know what's past naked? Can you guess? Do you have any idea?

Post-naked nakedness nakidity/nudity. Or if that's not far enough for some of you people then watch out I'm coming for you with post-post-post-post-post-post naked nakedness.

I'm trying to think of what moving past naked could be, post naked, after naked or next-level nakedness could be. It's not "more naked" or "nakeder." I think I already used "nakedest" earlier.

Going past naked does not take you to a never-before reached advanced plane of sensuality. That's not anywhere close to where I wanted to take this discussion, so get your head out of the gutter.

Is moving past nakedness an end to the naked phenomenon? Is moving past "naked this" or "naked that" a conclusion to the age we are in that attempts to describe things as they are not, purely for marketing purposes? Is a post-naked society clothed?

22

The First Black Comedian Who Was White Who Never Performed at the Apollo and Who Wasn't Really a Comedian and Who Likes Really Long Chapter Titles

It's healthy to write chapters about how you thought about but never did something.

■ ■ ■

Three weeks later
November 19

■ ■ ■

I have spent more time writing this chapter's title than writing the chapter itself. And if you peek ahead to see how long this chapter is, you might appreciate what I mean.

There is not yet an autobiographical chapter of this book. Maybe that's a good thing, maybe that's a bad thing. If "Now I Can Say I'm an Author" had been written by someone with name recognition, like Steve Jobs or Barack Obama, there would admittedly be a much higher interest in reading by the reading masses. I'm convinced this book will be of interest to no one because this thing called name recognition. Another way of saying it is this book has no chance, so why would I talk about me?

I managed to write a bunch of stuff before chapter one and then kept going. Twenty-one previous chapters that generously pass as twenty-one incoherent thoughts. If you don't know me personally, and you wanted to know more about my life, I wouldn't know where to begin in telling you that story. Would I offer a chronological life story, or would I share themed experiences that could provide a cumulative sampling of what makes me, me? I really don't know. I've given this so little thought in my attempt to become an author. If I were to write more autobiographically, first inclination would be the chronological method, to start with ancestors, a chapter or two on grandparents and parents, and then hit the ground running at birth and beyond. But as I know I'm repeating ad nauseum the book's purpose.

I'm not writing an autobiography. I'm writing a book trying to become an author. I guess I'm acknowledging that one of the many options for content that could be used to fill this book would be to write an autobiography, but that seems ridiculous to me. And to you.

All you should know about me by now is that I'm dying to become an author. A story of a dying wannabe author would make a better story than just a guy dying to become an author. And you know I like yogurt. A lot. And that you don't know what to think because this is a mighty strange book so far. On that note, I'm finally feeling hopeful that this strange book can someday get finished. I have actually gone so far as to outline what to write about next. Looking back on what I've written and estimating the projected word count using the current word count, I think I'm halfway there. Being halfway is amazing. It feels good. It feels so good that I need to remind myself to be careful. This is usually the point when I leave a project behind. I typically become content with being halfway through a project. What I need is for my contentment to not stand in the way between me and authorhood. I simply can't stand between me and me. I mean, enough is enough, self!

The target is to write about twenty more chapters, which, looking back at the current average, should get me to 60,000 - 70,000 words, or novel length. While this isn't a novel, it is for sure "enhanced nonfiction," i.e. a new genre I just invented. It's actually called creative nonfiction or literary nonfiction. I think. Or it's all bogus fiction. Whatever it is, this work, in its entirety, is not an autobiography.

Speaking of unfinished projects, incomplete wishes, unfulfilled creative goals, have I mentioned anything about when I was an early teen in Pennsylvania? I don't think I have mentioned that era of life. At that time, I was skinny, awkward, and never able to finish what I started. Thirty years later and I can honestly say I haven't changed a bit. "Now I Can Say I'm the Same" could be the aptly-chosen title of my autobiography.

In the middle school years growing up poor in Pennsylvania, I had a little old TV on the floor of my bedroom where I watched about ten and a half channels of whatever happened to "stream" via the UHF/VHF antenna. I think it was a black and white set. Pretty sure it was.

I watched a lot of sitcoms, probably all of them, a lot of Arsenio Hall, Garry Shandling, Joan Rivers, Howard Stern. At first, I tried to laugh at most *Saturday Night Live* skits but subconsciously taught myself to laugh when it was truly funny, which was maybe twice in 90 minutes. I craved watching comedians who were truly funny, and I was very picky. I don't remember being drawn to the news or drama. Just liked comedy. I liked the weather, too.

The first episode of Seinfeld, season two, began over apple cinnamon herbal tea with my secret ingredient of a half cup of sugar, sitting on the floor of my upstairs bedroom in the home of my youth, a rental originally built in 1830 for flour mill workers. The home's upgrades were modern plumbing and electricity. Our upgrades were rodent guards, the plastic milk carton pieces nailed to the floor to cover holes.

I would follow the same herbal sugar drink ritual watching his show every week. I loved it. The comedy of the show spoke to me. Unlike everything else I had ever seen, it seemed more real. The comedy enjoyment lasted the first few seasons until one day in biology class when I heard someone quoting the show. Then I stopped watching it. Always a little odd like that.

While watching comedy in those days, long before the YouTube era, and a few years before the internet went mainstream with Windows 95, I never schteriously entertained the idea that I wanted to write or perform comedy as a profession.

I first caught the bug of wanting to try out stand-up once when I was twelve watching an old Bob Hope Christmas Special, trying to memorize the jokes so I could tell them in seventh grade to be catapulted toward instant popularity. I forgot them all, and therefore did not become popular.

I caught the stand-up bug again when I became completely enamored by a late night show filmed on a famous stage in Harlem.

After *SNL*, at 1:00 AM early Sunday morning, I would stay up to watch Showtime at the Apollo, when amateur comedians and singers attempted to launch new careers at Harlem's Apollo Theater. I had never been drawn to talent shows like Ed McMahon's *Star Search* or the *Jerry Lewis Telethon*. But the Apollo stage somehow grabbed me by the ambition gland and wouldn't let go. If I could perform anywhere, the Apollo was the place for me.

Why would a young white kid dream of performing before a mostly all black audience?

The answer is simple: It's because I thought of the perfect act I felt I could perform there.

I still remember bits of my act:

I would get on stage, meet the host, which at the time was Sinbad, one of my stand-up heroes who I've seen three times:

1. Most recently in Sacramento at Tommy T's Comedy Club.
2. On a Philadelphia stage for an hour and a half in 2008 laugh-

ing so hard it caused me to BMJ.[103]

3. Standing behind him in line at a Sam Goody in LA in 1994. I was buying Ride's new album "Carnival of Light" on cassette while he was buying a stack of at least a hundred CDs.

The man is hilarious. Each time I saw him, I never talked to him. In my teenage dreams, however, I would approach and talk to him there on the Apollo stage.

I'd step on stage to meet Sinbad dressed in suit and tie — not Sinbad in a suit, but me dressed in a suit. I would come not as myself, but in character as the most stereotypical, out-of-touch white guy from the middle of stereotypical suburban white America. Arguably, I would be acting as me.

(If you are getting uncomfortable reading what you believe are racial overtones, please stop here, turn around, and walk away. I am 100% not racist, and never have been my entire life. Promise. However, if you find it difficult discussing that we all look different and that there is a spectrum of human skin color, I want to put out the warning to the racially hyper-sensitive that it's better for you to walk away now.)

My character would be an intensely serious, business-minded professional, slowly enunciating every syllable of every word in true out-of-touch white man form. That would be made clear as I talked with the black host.

(It's not too late to go.)

After the host directed me to the microphone center stage, I would stiffly and almost robotically walk up to the mic and then looking up toward the ceiling say, "Well, hello out there."

I would pause, as if I was expecting a crowd reaction, and then turn irritated.

"Don't you say, 'Hello,' back?" Still looking at the ceiling.

---

103 Instead of saying LOL, I'm trying to start new lingo that would replace LOL with BMJ = broke my jaw. It's not literal, just an expression. So don't worry, my jaw was fine.

And then looking down to closely examine the crowd, I would jump back and say, "Oh! Oh! Well! I admit I was prepared for a slightly different crowd tonight."

Jeering from the crowd, I'm sure, would have already begun.

And then taking notes from my jacket, I would say that I had jokes meant for people who were...more like me. I would say that as if I didn't know that was offensive.

(Why are you still here? It's okay to leave!)

Expecting the jeers to change to full-on boos by that subtly racist, closed-minded comment, I would shred the paper and say in thick white-speak, "Well, golly gee whizz [or similar expression], maybe I can let loose a little bit tonight. Maybe you will appreciate me for who I really am."

Then I would try to convince them that while I was very white on the outside, I was very black within. What would follow is a string of stereotypically white comments I would claim channel my "inner black," in hopes that they would be so thoroughly entertained that I would have a chance to perform again.

I came up with the act before *In Living Color* and well before the Bill-Clinton-is-the-first-black-

president era, by the way.

My act may have been inspired by Eddie Murphy's *SNL* skit I watched many times where he dresses as a white man for a day, going on to learn the advantages of white living, like parties on public transportation when only whites were onboard. Humor addressing racial stereotypes kills me every time.

McDonald's was a comedy laboratory for me as I tried out some of my aspirational Apollo material with coworkers, where I often found myself as the lone white employee. My black audience of coworkers laughed at almost anything I said, even if I was serious, so I grew pretty convinced I could have killed on stage at the Apollo.

A fellow former McDonald's employee (at a different location in a different time) who actually did perform before an all black audience, is none other than all-star comedian Jay Leno. He used to open for Rahsaan Roland Kirk, a black musician who found fame for playing a flute while singing. He played the flute and sang. At the same time. He was also blind.

On comedian Jay Mohr's podcast, Leno explains how the visually impaired Rahsaan would energetically announce to his all black audience,

"I wanna welcome you brothers! We've got a brother here! He's gonna talk about the white devils. He's gonna talk about…" And he would just do this whole black militant rap thing and he'd get the crowd all worked up."

Then Rahsaan would say, "'Please welcome brother, Jay Leno.'

"So I would walk out [and whisper], 'Shhhhh, shhhhhh. He doesn't know I'm white!"[104]

Of course, the crowd ate it up, and so did Rahsaan, which is why he liked to travel with Leno.

I LOVE this style of humor. Why, you might ask? I'm not sure. Maybe it's because I hate racism, especially racism between white and black Americans. I hate it, hate it, hate it, hate it. I've seen it up close and lived it. Maybe a little more comedy can bring us all together, improve race relations, except for the kind in chapter 13. I don't know.

Long story short, I never performed stand-up at the Apollo Theater. I never performed stand-up as I grew up. I've stood up and I can stand-up, but I don't do stand-up. You might ask if I have ever wanted to do stand-up since my youth. I have wanted to do stand-up many times

---

104 *Mohr Stories* podcast, Episode 78.

since then. Not so much in my 20s, a little more in my early 30s, and then the interest began to rise in my late 30s into my 40s. In fact, the last time I wanted to try stand-up was last night.

Before I share what happened last night, I'll add that all these years have passed thinking about trying out stand-up but the internet has offered some alternatives to putting yourself before a crowd. I've tried out some of these options, becoming a sit-down comic through my writing on a blog and talking to myself on a podcast. Not quite the same as standing before a live audience. Maybe someday.

Last night, my wife and I drove downtown without any plans. As we arrived downtown, we passed a comedy club and decided to do a U-y[105] [how is that spelled, anyway? Yewee? Do people still say that?] to check it out.

When we walked into the club I asked when the next show would go on.

"Nine o'clock but it hasn't started yet."

"What time is it now?"

He didn't answer me. I took out my phone and saw it was exactly 9:12. This place isn't funny at all, I thought.

Even if the show wouldn't be funny, I was about to watch amateurs try their hand at stand-up. I was so excited.

We paid $30 for admission and our hands were stamped with the word, "Insufficient." I changed my mind. This place is definitely funny.

We took a seat when my wife remembered she had left her phone in the car. So I left quickly to get her phone before someone broke into my car to steal it. I'm paranoid about that sort of thing. I saw a car with a Macbook Air in the backseat the other day. I came so close to stealing it and selling it on eBay.

By the time I got back, an improv group was in the middle of their act. Everyone was laughing. Unfortunately, I missed just enough of

---

105 Short for U-Turn.

it that I couldn't laugh, as I learned to do during the unfunny *SNL* watching days. Before I knew it, they were finished.

As the night wore on, I decided that typing is so much more comfortable than my fear of standing on a stage.

So here I am, writing a book.[106]

------

106 This chapter qualifies as the second worst of the book.

CHAPTER

23

deadbob

I can't believe I let more than twenty chapters go by without sharing this story.

■ ■ ■

Several months later (five and a week)
April 26

■ ■ ■

He was on all fours, underneath a desk, with a thoughtful though slightly panicked and perspirated expression on his smooth, wrinkle-free, glowing face. He had a purpose, but he was running out of time. He turned his head leftward as far as he could out of the corner of the utmost bounds of his beaming left eye to see if his boss was approaching, beads of crystal-like sweat forming on his translucent forehead.

Just a few inches above his back was the desk that, like the man's entire countenance and being, was like nothing found in this world, and just a few inches below the desk was where he was sprawled plank-like on all fours, propped up by two elbows so his hands and fingers were free to hold with one hand a cylinder-shaped contraption wrapped in protruding inch-long, old typewriter-looking keys, with a box resembling the old Texas Instruments Speak & Spell toy from the early '80s dangling on the floor from the bottom of the cylinder, attached by a two inch long cable as thick as a garden hose.

The unusual apparatus was connected by a root-ball patch of brightly colored wires spliced into a large network of glowing cables on the other side of the uneven cut-out hole of three-inch thick drywall just behind the darkest corner underneath the other-worldly desk.

The pattern the man followed as he attempted to type on all fours was to input a few keys at a time using every available finger made somewhat free in that awkward position. Then he would immediately stop, quickly scanning the room to make sure he was still alone, repeating this type-scan, type-scan process many, many times, until, unbeknownst to the man, he was suddenly discovered by the desk's owner, a very important person. I'm not talking a very important person in our earthly ways. This was more than a Very Important Person, or VIP. This was a **VERY IMPORTANT PERSON**!

At about the same time, the man heard a familiar sound while underneath the desk, so he stopped typing immediately. The sound was from a heavenly voice that struck his soul and filled it with unspeakable joy each time he heard it. The man was calm as he listened and his message was nearly finished, but not completely. "They'll know what I wanted to tell them," he thought as he backed out from underneath the desk. Soon, the man stood eye-to-eye with his Superior. No words were exchanged.

The guilty man was never heard from again in those parts.

What was he doing under that desk, you ask?

Well, in short, the man was a hacker. One might call him a computer hacker in our world. In his world, he was more like a "world hacker."

You see, he was hacking from his world into our world. He world hacked from his world's Whole-World Wisdom network. As the name suggests, the W-WW network was infinitely more wise than our own world's mostly junk-filled World Wide Web, and somehow, of all the millions and millions and millions of available hacking destinations for an accomplished hacker from another world, this man hacked from the obscure corner of his world into an obscure website at the farthest outreaches of our world's World Wide Web of interwoven websites.

Having accomplished his task of breaking into our world's internet, he very randomly chose to hack the website joshrolph.com, or my own, not because he was looking for it but because it seemed like the weakest link of the entire internet.

He seems to have hacked into the admin login of my Wordpress-based site, apparently through some crafty coding that got him into the config.php file. He then quickly developed his own username and began to type the very first message ever received in the world of the living from the world of the dead, and this is what he chose to say:

[[[Transmission initiated]]]

Hi, I'm Bob, and I'm dead. I'm a dead Bob. People over here actually call me "Deadbob," all one word. Everyone in my death support group thinks Deadbob sounds hilariously funny. Sure, it's funny. But it's not hilariously funny. And it's nowhere close to being twenty-two years of hilarious funny, like they think it is.

This is more than likely strange for you to be reading a message from a dead guy who is writing this while dead. You probably feel uncomfortable. Don't feel uncomfortable. You probably don't believe I'm really dead. I ask you to trust me. You may feel a little sick to your stomach. Just take a few deep breaths and keep reading. Where you are, I once was. Where I am, you will be.

This won't take long because I don't have much time. The Boss is away from his desk and when he finds me, it's all over, so to speak.

Let me first clarify that my death support group mentioned above, the one that calls me "deadbob," has nothing to do with death support, which isn't a thing. Death support isn't like life support, either. Life support tries keeping you alive. Death support doesn't try keeping you dead. There is no trying to stay dead. You're just dead. That's it.

My death support group is more like a focus group. It's sort of like a focus group of friends-in-death sitting around, talking about death's purpose and meaning while participating in some intense high-stakes poker.

Our philosophical system we in the death support group spend so much time discussing is what we call non-existentialism, which kind of makes sense, right?

There are some who call themselves the existentialists – mostly the dead French, ever the contrarians – but we keep reminding them existentialism deals exclusively with existing in life. Huge difference between life existence and death non-existence, we remind them, but they're stubborn 'til the end, as it were.

In short, I don't think the deadbob moniker sounds funny at all. Dead people, and you, should just call me Bob, since that's my name. I don't need a nickname in death. Believe me, over here, a nickname can get really old, really fast, sticking for hundreds of years. Nicknames are like a second death sentence.

That said, I haven't been over here for hundreds of years. Any guesses on how long I've been dead? I gave a clue earlier.

My twenty-second deathday is coming up. I was deathed in April, 1995. That may seem like a lot of death experience to you alive people, but it's nothing when compared to the incredibly loud Cro-Magnon family down the street.

When I first died, there was never an initiation and no one ever picked on me for being a newbie. I've never been hazed, for example, by experienced dead people, like the tribe of ancient Sumerians catty-corner to my place.

Instead of focusing on my eclectic neighborhood, let's get back to death.

Right before I died, I was walking to the bus stop as I had for the previous 14 or so years when the next thing I knew, I was dead. I've told this story many times and nearly everyone born after 1930 interrupts at this point and says, "You got hit by a bus, didn't you?"

Invariably, that's the first question I get.

People who died before 1930 or so ask, "What's a bus stop?"

Anyway, I always answer their question with, "No, I died from a nuclear holocaust."

The reason I like to start my death story by saying I was walking to a bus stop is because it sounds so benign. Then I throw in the nuclear line and people post-1930 go "Woah!" And people pre-1930 go "Whuh?"

Of course, any student of history knows there was no nuclear holocaust in 1995. I say that to test whether they're up on their current events.

But that's far from the point I need to make in my limited time communicating with you.

The reason I'm writing at this very moment is because when I was alive I used to wonder on rare occasion what it was like after death. Would I keep on living or cease to be? If I was still around, would I have form or would I become memory or ether or some element the Alives haven't yet discovered or couldn't comprehend with their finite minds?

I don't wonder anymore, mostly because I'm dead, and the dead don't wonder much at all. When you're alive, you're always thinking and wondering and making decisions. The dead simply don't have need to wonder.

At more contemplative moments you Alives might think, "What's it all for?" or "What's my purpose?" Those questions don't directly involve death. At least, you're not thinking about death when you ask them. But in reality, those questions and all of life in your world revolves almost exclusively around what you don't know, which all revolves directly on the mystery of death, even if you don't realize you're almost exclusively being governed by death all along. Death is driving every single one of your choices, and you have no clue. There's no better way of saying it. You have no clue.

You're living for something that you can't explain. It's some abstraction you can never put your finger on. Why? Because you don't want to face the certainty of the mystery of death.

You're living in this continual anxiety-laced panic. Why? It's almost entirely because of the mystery of death.

You're trying to fit it all in. You're trying to put the pieces together. Why are you doing that? Calm down. You're gonna die.

I don't want to upset you, but wake up: You're asleep.

For me, it all makes sense now. It didn't when I was alive. I ignored death. I pushed it aside. I was a death denier. Sure, other people died, but not me. I was alive.

And then, just like that, you die.

I'll repeat that:

You die.

And there's really nothing more to have anxiety about or to be panicked about or even to live or die for, because you're dead.

You can't die again so there's no dying for anything.

You're not alive so there's nothing to live for.

It's really amazingly wonderful, the capstone of wonder or the fulfillment of wonder, which is why we in death don't wonder. We indirectly wondered about the mystery of death all our lives. Now we have no need.

And the only way to find death wonder-fulfilled is by first living.

That's what it's like to never die again. It's wonderful. And notice I didn't say "That's what it's like to live forever." I would never say "That's what it's like to die forever" because you can't "die" forever. On this side, we stop using the word forever. I said "forever" all the time when I was alive. I never say it here. No need; never.

Over on this side, there's nothing that could destroy me to make me dead again or more dead than I already am. I could swallow a nuclear bomb full of heroin-soaked syringes and anthrax-baked nails and electric eels wrapped around my chest and limbs while I'm sitting on the electric chair, and such, but not even that elaborate death-inducing death agent could make me more dead than I happen to be at this very moment. I'd still be just as dead as I already am. It's quite great.

So all I wanted to say in this message from the dead is not to worry. Sounds cliché, but it really does all work out in the end. Even if you're hit by a bus, like I w

[[[Transmission end]]]

SECTION 3
BEGINNING TO BELIEVE
I CAN BECOME AN
AUTHOR, KIND OF[107]

---

107 This section is so short you can skip it and not get lost in the story.

?24

When Should a Book Conclude? How Many Chapters are Too Many? Can a Chapter be a Question? I Think So?

What if Tolstoy's 587,287 word masterpiece War and Peace was instead written as a 30,000 word novella? How much longer should I keep adding chapters before calling this work a finished book?

■ ■ ■

A couple minutes later
April 26

■ ■ ■

This is plenty of book so far. I've definitely entered the stage of becoming a book author as opposed to a something-written-shorter author. I've graduated from brochure, pamphlet, short story, novella, heading straight into full-fledged book territory.

God bless America. And God bless your country, too, as long as it is making it possible for you to read my book.

I did it.

I entered the zone. The book author zone.

This chapter will be short.

This paragraph will be short.
This sentence will be.
This sentence, too.
This sentence.
This.
T

Readers don't want lots of long chapters these days, which is why chapter 24 is my gift to you. I mean, you did pay for it.[108] Think of this chapter as my way of being sensitive to your time.

Moving on to chapter 25…take your time getting there. Don't rush yourself. I know I won't. I might take a little break from writing. This has been the most exhausting activity. It's been chapters since my last break. I need a break. I need to come back to this fresh. I need to rejuvenate so I can write at the same level going forward. This book can't get worse by the page. It must get better. If I'm full of book writing anxiety while typing, the product will read poorly to the reader. The anxiety will shine through. We can't have that. I'll leave this book for some time in order to reward myself and come back when I'm ready.

---

108   I hope. If you stole it, repent.

SECTION 4

SECTION 4 MORE FILLER MATERIAL TO INCREASE WORD COUNT^{109 110 111 112 113 114 115 116 117 118 119}

---

109   This section includes some of the worst chapters of the book, which adds to the count from the worst chapters found in previous sections. This section's horrible chapters are identified by rank in a footnote at the beginning of each chapter. Kind of like what I did to previous chapters.

110   Because so many of this section's chapters are so bad, as opposed to so-so, feel free to skip ahead to Section 5 and I will have no choice but to understand why you've done so.

111   An idea just came to me: "The Author's Dilemma: Writing." – I should write about that subject in Volume 2 (the next book in this riveting series).

112   I sometimes wonder the true purpose of the footnote.

113   A footnote is part of a book, it's just not a necessary part of a book. The footnote is as necessary to the book as a foot is to a human. It's helpful, not necessary. Few people read footnotes. Lots of people have feet. The question is why? And I don't mean to ask why people have feet. I mean to ask why few people read footnotes. Do you know the answer?

114   Footnotes are ignored because they are boring. Footnotes are rarely interesting. If you want someone to read your footnotes, you have to spice them up.

115   I wish I knew how to spice up the footnote.

116   Anyway, back to this section, which is the section of the book containing some of its own worst chapters. Notice I said "some of the worst" because there are other awful chapters in other sections of the book, as mentioned in a previous footnote I won't footnote here.

117   It will be a true miracle if this book is ever published, let alone read by anyone living, other than myself, as I plan to read it at all hours of the day for the rest of my life. I wonder if deadbob will read my book. I hope deadbob isn't in purgatory.

118   [This footnote reserved as a placeholder footnote for a future footnote.]

119   "Footnote" is kind of a gross word if you think about it. It's the nastiest part of the book. The part where the author exposes their feet and rubs them all over notes and puts the final product in the book. Might as well call it the "sandalsnote" or "toenote." It's truly disgusting when you think about it that way. Makes me never want to write another footnote again.

SECTION 4 (cont.): [120] [121] [122] [123] [124] [125] [126]

---

120   This citation right here is not a footnote. It is the first toenote ever written.

121   What if there was such a thing as a toeringnote. As in, a ToeRingNote. Wouldn't that be revolting?

122   If anyone who wears a toe ring is reading this book, all I ask of you is that you stop reading immediately. I disavow you as a reader. I accept anyone and everyone who is interested in reading this book, except for you, the one who wears a toe ring. There has to be a clear line of demarcation to keep you away from this book. If you have invested your time reading this far into the book, I hope you forget everything you've read and simply leave it without continuing past this page. Thank you. Revolting. Thank you.

123   I just went to Wikipedia to learn more about toe rings. Some cultures use toe rings by tradition. As a multicultural individual open to and accepting of multiple cultures, including those who practice adorning their toes with rings, I accept you and embrace you. Those who wear toe rings with cultural significance or meaning are great and I wish them well as they continue reading this book. All others who wear toe rings for no particular reason are dead to me.

124   Arch supports, ankles, in-grown nails. Podiatrists don't have it easy. Let's take a moment of silence for podiatrists.

125   What if there was a podiatrist type of person dedicated to the betterment of all footnotes, everywhere. Podiauthor. Someone whose sole purpose is to write and edit footnotes, checking them for accuracy. Fixing and healing along the way.

126   I've never thought so much about footnotes. There is so much to say about the footnote. I think I'm falling in love with the footnote.

Two Weeks Notice

*When book writing, imagine you have an imaginary boss who imagines
you are imaginary.*

■ ■ ■

Written in an alternate dimension

■ ■ ■

After wasting so much time on this book, I've been strong-armed into finally phasing it out. It wasn't exactly by choice. After my last chapter on chapters, I got a call to schedule a time to meet in the boss's office for this blog. It had been awhile since we last held a work meeting in his office, so I was eager to hear what he had to say.

As I entered his ornate office, he told me to close the door, and he didn't even wait for me to sit down. I remained standing.

He began reading me the riot act – I did this wrong, I did that wrong, I used bad grammar, too many commas, book didn't make any sense – then he began talking about how he climbed some mountain I've never heard of and quoted a guy named Seamus who I think used to be his neighbor?

I was incredibly confused. An unintelligible mass of words spewed from his mouth. After a minute of nonsensical rambling it became clear he was actually going to fire me, especially when he said, "So it's time to start packing up your things. We don't need you anymore. You can't write garbage..."

I surprised myself when I interrupted my superior by coolly gracing a slight smile, as nonchalantly as possible, and asked, "You know what?"

He immediately stopped lecturing me. Amazingly still behind his mahogany desk, he gazed directly into my eyes.

I had asked a question, hoping he would answer.

Why did I hope he would answer me? I mean, the man was never at a loss for words!

Isn't "You know what?" an expression that tells the listener you have more to say?

"Oh wait," I thought. By asking the question, I believed at the time he would answer back! I thought he would tell me something he knows! I forgot how the expression worked! How did I do that? I can't believe I didn't realize that. It must have been nerves. No wonder he hates my book. I don't even know expressions.

At the moment, however, I somehow believed my "you know what?" question had thrown him. For a millisecond, he kind of had a look of panic, as if I had thrown him. He didn't look like my boss anymore. He looked weak.

He looked like me.

This realization gave me a dose of much needed confidence, but I was still at a loss for words.

"You know what?" I repeated, still thinking he would answer the question.

I continued to endure unbearable silence for over a minute. He seemed to endure it effortlessly, making him look like my boss again.

I thought of my options. There weren't many. He was essentially firing me, but he hadn't yet said, "You're fired."

Ever the competitive one, I didn't want him to beat me to it. So I yelled at the top of my lungs, "I QUIT!"

Motionless, emotionless, and in his thick Colorado accent, he said, "You're an idiot."

I said, "Don't sugar coat this. You heard me, I quit! I'm not sticking around slaving away for you anymore!"

"You can't quit."

"Why can't I quit? I can do whatever I want!"

He told me I was correct about that and then added, "When you quit, you won't be able to collect unemployment insurance."

"I don't care about un–"

"Josh," he insisted, stopping me mid-sentence. "Do the right thing."

"What 'right thing?' I said I'm out!"

I put my hand on his office door knob, but surprised myself again when I didn't turn it immediately to open the door and leave his office for good.

He was right, I considered, hopeful to get a hold of that unemployment check. Maybe receiving unemployment was a way I could start earning money on the book I might never finish, I thought. How ironic.

I laughed to myself, my back to him. Then I heard him say words that were as if a knife had been thrown into the center of my back.

"You know I don't need you," he continued, evilly calm. "You know I don't like your work. To be blunt, it's pathetic."

I turned around, facing him, quickly checking my torso to see if the knife had passed all the way through. It hadn't. Then I remembered the knife wasn't real. "Knife in the back" is a figure of speech. I had forgotten.

Confidence waning.

No longer looking him in the eyes, I said, "I thought you wanted me to do the right thing and stay."

He was listening. I garnered a little more courage. "Instead, you mock my work. You know I'm the best author in my mind!"

I'm sure my face was bright red, a genetic characteristic attributed to my Nordic roots. I tried to cover as much as I could of it with my hands. Maybe he would think I was about to cry.

I was about to cry.

"Do the right thing." He paused. "Give me two weeks notice."

"Oh." I hesitated, trying to understand what had happened. "Oh!"

So he didn't want me to collect unemployment! He wanted me to earn my pay for two more weeks.

I knew he would counter-offer, just not so soon. It was instantly clear who had won this dance.

"Then fine!" I said, acting disappointed.

I left his office and headed to mine down in the basement of the large office complex. It was a mess down there, as usual. I faked being mad. I threw things around and then I cleaned things up.

And that's basically how it happened.

I have two more weeks to write the book. Then I'm back on the street. At least the way it feels to me, I have never not been writing this book, so this transition will be a real transition for me. I ask for your understanding as I transition to becoming a normal person, which will be so difficult.

There will likely be normalizing pains, but I'm willing to do whatever it takes in order to no longer write a book in two weeks.

If you are confused, read below the "***" if you want to understand what just happened in the area that is coming up after the period that is a little lower and to the right of the point of this arrow →

***

Very good. You are good at following instructions. Now look for the "&&&" below, and read what comes next.

&&&

Excellent. You are learning quickly. Now look for the "%%%" and see what follows.

%%%

Ok, now that you have carefully followed my instructions, I'm going to give it to you straight from the heart. By going through the exercise above, the one where I have a boss who is firing me, I'm now, in essence, giving myself another method to hurry up the book writing so I can wrap up my dream of becoming an author. Everything in this chapter is psychological. It's a psychological method of motivating myself to write. Time to move on to the "###."

###

You know what? You are so good. You should buy more copies of this book, assuming I ever finish it. And for those who have reached this part of the book, tweet this book's store link with the hashtag #twoweeksnotice.[127] I have no self-esteem and don't take medication for that ailment, so a click or a share goes a long way toward helping me guilt trip people into doing what I tell them to do. By buying or sharing, you and those you love will have something to read for many years to come.[128]

---

127 Ignore chapter 12.
128 Without question, this is the 3rd worst chapter of the book.

26

How to Sit

This chapter is self-help and autobiographical rolled into one.

■ ■ ■

Written after returning from an alternate dimension

■ ■ ■

I carry a slim wallet around. The slim wallet has improved my quality of life ever since it was gifted to me, far outliving its life expectancy.

I love my slim wallet because the slim factor makes it barely noticeable in my back pocket when I sit for long periods of time and also for short periods of time, especially compared to the fat wallet days.

Not only is the slim wallet good for carrying the essential cards and cash, it is also a good door opener when I'm trying not to touch germ-infested door handles in public places. It doesn't work well trying to open the doorknob variety, though. I use the shoe method for that.[129]

Since I can't easily feel my wallet anymore after going with the slim wallet, I have developed a habit of giving my rear end a subtle pat to see if my wallet is still there. I try to be discreet about it. Sometimes it's

---

129 Involves opening the door with your foot.

not there and I get a little panic, until I realize that it is conveniently placed in my shirt pocket.

I find myself checking my rear end and shirt pocket fairly often, giving taps in both places with a hand that may look unusual to the outside observer.

Future Biographer: Title this chapter of my biography "His Wallets."

I didn't verify, but this gentleman in the above picture definitely has a thick wallet in his rear pant pocket – most likely the pocket on the right side, though it could also be on the left side. If it is on the right side, by sitting the way he is over one and a half chairs, he avoids tilting Pisa-style into the woman to his left. He has great hair, by the way.

For the ten or fifteen years prior to discovering the slim wallet, I carried the classic billfold wallet in my back pocket. The problem was that back pant pocket would quickly wear out, long drives became uncomfortable, and the see-through plastic card-holding insides would fall apart or become so seared, scarred and sticky with black ink impressions of their former contents that they would become virtually unusable.

Worst of all, I even appeared to lean a little to the left while sitting, which was always embarrassing.

In the early days of wallet carrying, I didn't have enough cards/pictures/etc. to fill the plastic inserts. I didn't have a bank account either, which meant that the money I earned entered my wallet – cash, coins, and all.

Through my teenage years, my wallet began to be a place I kept notes, cards, and keepsakes. It became the home of a dollar bill signed by musicians that toured through the more indie theaters in Philadelphia.

I kept a strand of Morrissey's shirt in my wallet for a long time. The inch-long string of shirt is now ashes below a smoldering heap of trash somewhere in Landfill, PA.

I'm sure I spent the dollar bill sometime later when I began to value food more than autographs. The vending machine's Famous Amos chocolate chip cookies were totally worth it.

My wallet also became a place I kept more motivational things to remember.

In my early teens in the backseat of a police car, I admired my friend who boldly showed the cop through the glass partition his wallet-sized list of principles he got at church and said, "This is what I live by," as we tried to convince the cops that we were innocent of planting bags of cocaine along a trail in a nearby park.

It all began when we decided to call the police after noticing suspicious looking bags on a trail. We weren't idiots – we were probably hoping for careers in the FBI – but apparently the police thought we were better candidates for the Police Academy films.

...Or they were better candidates for those films.

"You boys better come with us, ya hear?" as they picked us up from my home. Five or six cop cars waited for us at the trailhead.

Later, the older cop was getting frustrated. After splitting up me and my friend, they saw inconsistencies with our story. The older cop said, "Son, you lie to us and you will have to ride behind a mule picking up its shit." He thought he was terrorizing me.

That line worked well in 1642, I hear.

It must have been a slow day, because a couple hours of amateurish interrogation later, trying to break us, their case fell apart when they saw that a small patch of dry skin on my earlobe was in fact dry skin and not remnants of flour we allegedly used for cocaine.

I know what you're thinking, "That's an unusual place for dry skin." I agree. But it was a blessing. Today, I could be in rural Arkansas riding behind a mule.

After the cop incident, I began to carry that church pamphlet around in my wallet.

The problem with slim wallets is they are so expensive. I used to buy a wallet for ten bucks. My Ralph Lauren slim wallet retails for $80. But it still looks great, even after floating down Independence Avenue.

Shortly after receiving my new wallet when I lived in DC, I got a call from the National Chicken Council, a real entity representing poultry farmers, saying one of their employees had found my slim wallet floating along the curb toward a sewer vent on Independence Ave. Retracing my steps, I had left my wallet on my lap as I paid a cab driver before exiting at the curb for my office during a significant rainstorm.

Point is, my slim wallet has been through a lot and it still looks great. I've titled this chapter "How to Sit." Here's my advice:

- Don't sit with the wallet in your pants pocket.
- Don't sit with the wallet on your lap.
- Slim wallets will help with the leaning factor while sitting in a convention workshop (if you missed that, see above image of man sitting)
- Carry something uplifting in your wallet.
- Don't hurry out of a cab on a busy street when it's raining hard and you have a lot of stuff in your hands.
- Don't call the cops unless you have dry skin on your earlobe.
- Oh, and sit up straight. Don't slouch.[130]

---

130   Easily the 4th worst chapter of the book.

The Pizzazz Challenge

If you're like me, you thought "pizzazz" was spelled "pizzaz" or "pizazz."
I was surprised to find that it's spelled "pizzazz." In any case, you may
have never been told this, but you've got some serious pizzazz.

■ ■ ■

On a roll. Still writing only 3 days later.
April 29

■ ■ ■

Did you know that Marvel Comics ran *Pizzazz* magazine for 16 issues from 1977 - 1979? You probably didn't know that trivia gem. There is no question the word "pizzazz" lost its pizzazz in popular media since that time. I want to change that.

I fell for this word on Saturday night when it somehow came out of my mouth from literally nowhere during conversation.

Once I said the unique word, I knew I had hit a word nerve. Those nerves are hit when you come across a really cool word. Pizzazz is exactly that: a really cool word. The more I think about it, the more I want to say "pizzazz."

It hasn't always been this way. From what I gather, pizzazz had its moment of fame in the '70s, followed by a slow death after 1980. It's still lingering out there, it's just more difficult to come by in spoken language, although apparently a growing number of books that are on Google Books use the word.

Let's look at the word more closely to make sure we're on the same page. Pizzazz is pronounced: pə'zaz.

The z's in zzazz are important when you say the word out loud. As you can see, all four of those z's land in just one syllable (play along with me here).

FOUR Z'S IN ONE SYLLABLE. Tell me when that happens.

Never.

Okay, there is zazzle, pizzazz's 1st cousin. But as you can see, zazzle only has three Z's.

Pizzazz begins so unassumingly with the opening syllable pronounced "pə-." Like in the word "pedestrian." It's unbelievable to me that of all words, the unimaginative word "pedestrian" begins the same way as PIZZAZZ. Point is, let's not underestimate the importance of the pə-.

The accented second syllable lets out a pə-nultimate bang as the "-ZZAZZ" shatters any notion that the word beginning with "pə-" would be dry, empty, and void of pizzazz.

What's incredible is how the two pairs of Zs can be held for as short or as long as the pizzazz-speaker wishes. The longer the Z is sounded out, the more the pizzazz. It's that simple.

NOT ONLY THAT but the A in the second syllable can be said with a Wisconsin "eh," the Philly "uh." the Southern diphthonged "eh-uh," or the British "ah."

Try saying it aloud in each dialect.

With that out of the way, I issue a challenge to you.[131] This is a real challenge (unlike those fakes ones) so if you're not up for it, please stop reading this and go read something much less interesting.

____

131   I hate challenges.

I challenge you to use the word "pizzazz" in your very next live conversation with another human.

You can use it as much as you want on social media (Twitter: #pizzazz), which will be too easy to do. But challenges aren't meant to be easy so I will not count your use of pizzazz in social media as meeting the challenge.

Instead, you absolutely must, must, MUST use pizzazz while talking to a person or group. Yes, conference calls are fair game. No, saying it to a telemarketer is not. Again, leave your comfort zone. Do the right thing. Say pizzazz like you mean it.

1. The rules for this challenge?
2. Don't look up the definition of pizzazz.[132]
3. Don't be pedestrian.

For some accountability, I ask that you please share on Twitter how you said "pizzazz" in your conversation.[133] Share the reaction from the recipient as well, if any. If there is no reaction, share what you think the reaction was in the hearer's mind. I expect zero, maybe one tweet from this exercise.[134]

I already used pizzazz in real life on Saturday night. I will likely never use it again. It came to me while referring to my youngest son and speaking about myself in the third person to my wife.

Here is the overly-dramatized version:

"From his mother, he inherited a broad smile that exuded charm. From his father, he inherited something that was...how do I say it in words? He inherited a quality of...of...it's almost impossible to say. I'm grasping for the word. It's at the tip of my tongue."

---

132 I think pizzazz is only generally definable, anyway. The word pizzazz is almost more than a word. It's one of those rare words that says more after it's said than when it's actually said.
133 Challenges that ask for accountability are extremely annoying and are probably pizzazz counterfeits (otherwise known as foolzpizzazz.)
134 Will yours be that tweet?

I groaned slightly, unwilling to admit to her there was no word in the English language that could possibly say what I was trying to say.

I was sweeping the floor. She was organizing the spices in the cupboard.

"Oh, I think I have it. I think it's – I think I know what to say."

But I didn't know what to say. I was stumped. Words were swimming toward the drain of my mind like bathtub water heading down that whirlpool tornado vortex thingamajig.

"From his father, he inherited..." I paused, when suddenly, it came to me.

I stopped sweeping.

"He inherited," I paused for effect, "pizazz." (That's back when I thought it was spelled with three z's.)

If I ever publish more than this book, I would love to use pizzazz in a story line.[135]

---

135 No other chapter qualifies as the 5th worst book chapter as much as this one.

Why I Drove With My Brights on For Nine Years

Are they High Beams, Brights, or Hypno-Aggressifying-Stimulights?

■ ■ ■

Eleven long months later, on the Ides of March
March 15

■ ■ ■

I used to have a problem. I don't anymore.

While driving home tonight, a compact, highly fuel-efficient-looking vehicle pulled in front of me in such a way as to indicate that the driver was either drunk, high, manic, texting, or enduring the funky music in-between news reports on NPR.

The car's body was covered in professional artwork advertising a local solar company, so much so that I couldn't easily discern its make and model. The driving of that car was so awful I almost memorized the phone number on the rear window to report their reckless driving.

Before I had a chance, the car changed lanes and I happily passed to the right.

The gears of my mind automatically shifted back to Autopilot Mode, a trance-like state I enter while driving, bathing, and karaoking that somehow gets me to my destination with little memory of what happened along the way.

A few moments later, I again snapped out of Autopilot Mode when I noticed through the rearview mirror that a car was flashing its headlights at me. Their lights flickered on and off several times.

I was surprised to find that the solar company car was the flasher when it passed me again. A young man was driving. While passing, he flashed his lights and made pointing gestures toward the front of my car.

It took me a second to realize that my brights were on. I turned them off. He then drove away into the night.

Yes, I call the brightest light setting on a vehicle "brights." You may call them by the more correct "high beams." I never liked "high beams" because:

1. It's one syllable longer than "brights."
2. When someone calls them "high beams" they sound like a DMV driving test.
3. The term "high beams" draws attention to another term I don't like, which is "low beams."
4. "Low beams" suggests to me that the light isn't that bright. Fact is, low beams are very bright.
5. I think "parking lights" should be called low beams and low beams should be called "just right beams."
6. High beams should be called "brights."

As for the driver tonight who put in a lot of time and energy to tell me I was using my brights, little did he know my story.

I am intensely familiar with irritating drivers who use their brights in the wrong places because I used to be one of them.

Post-Thanksgiving Black Friday 2003 was my most memorable Black Friday shopping experience and my only Black Friday shopping experience event to this very day. It involved shopping for a new car.

I'm one of those weird people that enjoys the car buying process because I'm really, really good at it.

The new car I was shopping for was to be new for me, not brand new. The car I settled on was a few years old and had a sleek, modern look.

I found two cars of the same model, year and color: one in Maryland and the other in Virginia. I worked the salesmen at both dealerships into the ground. Ultimately, we went with the car in Maryland because I negotiated an incredible deal even I couldn't believe.

Turns out, the car I drove off the lot that day had sustained significant front-end damage on the dealer's lot that had gone unreported, which is how I realized I'm really terrible at negotiating for cars.

One night soon after my purchase I noticed a car in the opposing lane flashing their brights at me.

A few days later, the same thing happened at a red light when a car flashed its lights, again, at my direction.

Not long after that, a car I was driving behind moved behind my car and began flashing their lights.

As dumb as I am, I began to notice a pattern.

I began to get a complex so I tested the lights to see what was the matter – if I was truly the problem – and found that my low beams were actually as bright as high beams.

Even more amazing was the fact that the high beams were so bright they could have lit Dodger Stadium. I say that because during a southern California power grid failure in 2004 my car was actually used to provide light to Dodger Stadium.

After I made the discovery of my vehicle's defect, I prepared myself for a glorious defensive measure that would teach every brights-hater not to mess with me.

The next time a driver flashed their lights at me, I would flash my true brights back to show them they were flat wrong.

Soon thereafter, when confronted with a light flasher, I was reflexively unprepared, unable to get to the brights-flashing lever fast enough. Angrily, I slammed my fist against the steering wheel, accidentally honking the horn.

The time after that when a driver, in a fit of rage, flashed their lights at me, I again wasn't fast enough to react. Right after they passed me,

I flashed my ultra-brights back. But it was too late. All that saw them were the inanimate trees, a mile marker, and an owl, probably.

As the sun fell beneath the horizon and shadows of the night replaced the once-illuminated drive-time scene, I began training myself to drive with my right middle finger wrapped around the lights lever, ready to pull it when a good oncoming belligerent driver citizen flashed their lights at me. It must have been nearing the Christmas season because for at least a week-long period, no one did.

Then one day, I remember it as if it were more than a decade ago, driving well after sunset on Magarity Road in northern Virginia, an oncoming vehicle flashed their lights at me several times. Not just once, but several hate-fueled times.

Boot camp had ended. I was no longer an amateur driver. I was thoroughly skilled and more than prepared for the moment to shine, both figuratively and literally.

I flashed my lights back at them. Several times. Over and over. I couldn't stop. I shouted an unintelligible battle-cry.

I won. They were defeated. As they passed me, I could almost sense the slumping shoulders of a losing former foe, soundly trounced and deservedly so. This was my time. I was the new master of the road. I was unstoppable from that point on.

For nine more years until my car passed away peacefully in my garage three days before Christmas in 2012 surrounded by family, I flashed hundreds, perhaps thousands of times at the kind of people who want you to stop driving with your brights. I grew to consider these people as my mortal enemies. And while looking back, I admit I acted somewhat immaturely at times, I was left with no choice but to defend my car from such vicious attacks.

Because it was always dark during these encounters, I never saw my enemy face to face.

I learned there are so many people in the world who feel it is their divinely appointed duty to take action when driving in front of or facing someone who has their brights on. So many modern day warriors driving these fast, heavy machines. It's something not widely discussed. It's something never discussed.

I don't know who they are or why they hate brights so badly.

Are you one of those people? If so, I come to you in peace. I want to know more about you. I want to understand you.

What are your motivations? Do bright objects startle you? Do people find you irritating/annoying in person?

If you were one of the hundreds of people I flashed back with my ultras and you're just now discovering who I am, how did you feel when you found out I wasn't technically driving with my high beams?

Can we set aside our differences and begin anew?

I Love Allergies

This chapter is lovingly dedicated to my allergies.

■ ■ ■

Three months later
June 15

■ ■ ■

In case you missed it above, this chapter is dedicated to allergies. My allergies.[136]

The book isn't dedicated to allergies. This chapter is dedicated to allergies.[137] If I decided to rewrite the book's dedication page and instead dedicated this entire book to allergies,[138] I might get into some trouble. Allergies aren't really worthy of an entire book's dedication. Name one book that dedicates itself to allergies. I bet you not one book has attempted it, even the most fringe-y, outrageous, absurdist, crazy, wildly fabulist book there is this side of the Tehachapi. I am confident this is the first chapter ever dedicated to allergies.

By allergies I should describe the kind I mean: Seasonal, non-food allergies. Not drug allergies. Not pet, bee sting, latex, mold — I'm only referring to the kind imposed on humans by the earth. Pets and bees

---

136   No offense to your allergies.
137   No offense to allergens.
138   Great. I forgot what I wanted to footnote for this one.

and mold come from the earth, too, but those things aren't everywhere. Latex is made by humans from elements found in the earth. Food allergies can be avoided - they're mostly man-made, except for peanuts. But peanuts do have to be farmed by humans. I've never seen a wild field of peanuts.

Anyway, my point is Mother Earth makes these allergen-infused plants that are everywhere humans can dwell. It's impossible to live in a non-allergen environment for too long without dying, like if I lived on the moon. It would be great to breathe for a half a second before I died. Similarly on earth, if I lived on the ocean, I wouldn't last too long unless I was on a cruise ship with unlimited buffets. I hear Antarctica and Mount Everest aren't too hospitable. But everywhere else has trees and grass and ragweed. Those are the main sources of seasonal allergies for me and millions of other humans.

Grass is everywhere!

Trees are everywhere!

Allergens like pollen are everywhere for a good chunk of the year. We have to live among this stuff that is absolutely delightful and beautiful to look upon and roll around in and absorb but it's slowly destroying our bodies each time we inhale, or to put it a little less dramatically, these allergens, at a minimum, are super annoying.

I sit in my air-conditioned car or home or office and think of my ancestors who biologically passed on to me these allergic traits and it leaves me to wonder how they did it before Kleenex and handkerchiefs and air conditioning.

My thought today is this: Why does the earth also inflict pain on us? Why can't the earth make life a little easier for us? Humans are already in conflict with one another. Humans are polluting the earth. Humans are pooping constantly. Humans are naturally different from person to person and some of us are highly judgmental and don't like you. I mean, I like you. But others might not. It's just how it is.

Then the earth steps in and yes, while there are tornadoes and hurricanes and earthquakes and volcanoes and avalanches and tsunamis and lightning and hail, there are also allergies. It's like a severe weather event on a clear, sunny day with the unseen pollen floating around searching for your nostrils and eyes to inflict pain and suffering on you.

It's sad. My body responds so violently to the earth during about half the year. I mean, if you could only hear me right now. I'm stuffed up. I'm tired. I can't think straight. I'm more irritable. All because of the earth.

Now, the earth's probably thinking, "You know what, buddy? You were talking about the moon a little earlier and how it would kill you in half a second. You know what, go somewhere else. I could make some ever so slight changes to my rotation, my orbit, jump in front of a meteor, and you'd be an instant goner. Keeping you attached to me is a matter of extreme generosity on my part. You flush and you don't think for a second about the kind of mess I have to put up with."

Allergies.

I'm not taking anything for allergies. I'm waiting it out. I'm trying to sleep a little more. Avoid being outside if I don't have to be.

You can do the shots but they're so unbearable and they take years and years. I'm waiting for the technology to improve so it's just a pill or a nasal spray that isn't the others that dry me out, knock me out, and don't work at all.

What if allergies were helping me? What if allergies were helping me to be healthier? Sleeping more is perhaps a good thing. Drinking more liquids? Adding days, weeks, months to my who-know-it's-a-mystery-length life. Allergies could be testing my resolve - somehow making me stronger. If I feel angry because of them I can choose to not act out on the anger. Making me stronger.

Allergies create some solidarity with others who have allergies.

"You have allergies? So do I!" and next thing you know you're soul-mates with a wedding date.

Or they are your kids and you know how to take care of them because you have allergies, too.

Allergies could be the answer to world peace. What if every bad event in history could be tied to someone who had allergies. Kim Jong Un, the North Korean dictator who wants to go nuclear on the entire world – what if he is actually suffering from terrible allergies to Bermuda grasses? I don't know. The UN should maybe explore that one.

Allergies. I could have the entirely wrong attitude about allergies. I could be doing this all wrong. What if I looked forward to this time of year? What if I changed my hatred of allergies into a deep, profound, and lasting love of allergies? The change in affection could be a reason to dedicate this entire book to allergies. That could do it. Loving allergies could change my life. What if we loved allergies and stopped cursing the earth for inflicting them upon us? What if we accepted them and made allergies cool? What if it was cool to sneeze all over the place, because it's certainly not cool now. Okay, so allergies could never be cool. But you can still love them. I can still love allergies.

Allergies and authors. Do authors get allergies? Come to think of it, I have never seen an author blow their nose. What if my allergies miraculously go away when I become an author?[139]

I want everyone who has allergies to repeat with me now the words: I love allergies. See what that does to you. See if that helps your suffering to improve any. I love allergies. I love

---

139 This could really help me during book signings or while in the ceremony receiving the Pulitzer Prize.

allergies. I love allergies. Increase word count. I love allergies. I love allergies. I love allergies. I love allergies. I love allergies. I love allergies. Just a few more words. I love allergies. I love allergies. I love allergies. I love allergies. I love allergies. I love allergies.

Thank You Notes

Caught in a thank you loop.

■ ■ ■

Mere weeks later

July 8

■ ■ ■

Cleaning out a dusty box the other day, I came across this memory between an Anne and a Josh...

Oct. 13, 2006

Dear Anne,

Thank you for your time this morning to discuss the senior manager position with your firm.

I believe my experience is a great match for this position, and I look forward to meeting with you if I am selected for the second round of interviews.

I appreciate your thoughtful consideration.

Best regards,
Josh

. . .

Oct. 13, 2006

Dear Josh:

I was pleased to receive your thank you note this afternoon. Same day courier service is unheard of in the thank you note tradition.

I hope to be in touch soon on whether you advance in the interview process.

Kind regards,
Anne

. . .

Oct. 18, 2006

Dear Anne:

Thank you for your thank you note. I am so glad you appreciated the courier service I selected. I thought that would be a nice touch. It says a lot about you that such a gesture would not go unnoticed.

I am poised to bring similar unique systems and strategies to the table should I be selected for this managerial role.

Kinder regards,
Josh

■ ■ ■

Oct. 23, 2006

Dear Josh:

I was pleased to receive your thank you note. I see that courier service was not an option this time?

Still, you can never go wrong sending a thank you note. The home-made salsa was a nice touch.

Kindest regards,
Anne

■ ■ ■

Oct. 25, 2006

Dear Anne:

Thank you for enjoying the homemade salsa. I'll tell my mom you liked it.

Most sincerely,
Josh

■ ■ ■

Oct. 31, 2006

Dear Josh:

I never said I enjoyed the salsa, but I thank you nonetheless for your note.

Best,
Anne

■ ■ ■

Nov. 2, 2006

Dear Anne:

I apologize for reading too much into your second-to-last thank you – so thank you for that. I need to be better about not assuming things. I assume that's the primary reason I didn't advance to the second round of interviews?? But I thank you for the correspondence.

All the best,
Josh

■ ■ ■

Nov. 7, 2006

Dear Josh:

Thank you so much for thanking me in your apology. You are perhaps the most considerate former job candidate I have ever encountered in my 4 years in Human Resources.

All the best,
Anne

■ ■ ■

Nov. 9, 2006

Dear Anne:

Thank you.

With gratitude,
Josh

■ ■ ■

Nov. 13, 2006

Dear Josh:

Thank you for your last thank you.

Anne

■ ■ ■

Nov. 15, 2006

Dear Anne:

No. Thank YOU.

Josh

■ ■ ■

Nov. 17, 2006

Dear Josh:

No, no. Thank YOU.

Anne

■ ■ ■

Nov. 20, 2006

Dear Anne:

No, no, no! Thank YOU!!! (Oh, and Happy Thanksgiving!)

Josh
Enclosure

■ ■ ■

Nov. 29, 2006

Dear Josh:

Thank you for the holiday newsletter and family portrait enclosed in your last thank you note. I have placed it in your résumé file for future reference should there be an opening that best matches your skill set. In the event of such a match, we will notify you of our interest and provide you with the option to enter the candidate pool for employment with our firm.

Sincerely,
Anne

■ ■ ■

Dec. 4, 2006

Dear Anne:

Thank you for placing the picture of my family and holiday newsletter in my résumé file. I don't like putting the accents in résumé, but following your lead, I have made that choice.

Regards,
Josh

■ ■ ■

Dec. 12, 2006

Dear Josh,

Your note about the accents in résumé gave me pause, for which I thank you. I have never liked them.

Anne

■ ■ ■

Dec. 15, 2006

Dear Anne:

It is with great pleasure that I provide you with an updated resume (note the accent-free "resume") that includes a recent accomplishment under the "Hobbies and Other Interests" section. And thank you for freeing me of the accents in resume! One more thing – Mom wanted me to send you the salsa recipe for Christmas, so here you go!

Josh
Enclosures

■ ■ ■

Dec. 22, 2006

Dear Josh:

Thank you for the updated résumé and recipe to be added to your file.
Anne

■ ■ ■

Dec. 28, 2006

Dear Anne:

Thank you for adding the updated résumé and recipe to my file. Just to be clear, the recipe was for you and not my file.

I also noted in your thank you note that the accents in résumé have returned. I needed that correction. Thank you.

Happy New Year!
Josh

■ ■ ■

Jan. 4, 2007

Dear Josh:

You're welcome.
Anne

■ ■ ■

January 8, 2007

Dear Anne:

You're welcome?! You're welcome?!

Thank you,
Josh

■ ■ ■

January 23, 2007

Dear Anne:

I wrote you a thank you note a few weeks ago and have not received a reply. I'm just writing to make sure you received it.

Thank you for your kind attention to this matter.

Sincerely,
Josh

■ ■ ■

February 3, 2007

Dear Anne,

I would fail to be remiss if I did not neglect to unsuccessfully admit that I have almost been less than a little distressed. As you are aware, I have not as yet received any word from you. It may also be the case that you are unaware that I have not received any word from you. In either case, just know that I am okay with the troubling fact that you have not yet replied.

Thank you so much,
Josh

∎ ∎ ∎

February 20, 2007

Dear Anne:

I am not okay that you have not replied. By not replying to multiple thank you notes, you have crossed a line; I am, to be perfectly honest, furious.

But thank you for your time,
Josh

∎ ∎ ∎

March 14, 2007

Dear Anne:

It is with restrained passion that I urge you to immediately respond with a thank you note (to retain your honor and integrity as a fellow human being). That is the only reason I'm keeping up with this exercise, and I assure you that I am exercising a great deal of restraint at the moment. I also just finished exercising.
It is very disappointing to me that you have not written back. I'm trying to stay busy to help keep my anger at bay, mostly by exercising at the bay.

All the best,
Josh

■ ■ ■

May 24, 2007

Dear Anne:

This is my last thank you note to you, perhaps ever. I hate to be dramatic about it, but this is possibly the most dramatic thing ever. It has been eons since your last "you're welcome." If, by chance, you happen upon this note, I thank you for everything.

Forever thankful, forever grateful,
Josh

■ ■ ■

May 25, 2007

Dear Anne:

I forgot to mention one thing in my last thank you, but I won't say it until you write me again. And again, I'm not being dramatic.

Very much thank you, ever so kindly,
Josh

■ ■ ■

June 3, 2007

Dear Josh:

Thank you for so many messages over the last several months.

You understood the situation correctly when I responded with a you're welcome note in my last note dated Jan. 4, 2007. As everyone knows, you're welcome notes terminate all conversation. It had to be done.

Sincerely,
Anne

■ ■ ■

June 5, 2007

Dear Anne:

Thank you so much for clarifying the reason for our fight.

Kindest regards,
Josh

■ ■ ■

June 9, 2007

Dear Josh:

A fight? Please tell me how that was a fight?

Thanks,
Anne

■ ■ ■

June 11, 2007

Dear Anne:

It was clearly a fight! It was a thank you note fight.

Thank you,
Josh

P.S. Or was it a you're welcome note fight?

■ ■ ■

June 13, 2007

Dear Josh,

Will you please stop writing me thank you notes? You keep writing and writing when there is clearly an UNWRITTEN thank you note proto-col. Do you understand me? UNWRITTEN. Stop writing me. NOW.

Coldly,
Anne

■ ■ ■

June 17, 2007

Dear Anne:

Thank you for telling me to stop writing thank you notes.

Sincerely,
Josh

■ ■ ■

June 20, 2007

Josh –

My firm request for you to cease and desist went unheeded. I take back what I said in my last note about the UNWRITTEN protocol. The rule is written. It's PRINTED INTO HUMAN DNA how and when to write and respond to thank yous. You obviously are NOT human. If you were human you would not have written a THANK YOU NOTE when I demanded you NO LONGER WRITE ME A THANK YOU NOTE. Enough of this madness you sick, twisted thank you note MONSTER!

No regards,
Anne

. . .

June 30, 2007

Dear Anne,

You must have been having a bad day when you sent me your last thank
you note. I laughed when you suggested I wasn't human. I just looked
it up. I am very much human.
Your note made me laugh and cry at the same time. I cried because you
were having such a bad day; I laughed because a monster can't possibly
cry and laugh at the same time.

So thanks for reminding me of my humanity...by depriving me of my
humanity. ;)

Appreciatively,
Josh

. . .

July 1, 2007

Dear Josh,

There isn't enough room in the limited space available in thank you
notes unless you write really small like I am right now to say as much
as I want to say to teach you what your allegedly "human" DNA hasn't
taught you. Since the beginning, my DNA told me to show you common courtesy of continually responding to your thank you notes.
Your freakish DNA told you otherwise. You are more than merely

dysfunctional – You have a DNA defect. You should check yourself into an institution because you are NOT well.

Worst,
Anne

■ ■ ■

July 9, 2007

Dear Anne,

Thank you for thinking of me. Looks like the bad day continues but I really hope you're better by now.

Gratefully yours,
Josh

■ ■ ■

July 14, 2007

Dear Josh,

This is my last note. My last thank you note. Goodbye. Write me again and I'm calling the cops. Thank you for the privilege and potential opportunity to use the modern legal system against you.

Worst wishes for all eternity,
Anne

■ ■ ■

July 16, 2007

Dear Anne:

Thank you.
Josh

■ ■ ■

On July 20, 2007, Josh heard a loud knock on his front door. Answering, he was served a restraining order by an armed, uniformed policeman. Officer Wentzel stated that Josh should no longer communicate in any way with Anne [NAME REDACTED].

"If you have any questions about this notice, my information is on this card."

Josh returned to his kitchen table, pulled a small, blank sheet from a large stationary box, and began to write.

■ ■ ■

July 23, 2007

Dear Officer Wentzel:

It is with great pleasure that I write to thank you for the way in which you presented the restraining order…

■ ■ ■

To this day, the officer has yet to respond to Josh's thank you.

■ ■ ■

THE END[140]

---

140 It's the end of the chapter, not the book.

31

21 Steering Wheel Holds and What They Say About You

Learn to drive, if you don't know how already, so you can learn something about yourself you may not already know. Your driving style says a lot about your personality.

A lot.

■ ■ ■

Roughly 86 days later
September 13

■ ■ ■

Have you ever wondered what your steering wheel grasp says about your personality?

Through a clinical trial, scientists have discovered that the way you hold your steering wheel says more about you than you might think.

I took some selfies the other day to demonstrate each steering wheel holding method and what it says about you.

Before you begin reading, it might be helpful to drive around for a few minutes to determine your dominant hold.

1. "The Student Hold" – Risk averse, careful, intelligent

Using this driving method, you are screaming out to the world that you are a law-abiding citizen. This classic Driver's Ed hold places you at the upper end of the top 1% of drivers, making you a superior driver qualified for the lowest insurance premiums, and one the 99% despise.

I don't know anyone in this category, but if I did, I'd politely say, "If you call this number, you could save 10% or more on your car insurance."

2. "The Cool Hold" – Life of the party

You are cool and you know it. I try to drive like this when people are watching. When a cop is behind me, I quickly change to #1 above.

The key here is holding the steering wheel at the top, slightly to the right of the top of the wheel, with your left hand.

Part of me suspects that I'm a loser, and the other part of me thinks I'm God Almighty. - John Lennon

3. "The When's the Next Rest Stop? Hold" – Short-tempered, anxious, anal-retentive.

This hold looks like the cool hold but it's not.

I just realized this is the first time my arms have been photographed for this blog.

4. "The Medical Grip" – You'd make a great doctor

This steering wheel hold means business.

You are very bright and can hold a scalpel like a pro.

5. "The Medical Grip II" – You'd make a great nurse

I probably wouldn't make a great nurse, as you can see from my poor attempt at mimicking this hold.

It looks like I'm flexing here but I promise, I'm not.

6. "The Unsure Hold" – Inept decision making, would make a good ballroom dancer, was a nice kid in middle school

See #6 heading for all you need to know about this hold. If you're unsure what you just read, stop here and sign up with Arthur Murray or similar local ballroom dance instructor.

7. "The Chef Hold" – Great cook, home is straight out of every good idea on Houzz, Cocoa Puffs cereal mixed in peanut butter is guilty pleasure

8. "The Fingertip Hold" – Germophobic, even of your own germs, and that's okay

No further explanation needed.

With the shadow on my right bicep, it makes me look pretty buff in this image, which is good, because I'm worried I have an anxiety disorder in this image, which is not good.

9. "Anxiety Hold"

Notice how the hands are slightly apart and the chin is closer to the wheel than any of the previously mentioned holds.

A mathematical formula can be used to determine anxiety level with this hold, where the smaller the number the more anxious the driver. In this image, hands are 2.5 centimeters apart. Chin is 15 centimeters from steering wheel. Therefore, this driver is 2.5 + 15 = 17.5 centimeters anxious.

If you are 20 centimeters anxious or less, you may have an anxiety disorder. You also may not.

I promise I wasn't flexing in this image either.

10. "Lazy Hold" – Pure laziness

Notice how hands are even closer together than in the Anxiety Hold description above. But this isn't anxiety. It's pure laziness.

The Lazy Hold is marked by the hands just resting on the steering wheel as if they're taking a nap.

Ouch! I'm still recovering from this unnatural holding method.

11. "The Butterfly Hold" – Vague personality

Also known as the Carpal Tunnel Syndrome Hold in more technical circles, the Butterfly Hold is named after the insect that kind of looks like this hold.

What do you think this hold says about you? Scientists aren't exactly sure, so they are calling this the "vague personality" to describe the kind of person who is sort of there and not there at the same time.

12. "The Double Pinky Hold" – Fun-loving, very brave when dropped into a war zone in your dreams but not so much when dropped into a war zone in reality

What more can be said? Description says it all.

One weird thing to mention. Notice how the side mirror in this image is blank and the side mirror in image #11 has a tree in it. Conspiracy?

13. "The Knee Hold" – Careless; feigned fearlessness; extrovert; probably texting with one hand while the other hand is holding a 32 oz (or larger) cup obtained as part of a value meal from a fast food establishment

14. "Toonee Hold" (US), or "Two Knee Hold" (NZ)

A joint study is being conducted between US and NZ researchers to ascertain the personality type of this hold.

I just want to point out, as you can see here, that I was driving 58 mph when I attempted this hold. I crashed and rolled the car a few times shortly thereafter.

15. "Pinky Solo" – Independent, vivacious, forgiving, still watches Gilmore Girls and is noticeably angst-ridden after a multi-episode binge

16. "The Rude Hold" – Always pointing at others making them feel bad about themselves

This driver can't help but point even when no one is around.

17. "Psycho Hold" – You are certifiably nuts and should be institutionalized

18. "The Perfectly Normal Hold" – You are perfectly normal

You can distinguish yourself from the Psycho Hold with only a slight deviation. Notice any difference? Look at the above image (#17) and then look at the image below. What's missing? You guessed it! The right hand. The right hand is hidden during performance of "The Perfectly Normal Hold."

I sliced the steering wheel in half .000309 seconds after this picture was taken, earning me the coveted and seldom awarded Gray Belt.

19. Karate Chop Hold – Almost not human

It's a good thing my camera isn't better at capturing still shots during rapid karate chop movements, because I wanted to capture the blur caused by the rapidity at which I was chopping the steering wheel. I was so impressed at my chopping skillz without a single Karate class! I now say "Karate" with an accent.

20. The Unsuccessful Author Hold – Creative, social, yet a little too awkward for authorhood success

This driving method is really easy for me to write about. It consists of two karate chop holds without the chop (i.e. kept still) on the center of the steering wheel, indicating a unique and competitive driving style. This is the least effective of all driving methods. The car is much less responsive using this hold, and so is the reaction to the material you come up with for your books.

21. "The 'Good Job' Hold" – Eternal optimist, helps others, an aversion to CNBC

Because the thumb is pointing upward with this hold, this is one for very upbeat, positive people who wish to let their fellow passengers and fellow travelers on the roadway around them know that they are doing a good job.

The driver who uses this hold is happy in every area of life except while trying to relax watching some TV and some inconsiderate person comes over and changes the channel to something like CNBC.

32

5 Distinct Thoughts After Writing This Much So Far

It was two days of walking in the desert, looking for a sign of water, a sign of food, a sign of anything, before I came to a sand dune with what appeared to be a door. I approached and saw, as a matter of irrefutable fact, a five-foot tall wooden door with a knob. I opened the door, and inside I was greeted by a land more beautiful than any I had ever seen.

A voice from no identified source hit my ears. "Welcome to the land of milk, honey, and one dollar cheeseburgers," explained a clear, careful, pleasant sounding woman. "The milk is to the right, the honey is to the left, and the cheeseburgers are straight ahead."

As I walked in a straight course for what seemed like a half mile or more, I was met by another gatekeeper standing before a narrow entryway.
"Welcome to the land of one dollar cheeseburgers. To enter the gate, you must solve this riddle…"

At that point, I was so famished from my journey and the unfortunate delay. Knowing I had never solved a riddle before in my life, I turned around, went back to where I had started, and turned towards the milk.

When I reached the milk, I was approached by another gatekeeper who pointed in the direction of an obstacle course that appeared nearly impossible to achieve.
I again darted for the honey.

As had happened previously, I was confronted by a gate and the most unusual scene. Standing before me was a seven-foot tall woman holding a large axe in one hand and an empty bag in the other. She said nothing. I dared not pass her. Frightened, I asked her whether it would be any trouble to go back to the cheeseburger gate and knock it down for me, at which point she swung her axe powerfully in my direction, and that's the last thing I remember.

■ ■ ■

Roughly 8 minutes later
12:02 AM, September 14

■ ■ ■

1. "Ow!" As in, "Ouch, something hurts."
2. Is an incomplete author an "auth?" Is that what I am now?
3. Writing to you is lonely.
4. Word drought. Word flood. I never know what to write and then somehow, years later, it flows again.
5. Worst case scenario: after finishing typing the book on my computer, I forget my password.

The Forgotten Password

It's my children's usernames, emails and Twitter handles I'm worried about. Ten, twenty years from now, will there be any left? Or will usernames, emails and Twitter handles start looking as long as a crypto keychain?

■ ■ ■

Two months later
November

■ ■ ■

I've had some nightmares since starting this book. One nightmare is a very real occurrence experienced by an untold number of people since the dawn of passwords. It is the password nightmare. Perhaps the worst kind of password nightmare was experienced by those who purchased Bitcoin crypto currency back when it was priced well under a dollar. The surge in price of Bitcoin turned many of these individuals into overnight millionaires. Some, however, bought Bitcoin years before the exponential growth in value, yet failed to save their secret keychain password. To this day, the affect that password has had on them keeps them up at night, has caused them to attempt retrieval of the password through hypnotherapy, or spend large sums combing nearby landfills for their old computer.

My nightmare is similar. The draft of this book is located on a password-protected computer. What if something happened that locked me out? What if all this time and effort writing was lost forever because of a password? The book would have to be renamed from *Now I Can Say I'm an Author* to *I Can't Say I'm an Author Because I Lost My Password*.

Think of the lost passwords that have kept many in humanity from retrieving old bank accounts, photos, and memories! Passwords are a modern-day scourge on society and I'll just come out and say it: I hate them.

The reason I begin with this is I couldn't remember a much-needed password today. They gave me a few tries, which was sweet of them, but then they locked me out of their system. There was no way to get back in.

I like to feel in control when I'm online – like I'm the boss.

I can click and drag;

tap, post, open, close, minimize, maximize;

browse, skip, skim, stay, play, pause, swipe, buy;

unsubscribe, mute, uncheck the box, ignore the ad;

fill out the survey, send the message, add a comment;

and I really want to add another semicolon;

and one more semicolon after that last one;

;;;;;;;;;;;;;;;; If I wanted to, I could endlessly type a never-ending stream of semicolons? ;;;;;;;;;;;;;;;;

On the great and expansive internet, I am in absolute and complete control. I read, I click, I write. I do whatever I want, whenever I want. I honestly, truly believe that I am the the "I" in "Internet."

If I wanted, I could start a site called "Semicolon" and just type semicolons whenever I wanted. I checked and the domain Semicolon.

com is taken but semicolon.guru is available. Semi.net currently runs $5,400 a year.

The Internet is the epitome of freedom, liberty, and stupidity.

Basically, I own my online experience, one of my very few actual possessions. It's an actual possession I actually included in my will to apportion to my posterity upon my death, evenly distributed.

After the internet built up my optimism and personal confidence over all of these precious web surfing years, the password lockdown company took it all away. I was now helpless and virtually broke.

This company apparently doesn't use the internet. The internet is all about openness, transparency, sociality, friendship, and love. Being locked out of a website is foreign to the entire web experience. You would think everyone knows this, right?

Wrong.

Only an evil corporation grounded in closed-minded, rigid, inflexible, proud, insular, reclusive thinking completely out of touch with the times and modern reality could exact a punishment as severe as this. Too harsh? I'm just getting started.

I'm the poor customer who is merely trying to make the world a better place. Don't they know me?

"To not be known is death."

–Josh Rolph

I'm the poor customer who is trying to keep them in business. Don't they understand me?

"To not be understood is whatever comes before death."

–Josh Rolph

Perhaps Corporation Evil didn't value the fact that I needed to access their services more than ever before in my lifetime. I needed their online service immediately. I could not wait.

Over the years, so many other lesser-evil corporations had exercised a degree of patience and kindness with me. I couldn't even remember what later was like.

When I had forgotten a password with the lesser evil corporations, they would at least show a little mercy. They would allow me to change my password with a verified email already on file or give me ten or even unlimited chances to get it right. Or they would lock me out for a few minutes. Or they would offer some other two-step verification method using my phone number or asking a question like, "What was the name of my childhood best friend's dog."[141]

Corporation Evil offered the most conservative password option of them all: They offered only three tries. After three unsuccessful tries – not even three and a half – I saw the cold response:

"Too many failed attempts to login. You are now locked out of our website."

And that was it. No offer to help. No saving me from their password purgatory. To them, I was worse than dead. It was as if I never existed.

How could you do that to me? How could you just…leave? I spent many hours with you over the years and now, just because I had relied on my computer for a while to automatically fill in the password — just because of that — when my computer forgot how to fill it in again for some unexplained reason you wouldn't accept me anymore! How dare you! It wasn't my fault! It was my stupid computer's!

Listen, if you will do this to me, I can get you back. I'm not a hacker and I have no ties to North Korea, but I think I know a way to get back at you, you inhumane power-hungry pawn of the devil.

It is very possible these days for the modern, connected individual and business to need dozens if not hundreds of passwords of varying

---

141 Hermie.

lengths and configurations to access needed services from everyone and their dog. I need a password just to type on my own personal blog at joshrolph.com. (BTW – my blog's password is "WhyAmIdo!ngThis?")

Password-protected sites need to understand that the over 35 crowd was not formally trained to create unique configurations of upper and lowercase letters, numbers and symbols for every organization, product, or business they would ever use.

The younger generations are different. My one year old already has several passwords to his favorite sites: Lego.com, Huggies.com, and managing his 529 savings plan with MerrilLynch.com. For privacy reasons, he has made it abundantly clear on many a bedtime he will not under any circumstances divulge them to me.

The first time I forgot a password was when I returned from Christmas break in sixth grade and forgot the combination to my locker. My locker combination was three, two-digit numbers, six digits in all. That was my first password I used for all of middle school. I think I changed lockers only twice in high school. So three passwords memorized in a six year period. That was it. Oh, and I remember a bike lock with a three-digit combination from pre-drivers license days. So four passwords memorized as a teenager. Little did I know what was to come.

There is a better way. If we all band together, we can create a password-free world. It will take all our collective energies, but I am confident it can be done.

First, we have to deal with Corporation Evil. I came up with a two-step plan to accomplish this task.

How to Get Back at Corporation Evil

1. Tweet my problem with them so everyone can see.
2. That's all I can think of.

Next, we need to acknowledge that the password problem is a viral epidemic that must end. Here, I offer a four-step plan to defeat it once and for all.

1. Eliminate all passwords.
2. Require that everyone simply trusts each other.
3. Create a jobs plan for hackers where the government finds good-paying jobs to keep them off the streets, FDR WPA style.
4. Require Internet companies that have passwords to have satellite offices in every city block and rural square to get to know people personally; vouching for them so they don't need to use passwords. We will call them the Gentle Mafia.

I'm sure there are other possible solutions. I haven't thought this through too well. But I couldn't wait another minute without getting a proposal out there to the general public. If we begin working on this together now, we can share a common password-free future together. We can always retain our memories, our photos, our books, and our Bitcoin keychain.

34

Two Men on a Plane

Listen. Are you listening? While you listen, I'm typing. As you know, you can't hear me type anymore because I already typed. For me, I'm typing. For you, you're reading. I'm telling you to listen. Just listen. See what you can hear. I'm typing because I keep checking the word count and at the moment, I'm not too far away from achieving a word count milestone. So close. All I have to do is continue to type away, allowing my brain-to-hand combo to conduct all the work in order to reach the word count milestone I'm about to...okay I just passed it by nine words. I guess you can stop listening now and get back to reading. I was just trying to distract you for a minute.

■ ■ ■

The next day
November

■ ■ ■

Here lies a brief account of two men on a plane:

<u>Man 1</u>

We boarded the plane. I was the very last to board, as usual, because I really don't like standing in line. I really, really don't like standing in line.

Why's that?

Because I don't like to stand.

I like to sit.

Being the first to board a plane means more time standing in line, waiting for the gate to open. That's why I like to be the last to board a plane.

To get here, I had walked the entire length of the airport with no problems en route. Walking is fine with me; moving at a 60 foot per hour pace is not.

Think about it. Boarding first is great and all, but you stood in line for thirty minutes at the gate. Thirty minutes is a lot of standing for someone like me who likes to sit.

It may surprise you that I've always been this way. When I worked retail – my first job in the 9th grade – the first hour of standing was a shock to my entire system. In my entire life, I had never stood for so long. Never in my whole entire life. It was maybe a never-ending eternity of five hours. I had walked, ran, played, but never had I stood, like that first day on the job, stationary at a cash register. Forty-five minutes into that job, I thought, "this isn't right." About thirty seconds later, I found my boss and gave him the customary two second notice. I quit, vowing I would never again in my life stand still for so long.

First trip to Europe, I noticed at the grocery checkout that unlike America, they sat on a high stool while scanning and typing into the register. But no, we Americans have to stand. We have to stand all day long. Whether it's that blue collar job, standing in line at Disneyland, or watching the parade pass you by among the crowd on the city sidewalk, it's stand, stand, stand. No other country does this to its citizens. Not one. I've checked into it.

I know they say sitting is bad for your health. They also say a lot of things are bad for your health. At least, "they" believe those things. And who "they" are is whomever the mainstream contemporary science sages anoint as the seers of all human wisdom. Don't misunderstand, I have a reasonable amount of confidence in modern science, except for that time when my doctor gave me advice to have surgery after which I got a second opinion from another doctor who, just like the first, graduated from an accredited medical school and, like the other, practices as a specialist in exactly the same field, yet who somehow proposed the complete opposite approach to solve my health issue. One chooses surgery, the other does not. One suggests heavy-duty medicine, the other herbs. One a cast, the other amputation. One proposes nothing, the other euthanasia. I have a genuine interest and trust in the human pursuit for good science. But I also carry a healthy amount of skepticism.

I've read the articles: sitting isn't at all good for humans. It takes years off your life, they say. It's much better to stand, for your physical health and well-being, they say. But I don't always do what is best for my health, I say. I do what is best for my mind.

You see, the body scientists don't always factor in the best practices developed by the mind scientists. For me, the health benefits right there, on the decision of where I opt for good mind science over good body science, is, for me, the better choice. And while this is by no means scientific, the skeptical part of me is reminded of the fact that my rear end is the fattest part of my otherwise lean body, so I'm inclined to think that the purpose of that fatty area is not to help support the human body in a standing position. It's for sitting.

Which is why I am last to board a plane, without fail. I do it to reduce the time standing.

My seat was the never-coveted middle seat, way back on aisle 24. I sat comfortably. It was wonderful sitting there, staring at the backs of a hundred heads. For about 30 minutes, all was fine, all was normal. Then, all of a sudden, something happened in the row behind me. It happened directly behind me. It happened in the seat in the row directly behind me.

He began to snore.

It was a hearty, solid snore. It was as if, if he were awake, it was as if he was intentionally making pig snorting sounds. It was as if, if he were awake, his vocal cords were capable of producing an incredibly loud speaking voice. A voice so loud, very loud, that was without a doubt much louder than me on my loudest of days. It was a manly snore. A confident snore. The kind one might engage in in a more private setting, such as one's bed.

The woman in the aisle seat to my right turned around once, then twice, wondering who it was who could be making such a noise. The man in the window seat to my left also turned around. Both seemed so bothered by it, I wondered if either would get up to forcefully nudge the snorer awake. Neither did.

I've heard snoring on planes before. I've never heard snoring like this.

The snoring continued. It would regress to a heavy inhale, exhale. Then an aggressive violently loud full-fledged snore. The kind of snore that damages throats, that causes the non-viral kind of sore throat, the kind that causes throat cancer.

After a few minutes, sitting in sitting bliss, I would forget all about the snorer, because he stopped. He awakened, for all I knew. Until I again would be distracted by the noisy neighbor seated directly, as the crow flies, behind me. The one in row 25 and I was in row 24. The one I assumed was a man because of the snorer's subwoofer-like, subterranean-tectonic-plate-

moving quality snore. The one who was tearing apart his throat and the ozone simultaneously, shredding both to pieces with each passing CO2-emitting snore. Would he ever communicate verbally again, the one whose snores were louder than any I had ever heard on any plane in my lifetime?

The snoring continued, on and off, for hours. And hours. The man could snore and, quite remarkably, sleep through it all.

The rumbling, steady roar of the plane engine would be silenced by another Snore. A Snore with a capital S. This kind deserved to become a pronoun. It was alive.

The snore became white noise for the plane engine. In the battle of noise, the snore won. We forgot we were flying on a plane. We were now flying on a Snore.

Again and again this continued. And again and again and again. It wouldn't stop. Passengers became irritated. The irritated became anxious. The anxious became furious and the furious went mad. Flight attendants began throwing pretzels around the plane. Movie watchers could hardly concentrate on their movie. Pilots rocked the plane to and fro in hopes that the passenger would finally wake up.

Throughout this peculiar scene, sometimes I would laugh. Sometimes I would get angry. But for the most part, I sat patiently, staring ahead, watching American Sniper through the two inch crack on the iPhone of the person in the row in front of me.

The snore made me consider myself. I've been told on many occasions throughout my life that I, too, am a snorer. Apparently, I snore. And when I snore, I do so loudly. I do the kind of loud that vibrates the mattress, floor, and walls – the kind that can be heard in other rooms.

Not only that, but I've even slept on plane rides.

Which means I could have snored loudly at least once on a plane. Possibly even twice. Who knows, I could snore every time I sleep on a plane. I've never been told by anyone after I awaken that I've been snoring. I don't think I've ever been nudged. Fellow passengers may have let me snore away until I awakened, as we were doing for this man.

Which is why I lacked the moral authority to do anything about the snoring man in the seat behind me.

This snorer could have been me.

Maybe this man, I thought, like me, also likes to sit.

• • •
<u>Man 2</u>

I never know what to do because I care too much what other people think.

It's time to end it. It's time to not care what others think about me.

I just buckled my seatbelt on a plane and right this very moment I'm thinking of what to do next.

Suddenly, it hits me:

I could fake sleep.

I could fake sleep!

Why would I do that? What would that accomplish?

Here's what it would accomplish: I would see if I could fake sleep in the most annoying manner possible and not stop based on the desires of the upset people around me.

In case anyone was looking at me, I thought it would be a good idea to make it look as believable as possible. As the plane lifted off, I pretended to fall asleep, because that is usually when I fall asleep for real.

I closed my eyes and then began to jerk my head from side to side in an effort to effectively and artfully get the right sleep "look." By jerking my head from side to side, adding a head bob from time to time, I wanted to show I was an energetic fake sleeper.

As soon as I was fake asleep for about two and a half minutes, I decided that fake sleeping wasn't a problem. I would have to make some noise. So I began to fake snore.

At first, no one seemed to notice, so I thought I would make more dramatic snoring sounds. I can be a loud person when I speak, and so I tried to snore as loudly as I possibly could.

Still nothing. I sensed no reaction whatsoever.

I thought I would try making a pig sound. I would make my snores more dramatic. I would "saw logs." I literally made a sound of sawing a log.

I began to hear people whispering. I was getting their attention.

The whispers turned to concerned voices. Concerned voices turned to yells. I was finally beginning to make a scene.

They wanted me to stop.

It was tormenting to not comply with their wishes. I wanted to stop so badly. I wanted everyone to be happy. I wanted everyone to be spared the pain of listening to my every snore.

I kept snoring.

Flight attendants were summoned. I kept snoring.

The flight attendants said they would wake me up, but they couldn't touch me to awaken me. The threat of a lawsuit kept everyone from touching me. They couldn't give me a nudge. Even if they did, I became more and more calloused to their wants, needs, and desires. I kept snoring.

The plane began to move back and forth, side to side. My snore must be penetrating the steel door separating me from the pilots, I thought. My snore could be interfering with the communications of the plane. I was becoming more determined not to be switched off to airplane mode. I kept snoring.

My snoring became snoring opera. I was performing a show of snores.

I could feel the thick emotional reaction from the crowd. They were all ears. I was all theirs.

"Sir, sir!" The flight attendants beckoned. I kept snoring.

"Wake up!" a toddler yelled from the back of the plane. Everyone laughed.

Others throughout the plane began to yell, "Wake up!"

After a few seconds, every passenger, in unison, began to chant: "Wake up! Wake up! Wake up!"

This went on for several minutes. It was remarkable. And they sounded great. But I ensured that my snore would carry above their chants. My snore dominated. It was the snore to rule them all.

I snored on for hours.

It was the last time I didn't care what other people think.

35

I Bring Out the Man in Men

For a reader, the best part of a book is the experience of entering a new world, learning new information, being transported from their existence into another.
For the author, it's the check. I think.

■ ■ ■

The day after that
November

■ ■ ■

I don't know why, but I bring out the man in men.

A very manly Texas rancher once told me "Josh, you're more man than I'll ever be." Calling me "more man" was his play on the word "Mormon" the religion I was born into. I'd never heard of that before he said it. Being told I was more-man than a Baptist Texan made me laugh. He was a pretty clever guy.

When I say I bring out the man in men, I don't exactly mean I make men more manly (though it's totally true).

What I mean is — well, let's take a step back for a sec. For one, the word "man" has a lot of meanings. I'm not talking about the man that deals with manhood or manliness or masculinity or mankind. Instead, I'm referring to the more informal meanings of "man."

First, there's "man" in the exclamation sense, like:

"Man! That's amazing!" & "Man-oh-man!"

Lastly, we have "man" in the fraternal/buddy sense, like:

"Totally, man," & "You alright, man?"

Of all "man" uses, these two are the most frequently used in the modern world.

Now here's where I'm going with this. Some men don't say the word "man" informally or casually – at all –

There are some men who NEVER say it informally. Never! EXCEPT WHEN THEY ARE AROUND ME.

I'm sure you know guys who never say, "What's up, man?" Or, "Man! Your book is amazing!"

There is one quick and easy identifier of these types who never use the word man: These are the same men who close their emails with "Best regards" and "Cheers!" You wouldn't expect a man who uses language like that in email to throw around the word "man" in informal conversation or otherwise. But when these men are around me, they say "man" a lot.

It's the oddest thing.

It's only odd because I have observed that these men become extremely unsettled at what is happening to them.

I can see it in their eyes as they say, "Josh, man, how are you doing, man?"

For some reason, when they are around me, they begin to create new, unnatural sentence configurations of "man."

"Man! I can't believe, man, how much, man, [unintelligible] man, man-man,an,ana,manamna\ dfnammann~maa..." [based on actual events]

It's like a virus, attacking their speech to the point that their words begin to lose all meaning. Their language becomes a mess of mans.

During these conversations, I can see in their eyes a simmering panic. It's hard to identify at first but I've seen it so many times now

I'm used to "the 'man' look." It becomes clear they are well outside their comfort zone. Most of the time they don't realize what's happening to them. Some of the time they do. In any case, I always feel for them, although I've become more numb to it lately. There's really nothing I can do. Whatever it is that comes over them causing them to say the word "man" is absolutely out of my control.

As I've said, I don't know why, but I bring out the "man" in men.

While I do casually use "man" in conversation, I don't use it regularly.

I could see a situation in conversation with these men where I, like a mentor, used the word "man" many, many, many times. Doing that, one could assume, would lead men to respond in like manner to me.

But I promise you, women and men, I don't use man all that much. I do use it sometimes. After all, I am human. I'm not some superhuman superman. I'm more like a freshman specimen in the school of life. I'm no spokesman or statesman with the acumen to provide any sort of omen, like foretelling an amen to my saying "man."

And don't think from the paragraph above that I'm losing my mind: I'm no manic attempting to manufacture this "man" problem. I'm not crazy.

You could call me "mental" as much as you could claim a manhunt for a mannequin from a Manhattan manor whose manipulated manslaughter charge lies on a mantel in a manila envelope emitting the faint yet menacingly potent scent of manure.

You could call me maniacal as much as you could claim a mansion owner with a manscaped abdomen is in a pool of mangoes munching menthol-mandarin flavored Mentos while working on a manuscript for a manual called "Manhandled Manatees with Meningitis" during a manicure.

Point is, I'm trying to make this happen as much as I am maneuvering a mandate to play the mandolin in Manila, which I can assure you, is as likely as me going menstrual or menopausal – it's simply not on the menu.

Anyway, don't worry. Whatever this is, I can manage. I refuse to serve as anyone's malefactor.

But this strange phenomena has led me to wonder why. Why do so many men say "man" around me?

Maybe they say "man" around me because I am a man.

Maybe they say "man" around me because I bring out more fully their inner-man.

Maybe they say "man" around me because I am so manly they can't help themselves.

Maybe this is what it means to be "a real man's man."

Maybe I am a real man's man.

A man who brings out the man in men.

SECTION 5: REFLECTIONS[142]

---

142 If you skipped the last several sections you're pretty much done. Flipping through a book is better than not reading it.

How to End a Book

[Insert motivational quote about finishing the job, sticking to your goals, fighting against the grain, or just keep this part in here because researching for some cheesily [sic] perfect quote sounds hard.]

■ ■ ■

I can't figure out when I wrote this

■ ■ ■

I have to admit: I've been at the airport for far too long tonight. I got here at 3:45 PM. It's now 10:21 PM. My plane may not take off for another hour, at the very earliest, severely delayed by a snowstorm, if it isn't canceled.

I've been writing and writing, which has been oh so good. What's bad is how badly I want to end this book.

Yes, it's now come to this: I want to end the book.

There. I said it.

At the very beginning of this book-writing journey, I shared with you that I would be honest. That was part of the useless acronym I developed way back in chapter one, the part where I undertook the job of lecturing myself on how to write a book I didn't know how to write. Let me tell you in acronym form what I've learned from this god-forsaken process:

This Is Nothing But Thankless Work. TINBTW.

I don't know how authors do it. So much time spent writing. So much time. So much. Maybe they're faster at typing than I am. Maybe they can kick out a book faster than I can. Maybe they are better look-ing than I can ever be.[143]

I will persevere. I will endure. I will overcome. I will conquer. There is nothing I want more than to finish this book. Nothing. Even though there is nothing I want more than to *not* not finish this book.

There could be truth to the previous sentence. That could be Gandhi-level wisdom I have gained since first attempting to lecture myself on authoring with a ridiculous acronym in chapter one.[144]

"To end a book, one must first be willing to not end the book."

–Josh Rolph

That, too, makes no sense.

What am I trying to say?

One must be willing to go through the work required to fill in gaps, stick with the effort, make all the edits, polish it up, share the book with a well-read friend or expert editor for corrections and advice, continue to improve and move to finalize, all in an effort to produce the best possible product. Once written, then published, it's final. No more can be done to fix up the book. It better be the way you want it to be when some stranger inevitably holds the book in their hand and says to their friend, "This book sucks."

I can't really predict whether the book will suck or not. The book could very well suck. Maybe I should accept that. This world is full of failing creative endeavors. Someone, somewhere, poured their genius into a product that tanked. Failure happens every day. Big companies invested billions only to achieve devastating losses of great proportions I may never fully comprehend. The question is whether I could endure this book sucking, and I'm pretty sure I can, since I've done a lot of

---

143   Chances are great. Most authors are better looking.
144   No offense to Gandhi.

things that suck in my life and I can still look in the mirror without completely turning the other way out of shame. The key here is that I need to be proud of what I finish writing. If the world winds up going to war against me (World War Josh), I would hope that I could stand proud of what I accomplished, at least to myself.

37

My Superpower, Super Weakness

"With great power comes great responsibility."
—an uncle in one of the fifty recent Spider Man movies

■ ■ ■

November

■ ■ ■

I have a superpower. It's nothing close to easy to have a superpower, because as everyone instinctually knows, there are rules to superpowers. Just as in budgets, where an expense is offset by an equal amount of revenue, so goes the rule for superpowers: if you have a superpower, it is offset by a super weakness.

My superpower is that I can see about two seconds into the future. The important caveat is that I can only sometimes do this. But caveat or not, did you catch that? I can SEE INTO THE FUTURE.

Sometimes.

I don't personally know anyone who can see two seconds into the future, sometimes.

I did hear of a guy who claimed to see one second into the future, but I'll be honest – it was a little hard for me to believe.

My Super Weakness

So I guess now that I've divulged my super power I have to share my super weakness, which I'll do right now. I'll just come out and say it: my super weakness is that I'm on a two second delay.

A not-at-all famous *SNL* skit from the Mike Myers era illustrates my super weakness perfectly. Three 20-something friends in a diner talk politics, clam chowder, and other topics during their casual conversation. The only problem is one of the friends chimes in with a clever zinger well after each conversation topic has passed. Fortunately, he finds a solution in the men's bathroom: a time machine, allowing him to go back to the beginning of the conversation where he lands perfectly timed lines.

I had only seen this skit once as a teen before finding it online and I will tell you this - it struck a nerve when I watched it in the 90s and I still find it true today...

The skit especially rings true to anyone with the two second delay super weakness.

Another instance where my super weakness manifests is the conference call. Invariably, it goes like this:

I dial the 1-800 number I was given.

I enter the passcode, followed by the pound sign.

I rock out to the music as I wait for the conference call to begin.

"Hi, thanks to all of you for joining the call. This is Sal Slymaster. We have a number of people on the call so let's go around for introductions."

"Bob Beem."

"Jane Sewasassis."

Do you know any Sewasassis's?

"Rick Springfield."

"Hi, Rick."

"Hey there, Sal."

"Don Newgood."

Someday I'll tell you more about Don.

"Lester Harris."
"
Chris Patelli."

I'm making these people up.

"DoJonnsha–."

"I'm sorry, we didn't catch that. Can you say that again?"

"Uh, yes. Donna."

I don't think I know a Donna.

"Jo–"

"Thank you, Donna."

"Bajrtsh."

"Repeat that please?"

"Jo–"

"Bart Schlundunn."

And the call roster continues.

"Anyone else on the call?"

"Lucijondsh."

"Say again? I missed your name."

"Jo–."

"Lucinda Maretz."

"Ok, thank you. Well, let's begin the call."

If you didn't catch what happened above, Donna, Bart, and Lucinda won the conference call roster war against me. I was trying to say my name, but could never quite get the timing right. It's a war and I've come to feel warrior-like when this happens.

This happens to me every time I'm on a conference call. It is a source of genuine frustration.

All because of this two second delay super weakness business. There's absolutely nothing I can do about it. Nothing.

...

My Superpower

When I get really frustrated by all this, I try to think of things that make me happy, like my superpower.

I've noticed that sometimes, when someone is telling a joke and hasn't quite made it to the punchline, that I laugh about two seconds before everyone else does. Sometimes.

On the next conference call I hope to see into the future two seconds to know whether to say my name at the perfect time and not overlap with anyone. But the two second delay will most likely keep me from doing that.

A smart person might argue that my seeing two seconds into the future, offset by my two second delay, would nullify my power and keep me firmly planted in the here and now. I can see their point.

My Other Super Weakness

We've come so far together within the pages of this book. All these words, sentences, paragraphs. All this *time*. We've come so far together in time. As in, when we started our journey, we were at one point of time in the past. We now find ourselves here, in the present.

Time moves along at a most unfrenetic pace. It's controlled. It's too controlled. It waits for no one. I wish it was more self-accommodating. I wish it waited for people to catch up to it. Waited around, held up — you know. I wish it was less disciplined, like me.

I've spent so much time writing. You've spent so much time reading. We're spent. We're spending our time. If you do not possess monetary wealth, you possess the same amount of time I have. Sleep is the only thing we spend differently. I might need more or less sleep than you. I might be narcoleptic and rarely spend time awake. As I've mentioned previously, I feel so narcoleptic when I write.[145]

More time has been spent by me, admittedly, writing, than for you, reading. Typing out a paragraph takes forever when compared to reading a paragraph. This paragraph, for example, could take me fifty-five minutes to write and only a minute for you to read. I don't want to turn you away after coming so far together by lavishing myself with praise for the great sacrifices I have endured to write this paragraph, or even this book. But let's be honest, writing takes longer than reading. At least it does for most. If you're reading this letter by letter through a magnifying glass then yes, I concede, you could have given more of your time to this work. I'm talking about something entirely different, though. What I'm talking about, or about to talk about, or about to talk about right about now, is I wonder if you have the same type of problem reading that I have in writing. And by that, I mean that this problem has absolutely nothing to do with the act of reading itself, just as this problem has nothing to do with the snail-like pace I seem to be writing. It has everything to do with one simple yet soul-wrenching quality. Just one. The massive problem I have is one of pure, unadulterated guilt.

Do you feel guilt every time you sit down to read? If you do, then we share something in common. You may have been wondering if we have anything in common. I would assume that if you've made it this far it's because we do have a thing or two in common. All the people who have nothing in common with me are long gone. They didn't even buy the book. They saw the title and began throwing things around the room and screaming loud vulgarities.

The people who had a little bit in common with me saw the book title and said, "Huh." They then walked away.

Those who had a little more in common with me saw the book title

---

145 No offense to narcoleptics.

and looked at the back sleeve only to get distracted by something more interesting.

Those who had a little more in common with me than the ones who had a little more in common with me were intrigued enough by the summary or the recommendation or some other summary that they spent money or borrowed or invested something more of their time than the previous bunch, although they, too, didn't endure through much of the book.

Keep moving up[146] the in-common-with-Josh-Rolph scale and I would wager more than fifty cents[147] that those of you who have more in common with me stuck around longer, until we find ourselves here, to the ending of my first book, and I have to ask:

Are you me?

My point of saying all this is if you are anything like me, you feel guilt when you are using your limited time in this existence we call mortality in a way that isn't at all optimal.

For you, that may mean every time you go on YouTube watching a binge-allotment of videos calculated by the Algorithmic Gods to be binged by the masses. It may mean indulging yourself in another form of time wasting, and in our modern age, there are many time sucks. It may mean taking time to read this book. Let's be upfront and honest: this book will do nothing to add to your life. It contains no nuggets of wisdom. It contains no pearls of knowledge. It contains little of worth. It contains not a thing to improve your status, to motivate you, or to help you in any calculable way.

For me, the act of writing this book has been the exact same. I'm writing and writing for a mere title of "author." A title that once meant something but no longer means anything out in the great big world we call home. I am filling my time writing when I could instead be doing a million useful things.

---

146 (Or down)
147 And not a penny more.

In other words, for the last who-knows-how-long, every single instance I sat down to write this book, I have been filled with the most extraordinary, overburdening, nearly debilitating sense of guilt. Most people, when feeling guilt, either abandon the activity causing them guilt, seek to rectify the situation so as to resolve the guilty sensations, or do drugs. It is obvious to me that I didn't abandon the activity of writing this book. And I don't do drugs so I had no readily available resource to absolve the burdensome feelings of guilt I felt each time I opened this book on my computer or my phone attempting to fill words within it so I could someday become an author!

The guilt came because of the million useful things I knew I needed to do. I needed to be a better father. My kids are so great. I need them, and they need me. When I write, I write at night when they're asleep. On rare occasion, I write when they are wide awake, like right now. My kids want me to play with them. I'm not at work and I'm not traveling, so I feel that I need to spend quality time with them at the moment. But I'm writing instead. And I feel awful, dreadful guilt about it.

I love my family. I have extended family spread out across America and the world. I can't reach out when I'm writing the book. Every day is precious. You never know when contact with family members will be the last. But I choose the book today. For many hours, I chose the book, a thing that will give me no lasting happiness, companionship, pleasure, or lasting reward. Guilt, guilt, guilt.

There are friends all over and I love them, or at least, I think I do. There are friends who I can't talk to when I'm writing the book.

So much guilt.

I have a job and can't write when I'm working or traveling. There's just too much to do. There's guilt when I'm not writing at those times. If only I could write when traveling for work, at least, but traveling is all work. I couldn't write if I tried. It's a completely different mindset. I'm on the clock. Yet there is this guilt at those times for not writing.

That's right, not writing fills me with a level of guilt so debilitating I should probably seek medication for except it's not that debilitating.

TV. I love TV. Movies. I love movies. Not a movie or TV show watching moment goes by without feeling extraordinary guilt for not writing this book.

Housework. Yard work. Cooking, cleaning, ironing, showering, shaving, talking…even bathroom visits are all instant tickets to instant guilt. I'm doing all those things in order to build credit and goodwill with my family hoping to spend the credits for a few minutes here and there of uninterrupted book writing.

One truism is the guilt is there when writing and when not writing. I can't escape the guilt. It's entirely self-imposed. I don't have to be doing this. I don't have to be writing and I don't have to not be writing, and I don't have to be feeling guilt. Many authors have come before me and many will come after who all have life obligations they must fulfill. Whether they feel or felt guilt from beginning to the end is unknowable without talking it through with them and getting an honest answer.

All I know is this: writing the book "Now I Can Say I'm an Author" and not writing the book "Now I Can Say I'm an Author" is an exercise in guilt. And that never-ending sense of guilt, in addition to my two second delay, is my other super weakness.

38

Word Count Obsession

"Word count is the book writing topic no author wants to discuss as freely as I do."

–Josh Rolph

■ ■ ■

November 6

■ ■ ■

You may have missed something I've written very candidly about in the entire book. As in, the entirety of the entire book.[148] The book sections, book chapters, especially, and most recently, the title of this very chapter, contains a subject I'm hoping clued you in on a little obsession of mine. It is an obsession about word count. I check it constantly. Like, I just checked it. I won't check it again until it feels like I've been typing for a long time, which is right now and usually around three-minute increments or right now again or right now or let me just check again right now and also after the three minute dozing-off episodes that happen every three minutes before I doze off and then I am checking again right now. Checking

---

148 This is the part that tests whether you have been reading my book.

the word count is an obsession that keeps me awake a little longer but sometimes puts me to sleep, like right now.

Do real authors obsess over their word count? We will probably never know.

Authors don't want to talk about their creative process. If they do, they keep it high, lofty, and distant. They don't want to admit they are mere humans, as I addressed back in the opening pages of this work.

I'm on chapter 38. Amazing. It's hard to believe.

I tweeted several celebrity authors about word count and got the following responses:

NADA

So, I Facebook messaged a couple more and got the following responses:

NADA

So I gave up and thought, "This is a great place to end this chapter."

In case I haven't spoken of the book's word count enough, this chapter might make the reader shout, "Enough!"

National Authors Day

When I discovered authors are actually losers.

■ ■ ■

November 7

■ ■ ■

discovered that November 1 is National Authors Day as opposed to National Author's Day or National Authors' Day. Apparently, an author doesn't own the day, and neither do authors for that matter. They do, however, have a day dedicated to them.

National Authors Day, celebrated last week, brought about some feelings I am attempting to reconcile.

For one, I had never heard of this day before. All the time spent writing the book, all the people in my life who know I am writing the book, and no one has ever mentioned the day. All the research I've poured into trying to write a book and I never once came across any reference to the day. The people I've told I'm writing a book, the authors I follow, the interactions I've had solely on this topic, not to mention the many years I've been alive with calendars, planners, and the recent surge in awareness for the many national days for this and international days for that —— National Authors Day must be the most unknown of all of them. They might as well do away with the commemorative day altogether. It's meaningless. If no one celebrates, it shouldn't exist.

I began asking questions. Why, I wondered, is National Authors Day not a thing? Why do we not know about it in common society? Why are there no parties thrown, gifts given, songs sung, fireworks launched, flowers delivered, store discounts offered, federal holidays granted?

It could be that the day is so new to the world and authors so few and far between, scattered among the non-author public at such a low frequency that hardly a thought is given to recognizing authors.

Drawing from my own personal experience, it could be that what most people feel connected to in a book is the book itself, not the person or persons who wrote the book. A few famous authors who write more than one book get praise enough without having a day dedicated to them. For most, though, a book is read and then the reader moves on, not necessarily devouring everything the author of the book has written.

In my case, should this book ever be published, and should a reader like it enough to look into whether I've written anything else, only to find that I died a long time ago without writing so much as another published word, then…I forget where I was going with that.

Back to the idea of a national celebration honoring authors. I mentioned singing earlier and want to make up a song now. Here are some sample lyrics for National Authors Day, sung to the tune of "La Bamba." No, change that. The National Authors Day ballad would sing to the tune of "Macarena." No, no, the song would be an original rap, with lyrics that go something like this:

Let all the authors rise!
Put your hands up
Put your hands up
Rise
Rise
Yeah
Yeah
Uh
Uh
Ya thas wut ahm talkin bout
Yeah
Yeah
Put your hands up
Rise
Riiiiise
Riiiiiise
[woman sings "oooh" in high-G]
Yeah
Yeah
Oh I know
Know know
No, no
Don't chya go no
Ya know no in the no no ya rise ya rise yo

Let's get right to the point: authors are losers. They are. It's clear to me now. No legitimate rapper would ever write a rap about being an author. No rapper would write a book. Rappers are cool. So cool. It could be said that authors are the opposite of rappers. Both write, only one of the two is wrong.

How about a day of bookstore discounts celebrating authors?

How about a mandatory day of book clubs all across the fruited plain?

What if author parades were held where big floats and balloons heralded down Manhattan streets?

Do you see what I mean?

Authors are losers.

Now I Can Say I'm a Loser.

40

Almost There

Law school is a torturous form of reader purgatory.
Writing a book is a form of writer purgatory.

■ ■ ■

Who cares what time it was when I wrote this?
What is the point?
What was I thinking when I began that exercise?
Why does this book make me angry?
Why can't I own the fact that a book can't make me angry?

My anger comes from within.

■ ■ ■

We're at a party. Lots of familiar faces here. I can't help but look around the room while we talk.

You're asking me about my book. The book is out. No one has bought it. I may never sell enough copies to cover the $500 advance I received from the no-name publisher, but you don't know that and I'm not about to divulge the truth. I'm just going to run with the fact that I'm an author. A real author. Even though I'm fully aware I'm nothing but a big loser, I'm used to it now. I've accepted my place in society as a loser author. Where I once believed authors were cool, I now understand I will never be cool. I will never be a rapper, even though I can freestyle better than anyone in my suburban neighborhood.[149]

We get to talking about authorhood and the writing process. I'm yakking away like it's nobody's business. After a few minutes, I sense I am losing you, so I ask what you do for a living. You tell me you're a lawyer and I cut you off because I have a great lawyer story.

You see, I was on track to becoming a lawyer for about three months. Three years if you count the preparation in undergrad. Taking the LSAT twice. Applying to schools. Getting in. Quitting my job and moving 1,000 miles away. Three months later, I was out. I dropped out. I am a law school dropout. But you don't need to know that. What I did was I thought of a way to bridge the conversation from you back to me.

Writing a book is like becoming a lawyer, I explain. Preparing to go to law school and then slogging it out for three years if you go full time is exactly like book writing. If you aspire to become a lawyer, law school isn't enough. If you desire to become an author, writing a book isn't enough. Lawyers must take the bar and authors must find a publisher. The process for both is absolutely grueling.

You begin to talk about your job. I give you a few seconds before trying to tie what you say about you back to me. Let's just bring it back to me. I'm an author. Yes, you're a lawyer, but there's a lawyer at every party. How many parties have you been to where you've been in the company of an author?

Now, what if I wasn't nearly as rude to you during the party? What if I kept looking over your shoulder but I had a pretty good reason?

---

149 Full confession: I've never tried freestyling with any neighbors.

You may think I'm ignoring what you're saying when I look everywhere around the room but at you, but I could be looking away from you because...

1. I see through the window that a derailed train is heading straight toward this house but I want to appear calm so as not to frighten you.
2. You're on *Dancing with the Stars* on that TV over there.
3. You have a gross white spittle thing that suddenly formed and it's connecting your lips as you move them up and down while you're talking.
4. The person who saved me from drowning when I was a kid just walked through the door.
5. We're actors and it says to do so right here in the script.
6. I see dead people.
7. (I'm fully aware that saying "I see dead people" isn't funny anymore.)
8. I'm actually looking at you square in the eye but you can't tell because my eyes are slightly off-kilter.
9. I've found people are bothered by my tendency to not blink.
10. I'm trying to send you a not-so-subtle message.
11. The guy standing behind you has some incredible dandruff.
12. I see dead people.
13. I'm bothered that out that window is a lunar eclipse and you don't seem to care at all.
14. You have dandruff. Like, the really bad kind.
15. When can I walk away from you? I have to pee in the worst way.
16. For years I've been practicing to be the kind of person that looks away from you at a party, and today I have finally succeeded.
17. I have dandruff.
18. Every time I talk to someone I look away because I have no self-confidence.
19. Every time I talk to someone I look away because I'm trying to be dramatic. Do I look dramatic?
20. I see dead people. Like, for real this time.
21. I'm playing "Eye Spy." You're supposed to guess what I'm looking at, silly.

22. I begin to sing, "Life is but a dream, sweetheart."[150]
23. Your breath smells like dead people.
24. I really wish I was talking to anyone else in this room but you.
25. I really wish I was talking to dead people.
26. Maybe you are a dead person.
27. Maybe this is an M. Night Shyamalan film.

Okay, let me clarify. In #23 I didn't mean I don't like talking to you. As in, you, the person reading the book right now.

When I'm relaxed, the words in this book just flow from my mind on to the keyboard.

I do need to do the dishes. And I'm really tired. And I have to go back to work tomorrow after a long weekend break. And oh how the self-flagellation[151] of guilt whips are laying on heavy purely figurative stripes at the present moment.

Speaking of you, I haven't told many people I'm writing a book. For those I have told, the reaction is often, "Oh, really?" Then end of discussion. No one wants to know anything more.

If you were writing a book and thought to share with me that you were writing a book, I'm sure I would have a different reaction. I would probably say, "Oh, really?"

Aha.

I see now.

Now I understand.

---

150   "Sh-Boom,"song by the Chords, written by James Keyes, Claude Feaster, Carl Feaster, Floyd F. McRae, and James Edwards, labeled by Cat Records, 1954.

151   As opposed to self-flatulation, which isn't even a word, you weirdo.

CHAPTER
41

Umm, Yeah, And *The Little Paris Bookshop*

How many authors have worked as many hours as I have to finish their book, only to not like what they ultimately published?

■ ■ ■

Let's give a moment of silence for Time

■ ■ ■

Just a little more filler material to go before I hit my target word count of who knows how many words.[152] Hitting a target word count is purely subjective, I know. The book could have been 30,000 words or shorter and still counted as a book. No idea why I thought the book needed to be as long as this one. But I do remember thinking such a low book word count didn't feel like a book to me. I want to do this right by not cutting too many corners, like all the ones I've cut in order to get to where I am now. This chapter should add both to the word count and the page count. Very little thought has been given to page count, and I want a book with some significant page count. The book needs some serious mass to it.

<u>Umm, yeah</u>

Umm, yeah. I have absolutely nothing left to write. What happens then? What happens when there's nothing left to write?

---

152   I sure don't.

The Little Paris Bookshop

My wife is reading *The Little Paris Bookshop*.[153] She was telling me that part of the book is about a man who recommends books to people in order to help them work out a life issue.[154]

If this character was aware of my book, what kind of person would he recommend read it?

I would like to take an opportunity to diagnose the kind of reader this book might help.

This is a very difficult exercise, for me, but one I should start if I really am serious about not self-publishing. To find an agent and/or publisher, I need to know my "market." Unfortunately, that's what you are: a "market." But you are not a market to me. You are a human. I will not demote you to a market. You are special, unique, and one-of-a-kind. It's not like you are just like oodles of other people who all enjoy the same types of books. I mean, there are so many kinds of books. We like putting them in these broad, general genres, but one book isn't necessarily like all the others, is it?

I really don't think this book will be liked by most types of people. Non-English speakers definitely won't like this book because at least at this time, it's not written in another language. In other words, to them, the book would be completely foreign.

Anyway, I'm pretty confident my book will be enjoyed by a certain type of person who meets some of the criteria listed below. And again, I'm sorry to label you as a "type of person," although you may like to type, as I am doing, right now.

Whatever I am trying to do, whether it is to diagnose, type-cast, or plop you into some horoscope-like determinant of how you ended up becoming a match for this book, be prepared for me to exactly nail the kind of person you are.

----

153   *The Little Paris Bookshop*, by Nina George. Large Print Press, 2016.
154   This isn't some made up way to cover the fact that I actually read the book. Because I didn't.

This book is for you if:

- You've already read every other book and wanted to read one more, and came across this one.
- We are not related.[155]
- You have never met me before.[156]
- Before reading this book, you had this fantasy about becoming an author.
- You frequently check for social media updates against your will.
- Determined to make a life plan, you take out a notebook to record your wishes, desires and life goals, and then can't find anything to write with.
- You often end sentences in prepositions.
- During rapid eye movement in the night, your dreams sometimes take you to a place that is different from actual reality.
- You either like to cook, enjoy cooking somewhat, cooking is neither here nor there, or you really don't like to cook.
- Your heart is in the right place, but you accomplish very little.
- On a clear, moonless night, you look up at the starry sky and think, "Man, it's sure dark out."

It's probably time to refresh your memory on what these bullets are about. Thought I would check in again to remind you.

This book is for you if:

- While reading this book, you find yourself LIL'ing from time to time.[157]

---

155   I discuss this in a previous chapter, or maybe it was in the preface or acknowledgements or possibly the introduction. So long ago, I can't remember where I wrote that.
156   *Ibid.* [sic]
157   Laughing Inside Lightly

- You still write personal checks and often overdraw. You have a debit card and often overdraw. You're an artist and over draw. You're a kid and draw over and over.
- You have a really hard time enjoying yourself at Costco.
- You think the Olympics should go from every four years to every 40 years. Or not.
- You have more time on your hands these days.
- You like to say, "No kidding!" Like I do. Which means you have to space them out more, like I do.
- You're vanity plate would read, "NICS" for "Now I Can Say" if you were me.
- You've gotta friend in Pennsylvania.
- You keep your politics to yourself, and to everyone who will listen.
- After reading this book, you have a diminished view of authors.
- After reading this book, you have a diminished view of me.
- After reading this book, you decide to become an Egyptologist.
- After reading this book, you find yourself more charming and charismatic, able to influence people and encounter success where'er you may go.
- Truth is stranger than fiction, which it is.

I Think I'm An Author (Measured in Inches)

I settled some time ago that I would write forty-one chapters. Right now, I'm plowing right through that vow by going with forty-two. This is it. This is the end. I'm nearly finished.

■ ■ ■

Today

■ ■ ■

Now I Can Say that all I have to do is format the entire book, among other things, in order to get the book published. Proofread. Edit. Rearrange and reorder. Make a Table of Contents for people who use Table of Contents. Figure out what the genre is. I really have no idea what it should be. Start researching literary agents and publishers. Do more research. Decide which ones to shop and reconfigure the book to match each of their interests. Write a query letter. Rewrite the query letter. Send the query letter to the best agents. Wait for their replies. Deal with the rejections. Write more query letters. Write so many query letters. Pay a professional editor to help me rework what I got wrong. Make sure the editor understands what I'm trying to do and doesn't change the book so much that it's no longer in my voice. Send more query letters. Get more rejections. Give the book a rest for a decade or two. Try not to think about it. Save it for the next generation; a discovery for a curious great-great-grandchild exploring in an old trunk in an attic. Engage in escapist activities. Avoid embracing harmful escapist activities after embracing harmful escapist activities. Edit the book again. Scrap chapters I don't like. Rewrite others. Add a few more. Allow the dream of authorhood to fade into the night. That one escapist activity that seems to be the most interesting and best for me becomes my new obsession and replaces all interest in becoming an author. Forget about the entire thing and when reminded tell myself, "Authoring isn't really my thing," and "Look at how much more time I have to do all these great endeavors I'm doing." And then when I pass a bookstore or see books on my shelf I fall to the floor and sob like a little child that my book failed to become a book equal to one of those books. That I couldn't have my own book on that one shelf in that bookstore or at the very least on my own bookshelf. And when I look more closely at the bookshelf, I notice a book that is particularly thick in the spine – perhaps a 100,000 or greater word novel – at least two full inches wide – and I realize at that point in time that my book would have been so much slimmer, perhaps only an inch-and-a-half, taking up so little space on the bookshelf among all the rest. Would my book have even made a difference in the world? Taking up so little space on a bookshelf. Is all this effort worth it for only one inch and a little bit? Hours and hours, day after day, week, month, year and more all spent engrossed in the effort of book writing, only to achieve one inch of space? Is this what I wanted? Why did I think the result would have been so much greater?

Electromagnetic Pulse Bomb Social Media Toolkit

"I bought this book for the bonus chapter."
—You?

■ ■ ■

In this chapter, I reveal my age.
It's so depressing, really.
I should have finished this many years ago.
But oh well.
Maybe I still have decades of writing left in me.
Or maybe not if the EMP hits…

■ ■ ■

I know what you're thinking. "This book is supposed to be over by now! You said it would be over in chapter 42."

And I agree. I agree wholeheartedly that the book is supposed to be all wrapped up, that there should never have been a chapter 43. The problem is I turned 43 and decided to mark the occasion by adding a 43rd chapter. Few consider 43 years old to be a bonus year, except for those older who fondly recall days of better health. Anyway,

I'm tangentializing – point is I wanted to add one more bonus chapter on electromagnetic pulse bombs, which I think I've discussed in a previous chapter. Putting some time aside to cover the topic gives us an opportunity to think about the future and add it to the list of all the scary things that could go wrong.

If, and I repeat, "if" it comes to this, that we are hit with an electromagnetic pulse bomb, wiping out the power grid, we should put a plan in place. The plan should provide for food, shelter, and general survival. We must also prepare for the other life necessity: social survival. And by "social" I mean *social media* survival.

This book has talked a little about the world of social media, but not a lot. The following letter to public affairs staff of a large company may give you some ideas on ways to keep your game on in the event of such a catastrophe. For those of you much older than 43, it may not make any sense. I guess I'm now giving away that I will be marketing this chapter to young professionals who will get the social media lingo. Not that you super old people don't. I'm sure you know a lot of things. Unless you don't, in which case, no problem. Just keeping reading. Unless you don't want to. Bonus chapters may not be for you, and that's fine. Unless it's not.

■ ■ ■

Dear Public Affairs Staff:

Please see the enclosed Electromagnetic Pulse Bomb (EMP) Social Media Toolkit for use by your division in the event an EMP attack occurs and, about fourteen days after everything in the fridge goes bad, you are fortunate enough to survive.

For those unfamiliar with an EMP, it is a nuclear bomb detonated in the sky that knocks out the power grid, making it impossible to watch *The Handmaid's Tale*, but very possible in intervening months to experience the show for real.

The toolkit contains the following company-branded items you can use in order for us to remain social media communication leaders in a dystopian age:

<u>Yard signs and dry erase markers</u>: For display of social media posts and tweets in yards and on street corners. Please encourage employee amplification to improve reach and promote trending as we grow to scale to become yard sign posting leaders in unabandoned areas.

<u>Selfie stick</u>: For self-protection purposes while scouting out new social media posting locations. Be aware that all attacks will live stream, sort of like Instagram stories only they will become the real-time stream of real-life stories unfolding right before your eyes.

<u>Walking shoes</u>: Much easier on the feet when posting yard signs around town than your current pair of incredibly trendy but tough-to-run-away-from-bandits Nordstrom dress shoes. Will also come in handy while performing the Search Engine Optimization hunt for a functional combustible engine to usher in the post-EMP era.

<u>Paper, colored pencils, stickers</u>: All stock photos, filters, and screenshots will now be hand drawn. Sketch and cut out augmented reality lenses and bitmoji masks to wear around the office/shelter. Give out stickers to reward social achievements, like staying alive for six weeks, seven weeks, etc.

<u>Graph paper & crayons</u>: Sketch out Minecraft and Fortnite simulations when your post-EMP social media activities are interrupted by kids begging for food.

<u>Spray paint</u>: Ensure that graffiti posts are carefully sprayed by vetted street gang artists in high-traffic areas with evergreen content, as murals are permanent when lacking the assistance of a power washer.

<u>Beef jerky and iodine tablets</u>: For social media team nourishment and to avoid dysentery.

<u>Analytics Notebook</u>: Track all posts, goals, referrals, conversions, acquisitions, and other metrics that will be mostly meaningless and more about killing time when not participating in hunter-gatherer activities. Analytics assessments should always be placed on the agenda for periodic staff retreats to warmer climates.

<u>5 page notebooks</u>: Ideal for creating hand-drawn flipbook GIFs. Also great for swatting mosquitoes to prevent spread of Zika virus.

<u>Soap box</u>: To stand on while conducting AMA events.

<u>Seeds and exercise plan</u>: Since "going viral" will come to mean the spreading of human-borne biological viruses caused by a shortage of hand sanitizer and fitness apps, we are providing an assortment of garden seeds to sustain your colony along with printouts of YouTube workout screenshots. Any virus traced back to you will result in your immediate termination.

<u>Paper clips</u>: When you're stuck on how to pursue social media goals, those raised in the MacGyver era will feel empowered to overcome any obstacle through creative use of these elegantly shaped metallic objects.

Remember, "raw authenticity" is the gold standard in a post-apocalyptic era. As such, our current upbeat, overly-produced, while incredibly phony authenticity messaging will be replaced by a much more depressing variety. Make sure our company's sad stories stand out from the rest through original, cross-platform storytelling to improve social ROI.

And lastly, when you hear a tweet, it is the sound of your first prospective protein meal in days. Now you just need to figure out how to catch the damned thing and cook it.

A copy of this policy will be attached to the HR bulletin board.

Sincerely,
HR

P.S. This was written before COVID. Except for this P.S. part which was written after COVID.

All My Life I Wanted to be a Flight Attendant

Just in case I don't publish this 'til I'm 44.

■ ■ ■

Later

■ ■ ■

Full disclosure. All of this author business and what I really want out of life is — this was a worthy exercise to get closer to the truth.

All my life I have wanted to be a flight attendant.

The thrill of flying from one destination to the next, to exotic destinations like Portland and Omaha (I wanted to be a domestic flight attendant) on an airline with an endless supply of assorted juices and sodas and trying to pour scalding hot coffee during turbulence delighted me in a way I can't fully express.

I was six when the career aspiration first came to me. At that time, male flight attendants were becoming more accepted by the general public, even though the term "flight attendant" hadn't caught on. In the early 80's, the position was still commonly referred to as "stewardess." While male peers answered doctor-lawyer-fireman to the one question kids are most often asked, I answered "steward."

In those pre-adolescent years on days-long station wagon road trips with the family I would practice steward-ing by serving my younger siblings honey roasted peanuts in the backseat. As we left each rest stop in winter months, I demonstrated how to secure a seatbelt and how to roll down the window for oxygen in the event of a loss in cabin pressure. "First ventilate for yourself and then for young children," I would announce when the baby needed a new diaper but there was no place to stop for 52 more miles.

What's remarkable is I had never been on a plane and I had never seen a flight attendant in action. This all just came naturally. You could say I was meant to be a flight attendant.

When I was 12, the local grocery store offered a sale on airline fares. For $150, frequent customers could purchase a round trip ticket to anywhere in the continental U.S. My good parents, struggling to understand their first pubescent child, gave the green light for me to fly solo two time zones away into the arms of adolescent-parenting veterans, their own parents.

My only challenge was to raise more money than I had ever possessed in my young life: one hundred and fifty big ones. In today's dollars, that's about $4.2 million.

In my excitement to get started and track progress, I ripped a very uneven piece of notebook paper and drew 30 boxes that each represented $5. The torn paper looked a lot like the State of Arkansas. Interestingly, this was only four years before a U.S president would be elected from that very state! Coincidence?

It is now obvious even to me that I should not be writing anymore. I should be flight attendanting.

For each $5 earned, I would fill in a box on the chart. When I earned anything less than $5 I divided each little box five different ways and filled in a line for each of the dollars earned. I used blue ink, which meant no screw ups, and no spending. Man, I loved that piece of paper. It represented freedom, growing up, responsibility, goal setting, and another step closer to becoming a flight attendant.

In just a few months selling newspapers door-to-door, delivering the paper, pulling weeds, babysitting, and performing other odd jobs for kind neighbors, I earned the $150.

The day of my first commercial airline flight finally arrived.

Without going into great detail about that first flight, I will only say that after experiencing life in the sky, I was more certain than ever: I had a future in flight attendance.

Fast forward four years to age 16. President Bill Clinton is now in the White House and Kurt Cobain is dead. Still hanging on to my dream and learning more about flight attendant job qualifications, I passed my 5'11" father in height. That's when I began to worry that I would exceed the 6'1" drop-dead highest height requirement allowed by the major airlines (TWA's requirement was 6" even and we all know what happened to them).

I measured my height daily during those years. At 19, I hit my paranoia peak when I grew to 6" and a half inch. Almost magically, I stayed exactly at that height and felt confident I was finished growing. This job in the skies was going to happen. I was going to do this.

I patiently awaited my 21st birthday, the youngest I could be admitted to flight attendant training. First, I had to wait for an airline to recruit in my city. Three months later, on a surprisingly warm February morning, the recent snow melting away, I took a bus to the interview. As the bus traveled to the airline training center, I walked up and down the aisle, pretending to check that seats were in their upright position and luggage was properly stowed.

"Are you training to be a flight attendant?" A perceptive passenger asked as we approached the airport.

"Yes," I responded, "And is your seatbelt securely fastened?"

I breezed through the interview. It was surreal. Yet so real. And also surreally real. Just not surEltonJohn real, although my interviewer admitted he was a big fan.

The first round, second round, and then third came and went. The selections process was brutal, but I eventually received a formal offer to serve as a flight attendant for Delta Airlines.

Because of my height, charm, years of experience in a station wagon (I was told), and incredibly good looks (I told myself), I was assigned to the PHL – ORD and ORD – DFW on a Delta 727-200 which accommodated flight attendants of my height. I was told with excellent performance reviews I could move to a 747 by the time I was 30. By 40 – I could wear the coveted red suit.

Two weeks before my first flight they asked that I turn in my training gear, get sized for my official Delta uniform and go through one last round of physical checkups.

I went straight into my training exit interview and Ms. Kirschner asked that I sit down.

"Josh. You have been one of my best students in 23 years of training. Maybe even the best. I am so disappointed to learn that you have grown a whole inch since training began two months ago."

She didn't have to say any more than that. At six feet, one and a half inches, I knew I was too tall to be a flight attendant on anything but a cargo plane. I knew it was over. I would never wear the red jacket. I would never fly to Omaha. I would never point to the nearest exit or wear a deflated life preserver around my neck. I was too tall to serve the cause. I was too tall to serve the coffee.

■ ■ ■

This was a joke.

I have nothing against flight attendants.

Epilogue

How to Reach Me

Every amazing book has an epilogue, like mine. I wrestled with what to say here, and it just came to me. At the end of every book I've ever read, I've wanted to know how to reach the author. So here is my contact information. Except I won't just give you my contact information. There are rules about how to reach me. Here are a few:

WARNING: This epilogue is unlike any you've ever encountered. It contains a film script, my zero-tolerance policy for a surging salutation trend used in email, and the first ever picture of what a text looks like hurling through the air to your phone. I offer this warning now only because the part about when my phone is stuck under the driver's seat is rather long, but if you keep reading in this Epilogue, you'll learn a lot about HOW TO REACH ME.

TEXT

What a text looks like before it hits your phone.

The best way to reach me these days is by text. It's as close to an instantaneous way of getting in touch as being physically present, grabbing my attention, and then showing me a poster with words on it.

After many hours wondering how best to respond, which is what I do, I ended up sending Mrs. Obama a message that was respectful of her time. My reply simply said "text."

The beauty of the text is how it is delivered right to my phone, which is almost always in a pants, shirt, or jacket pocket or on my desk or on the kitchen counter or over the river or in my bag or through the woods. The phone is rarely anywhere else.

So if you text me, your transmission of characters will hurl through the wires and air until it hits my phone which will be located in one of those places.

One thing is for sure: there is a sixty-four percent chance I will get your text right away. And if you're trying to reach me, those are pretty good odds that you'll accomplish your goal.

Active vs. Passive Texts

When I drive or am walking in a parking lot or staring in a trance at the screws in Home Depot aisle 12 – three things I did today – I can't guarantee I will see your text as soon as you send it.

Okay. I will most likely see your text, but I won't always think to reply immediately. In other words, all too often I will not *actively* see your text. Instead I will *passively* see your text.

I forget texts I receive passively. I forget them as soon as I passively view them.

For instance, if you text:

"Can you meet up at 7pm?" and I passively read it, I simply will not respond to you because it's already gone from my memory. Just like that.

Let's say the next day you see me and ask, "Didn't you get my text?"

And I say, "Oh yeah, I meant to write back."

What should be said in situations like this one is, "Oh yeah, I passively saw your text which means I completely forgot about it and therefore failed to respond."

I share this with you so you will know how to react when confronted in this way. Let's be more honest with one another.

So, when texting me, take into account whether I am actively or passively seeing your text. You've gotta time it just right. Timing is everything.

When actively texting, I tend to like to have the last word. For example, you write me, I write back, you write, I write, etc., until I write and then you don't write back. I always have something to say to close it out, even if you've made it clear the conversation has ended. This isn't intentional. It's just me passive aggressively wanting to have the last word. But it's something I've noticed about myself and I have little intention of actively changing.

MORE ON TEXTING: The Little Door Handle Thingy Area That Doesn't Have a Name

I now turn to the little door handle thingy area that doesn't have a name. It's the part you grab when you're closing the car door. I've owned several cars and I think it's been in most of them except, I think, for one or two.

The little door handle thingy area that doesn't have a name is the place wherein resides my phone when I am in the car or sometimes when I'm not and I forgot to take it out with me. It is also the place wherein resides my wife's bobby pin which has been there for years. It's the same place wherein my phone doesn't quite reside comfortably so if I open the car door too quickly the phone may fall to the pavement below and crack and need a screen replacement. In addition to the little door handle thingy area that doesn't have a name, the phone also finds itself in the cup holder or seat or sometimes my lap. The phone is rarely anywhere else.

And how about this? Brace yourself because I'm about to explain the most frustratingly frustrating problem I have ever encountered in every car I have ever owned in my entire life since I've owned a cell phone.

■ ■ ■

CAN'T TEXT Because Phone is Under Driver's Seat

Okay, so you try to reach me, but what if I can't reach the phone? Has your phone, like mine, ever fallen under the driver's seat?

When the phone is under the driver's seat, monumental effort is required to retrieve it. I try to slip my hand in the tight areas on either side of the seat or even underneath the seat but there is hardly enough space to get in more than a few fingers. Even then, I can only reach underneath the driver's seat up to my second knuckle.

Since the phone is impossible to reach while driving, I have to park the car in a safe area (see Hollywood script below for why this is important), get out of the car, kneel on the ground, and twist and contort unnaturally with head under steering wheel trying to see the phone in order to get my hands to the right place underneath the driver's seat – the place with the best chance of retrieving my phone. And I have to do all these things AT THE SAME TIME.

I am not a multitasker, even though I put that on my résúmé (while patting my head with one hand and rubbing my stomach in circular motions with the other) early in my career because that's what everyone was doing at the time (writing résúméś while patting their heads with one hand and rubbing their stomachs in circular motions with the other).

I've learned so much since then, just one thing at a time.

But yeah, dropping the phone under the driver's seat........

It's frustrating. It's like everything going dark. My phone = my life.

So here I find myself searching for my phone, my temples pressed firmly against the bottom of my steering wheel, my eyes straining to look sideways but not being able to look sideways enough, my hand probing as much as I can underneath my car seat, when all of a sudden, my mind tricks me into thinking the tips of my fingers have discovered something resembling a phone, and instead of grasping my impossible-to-reach phone, I find relics from my children's past. It's like a precious time capsule of an event in history when my kids were with me in the car. The object may have found its way there during an outing last week or it could have been from an October 2nd three years ago.

But no. Nothing precious is found. Instead of finding sweet reminders of memories gone by, it's the crushed Happy Meal toy part or the perfectly preserved Skittle.

Dropping my phone under the driver's seat would make for a suspenseful film scene.

Imagine the protagonist who needs his phone during a high stake's situation – let's say a hungry prison escapee happens to see this guy – and let's call this guy "Josh" – searching for his phone, which has fallen under the driver's seat, à la this short film:

REACHED

Written by

Josh Rolph

California
555-1212
(please
don't try
to reach
me at this
number)

```
EXT. PARKING LOT - NIGHT

Strikingly handsome man in 40s frantically tries to search
under car driver's seat. JOSH's knees shift on the gravel,
his bloodied fingers reaching for an object. A long, eerie
SHADOW creeps slowly towards the car.

                    JOSH
                (panic)
            What was I thinking? Driving to
            this abandoned warehouse was a
            crazy mistake--

                    SHADOW (O.S.)
            You're out of luck...you are in my
            control now.

                    JOSH
                (whispers)
            I just need my phone. I need to
            call for help. I just need...

                    SHADOW (O.S.)
                (maniacal laugh)
            You will never get your phone! It's
            - it's - it's under your driver's
            seat!

Maniacal laugh gets more maniacal. Josh's fingers fail to
find the phone.

                    JOSH
                (hysterical)
            You're wrong! This can't be happ--
            I'll find it! I'll find it!

                                            CUT TO:


INT. UNDER CAR SEAT - NIGHT

Fingers continue search. The phone is propped against a
broken pencil, near eighteen cents in change, and to the left
of a half-eaten chicken nugget. All at once, fingers STIFFEN,
and then DISAPPEAR.

                    JOSH (O.S.)
                (screams)

                                        FADE TO BLACK.


            THE END
```

What I'm trying to say is if you need to reach me, I need to be able to reach my phone.

TEXTING EXCEPTIONS (and my self-esteem in meetings)

Sometimes a text can also slip through the cracks, as it were, like when I'm driving and I get your text and can't break the California hands free law at that given moment and I think of what to write back but then get distracted by turns that make it hard to text or brake lights that interrupt my text, or pedestrians that give me that look when I almost run over them while texting.

Still, texting is by far the best way to reach me, except when I'm in a meeting and haven't turned on vibrate – no, change that. Getting texts during a meeting makes others think "Wow, Josh must be working hard" as the phone sings its text tune every other minute. "I'll turn it on mute," I say to them. Buzz, buzz, buzz, buzz… and they all look on amazed that I have someone texting me. Buzz, buzz. "Josh is getting another text. He gets so many texts! He must have a lot going on right now."

In the times of day that I'm not near my phone, moments which have been known to happen, texting is not the best way to reach me. In that case, it's better to call.

Since I was just on the topic of texts in meetings, I find it funny how a call during a meeting is less likely to leave an impression of importance than a text. Anyone can call a phone: telemarketers, survey takers, those incredibly effective fraternal order of police that get me every time —————— But not just anyone can text.

There is still a lot more to say. Like when AT&T texts me or I get the unusual spam texts about free cruises or the misdirected texts in other languages with tons of emoji and how depressing that is.

So much more to say. But let's move on.

PHONE

Like I said, if you need to reach me, sometimes a call is better than a text. Calls can be quite effective. Like when it's an emergency, you could call. I may not pick up the first time and I may not see your text right away, but if you call and hang up then call and hang up and then call again, I will think, "Oh wait, this must be important. Hold on, people around me, I need to get this call."

Most of the time, however, it's not an emergency. In fact, I can think of maybe two or three emergency-level calls in my entire lifetime, and they weren't really emergency-level, though they were somewhat in that direction.

Most of the time, it can wait. Most of the time, just a regular call is okay. Except I prefer urgent calls more than regular calls. Although sometimes a regular call is better than an urgent call.

There's nothing as bad as an urgent call that ruins a relaxing moment. There's nothing worse than a regular call that ruins what I hoped would be an urgent moment.

I pick up calls maybe 40% of the time. I rarely pick up if I don't know the number.

And oh, I should clarify, when I say "phone" I mean my cell phone.

I have two cell phones, and I don't care which one you call. One is for work and the other is personal. While there is a wall of separation between both phones, where one does not infringe upon the rights of the other, there are times when one must be used for the other purpose and vice versa, but it usually works itself out in the end.

One more thing: If you are a telemarketer, don't call my cell phone.

Lately, my phone has been resurfacing here.

HOME PHONE

If you are a telemarketer, it's best to reach me by home phone. This section is about my home phone which now is limited to telemarketing calls, only. We feel it's important to keep an open line of communication between our family and the telemarketing industry. I feel a sort of bond with the telemarketing industry, having spent valuable time in my career working within it, once selling Martha Stewart subscriptions about a day after she had been indicted for securities fraud. While I did ultimately quit (after two and a half hours), I feel tremendous empathy for telemarketers, so they are always welcome to my home, through my home phone.

VOICE MAIL

There have been ample articles in recent years discussing the death of voice mail. Apparently, not many people check voice mail anymore. I happen to be one of the few who still checks his voice mail as soon as

I can retrieve it. I happen to enjoy voice mail. I may not listen to it all the way through if I'm distracted, so please enunciate and ensure you are leaving the message indoors – away from a noisy environment – using a landline or a cell phone with a strong signal and getting out your main idea in the first four or five seconds of the message. Don't just say, "Hi, it's so and so, call me back." Tell me why you are leaving the message. Like you, I'm not a fan of obscure voice mails.

Obscure voice mails are totally different than obscure Facebook posts.

I need to know a little about why you called before I decide if and when I should call you back.

EMAIL

If you can't reach me by any phone and it's not an emergency, then email is best. Emails should follow certain guidelines. Not too short, not too long. I appreciate decent spelling and grammar. A little thought and care goes a long way. I have a hard time with emails that address me but don't use any punctuation after my name in the salutation, like this:

From: robertbob@neither███northere.biz
Subject: Such and Such
To: "Josh Rolph" bad-dawg████ @███biz.biz
Date: Mon, 20 Jul 2015 21:11:01

Josh

Per our conversation, can you check to see if so and so can do such and such here or there from time to time, and if he or she has come and gone on this, that, or the other thing?

Robert Bob

In the above case, see how my name just hangs there? It's just "Josh" with nothing holding it up. Please avoid the hanging salutation with no punctuation after the name. You should include a comma or colon or hyphen(s) following my name to support it up there at the beginning of your note and not allow it to float alone like that.

I can get a little picky about the emails I receive. In other words, I'm judging you by the content of your emails to me. Just don't try to sound smarter than me in an email, because then I won't judge you, I'll judge myself and realize how much dumber I am than you.

FACEBOOK MESSENGER

Sometimes email doesn't work and texting can be too slow. If you need to have a quick, fast conversation over instant messaging, I've been enjoying Facebook's Messenger. It's a quick way to get back to me but understand that it can also be an easy way to send friend spam. Friend spam is when you send me that quick link without commentary. And if it's a link to a video about COVID, Democrats, or Republicans, it's much more likely that my brain will unconsciously classify it as spam, even if I fully agree with you.

SKYPE/TEAMS/WHATSAPP/ZOOM

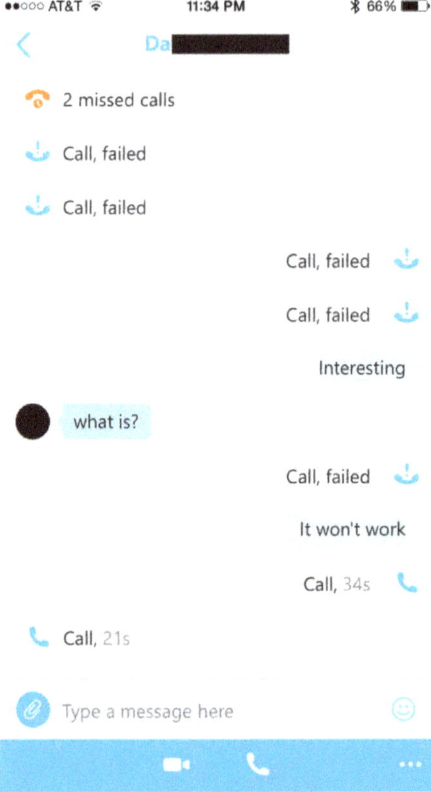

I didn't feel like asking the person for permission to use this screenshot so I blocked out the name.

There was a time not long ago that Skype was great for IMs, especially if I was sharing attachments from a laptop or desktop, which Facebook Messenger isn't that good at. I reserved Skype video for business and family calls, though it wasn't that reliable, especially on Sundays and holidays. And if you wonder why I'm

"To skype" quickly became a verb. Think about that for a moment. It's an odd word. A really odd word. If the Internet didn't exist and a friend said "let's skype," what would you think it meant? To me, it sounds like a fishing expedition or a game one might play in the backyard of an Eastern European family's BBQ.

Barbecue is a weird word.

Then came ZOOM during COVID and everyone forgot about Skype. Now we "zoom." Think about THAT for a moment. What if the next think was called "THAT?"

Except it is! WHATSAPP is also a thing used by tons of people, as in, so many. And the whole name for it is a question. What's up? What's app? Wut?

Unlike the words "skype" and "barbecue," "what's app" doesn't sound as weird. Not nearly as weird as the word "word."

Gotta say, "word" is a weird word.

Word.

GOOGLE HANGOUTS

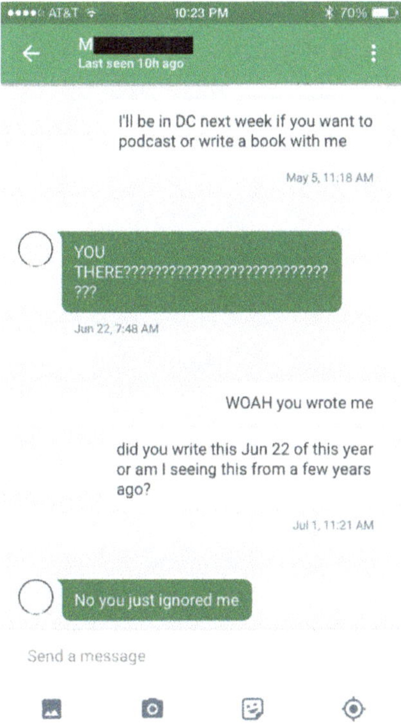

I didn't feel like asking the person for permission to use this screenshot so I blocked out the name.

Google Hangouts is great as well, both the video and chat features. You can reach me there except be aware of the 5% chance I will get back to you (unless we initiate the video or chat at the same time (assuming the call goes through (often it doesn't (but sometimes it does (does not (does too (does not (does too (does not (etc...)))))))))).

LETTER

huh

TWITTER

This is the social media platform that shares in common the last three letters of "letter" and the first four letters of "twit." Never thought of that 'til now. I don't use Snapchat much (except for a few days where I got addicted to earning their points), but I do use Twitter on occasion. Not sure how Snapchat is relevant here. Forgive me for bringing up Snapchat. Twitter: don't try to start a conversation with me on Twitter, but do favorite and retweet often. I mean, you can always try to start a conversation. It's the debates that don't work. Limited character debates are like – well, they're really fun – but don't get me sucked into one because I may obsess over it for too long and get distracted from what I was doing before it got super fun. In other words, don't take advantage of my lack of self-control when Twitter Debating.

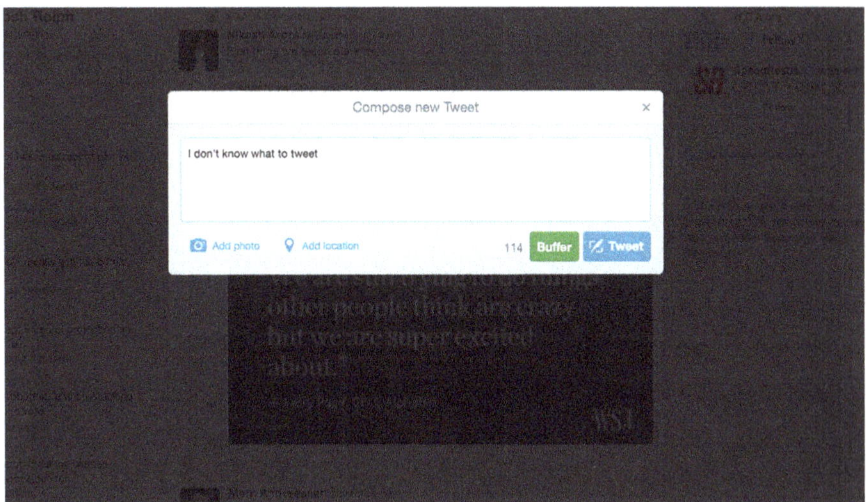

FACEBOOK POSTS & INSTAGRAM INSTAGRAMMES

I can't think of a way to reach me on Instagram other than to share a photo with me you think will send me some sort of message. Most likely I won't understand unless words are attached to the image, which is easier to do on its ad-heavy sister-site: Facebook. I don't react well when I'm tagged in pictures on either site. You can always tag me in a photo, just use caution when you do because there's a chance I don't want to be tagged at all. In fact, there's always a good chance I don't want to be tagged at all. If I want to be tagged, I will tag myself. Please don't tag me. Unless you think I'd like to be tagged. But chances are, I won't, unless I do.

A scientific comparison between the reaction on Instagram and Facebook of a revolting photo of a sock on a toe. Oh, and I didn't feel like asking the people who commented for permission to use this screenshot with their comments so I blocked out their names.

FACETIME

FaceTime can be useful if you're not comfortable with Hangouts, Skype, Messenger, or Twitter. The reception isn't as clear and if we don't know each other well, an unscheduled FaceTime call from you will be a tad awkward and I will ignore it and when we next see one another in person I will pretend I never saw it. If I'm calling you on FaceTime and we haven't planned the call beforehand, chances are it's my kids calling you on accident. That's happened. Mostly to the names that start with "A." Sorry, friends named Aaron.

JOSHROLPH.COM

And you can always comment on a blog post. That makes me feel good. I usually don't respond because I'm not sure you'll check back but on occasion I will respond if I'm feeling especially friendly. If I don't it's because your comment either didn't require a response or I didn't know how to respond back to you. I may have tried to reply to your comment once, twice, or many times spending a few hours writing, editing, writing, drafting, erasing, and then ultimately writing "thanks!" It's hard to write, especially when you're not sure what to say. And a lot of times I just don't know what to say after practicing a few dozen things to say.

APPLE WATCH

So, I have this little device on my wrist that other people with the same device can send heartbeats and draw pictures and send animated emoji and hearts. Except don't do it. There is a certain middle-school-yearbook feeling to these types of messages. Unless you knew me in middle school, please don't "Apple Watch" me.

OTHER

The other way to reach me is to see me in person. This could be at work, at my home, or at a meeting or event. You could reach me in the store but that would be an unplanned-reaching-me. In any case, in-person reaches are the way people reached each other for thousands of years before phones, texts and blogs.

METAPHORICAL

What is "reaching me," anyway? Is it as simple as simply getting my attention? Or is it more than that? When I'm "reached" is it possible that I don't think I've been reached, or that I am not even aware of the reaching? Could it be that I think I've been reached when I haven't?

To ask these questions, am I reaching?

COSMIC

Definitely reach out cosmically. Totally down with that.

SUMMARY

Anyway, if you want to know the best way to reach me, I would really appreciate it if you please consulted this simple guide first.

And if you want to do something different, next time you see me, hold a poster board in front of me with the words you want to say. Just don't be alarmed if I take a picture of it on my phone to read later because at that given moment, it might not be the best way to reach me.

Book Audit

I, ███████████, Certified Public Auditor, as requested by the book publisher, and following all rules, guidance, laws, and audit accreditation standards with which I am accredited, performed an actuarial audit on the chronological truth claims made in this book.

The author claims a certain chronology with intervals between chapters. I have determined that if all of these time and chronological claims are accurate, then Josh Rolph began writing this book in approximately 1632 BCE.

{This page left intentionally blank except for these words. Now go on and live your best life cuz that's what you do after you finish a book.}

www.ingramcontent.com/pod-product-compliance
Lightning Source LLC
Chambersburg PA
CBHW040854010826
48978CB00013BA/1012